C000051304

THIRD COMES VENGEANCE

A MAFIA REVERSE HAREM ROMANCE

PROMISED IN BLOOD

LILITH VINCENT

From purest pain comes sweetest vengeance.

The city of Coldlake, where everything appears bright and sunny but beneath the surface is blood and darkness. A city where killers hide in plain sight and the ones you trust can turn on you in a heartbeat.

My heart has endured pain, but in the arms of the Coldlake Syndicate, I've known only sweetness. Their kisses are my joy and their love is my salvation. When their pasts collide with our present, nothing will ever be the same.

My four men have suffered at the hands of an unknown killer, and I'll do whatever it takes to heal their broken hearts. I see him, and he will tremble at my coming.

Vengeance will be mine.

Author's note: Third Comes Vengeance is the final book in the Promised in Blood series. These books contain dark themes, violence, and a Why Choose romance with ruthlessly possessive men. The story is dark, dirty, and delicious, so please read at your discretion.

1

Chiara

My harsh breathing echoes off the walls and the air feels heavy and damp. Water is dripping, and there's broken concrete beneath my bare feet. All other sound is muted. Like a coffin. Like a crypt. I strain for the sound of traffic, voices, music. Anything.

Alone.

I'm so alone.

The last thing I remember is Acid pressing a cloth over my mouth and struggling with another man. I lift my head and stare around me. There's a thin shaft of daylight from a vent high in the wall, but most of the room is in darkness. The ghosts of four murdered women cluster around me, and I can feel their sorrow and hear the echoes of their screams. There are ropes around my arms, waist, and legs intricately crisscrossing my body, like whoever did this took their time, their heart full of sadistic delight.

Lorenzo described this place as he sat, hollow-eyed, over a glass of vodka. An underground room, their sisters all alone and tied to chairs.

Then a killer entered and ripped them apart.

There's a sharp pain in my heart. Acid is probably recording me right now, and when this is all over, he'll deliver the video to my men. A sob rises in my throat as I picture Lorenzo in front of his laptop with a pen in one hand and a bottle of vodka in the other. Shoulders slumped. Defeated. A gun lays on the table nearby, tempting him.

"No," I moan, yanking my body this way and that, trying to loosen the ropes.

How could Acid look Lorenzo in the eye day after day, week after week, year after year after what he did? There was always something crafty about Acid, but I assumed he had to be that way to survive in one of the roughest parts of Coldlake. All this time he's been concealing a psychotic hatred of the men he takes orders from.

I twist my wrists, but I'm bound so tightly I can barely move. My only hope of getting out of here is that one of Lorenzo's guards survived Acid's attack and recognized my kidnappers. They'll be able to tell my men who took me, which will give them a place to start looking.

But where are my men? They all disappeared in the

middle of the night without telling me, and the only clue I have is Cassius' cryptic text, *I'm in position*. That sounds like they were watching something, or about to attack someone. The Black Orchid Killer? My father?

Whatever happened next, something went wrong. Every single one of Lorenzo's men turned pale as they received a text that read, *Orchid Protocol*. I have no idea what Orchid Protocol is, but the guards did. It was a signal to take me from Lorenzo's home to a different location. The safest place for me in Coldlake was Lorenzo's own fortress-like house, with its high walls, armed guards, and security cameras. I don't understand why they needed to get me out of there.

Lorenzo, where are you?

Are you still alive?

Is Nicole alive?

Why did she answer the phone when I called you?

If that even was Nicole. Whoever it was, she was whispering and slurring her words. A girl who was drugged and afraid, and she was trying to warn me about something.

It's a trap.

Dead.

And then... *Blond. Scary.*

The blond, scary man is dead.

Or was it *Dad*?

Could it be that her father was leading my boyfriends into a trap? Other than disliking my men, Mr. De Luca has no reason to personally go after them. Or was the woman on the phone referring to *my* dad? That makes more sense. Dad absolutely wants the Coldlake Syndicate destroyed.

And I'm stuck in a basement, tied to a chair while God knows what happens out there to my men.

"I'm going to kill you, Acid," I seethe.

A deep chuckle emanates from the darkness, and all the hairs stand up on the back of my neck.

I lift my chin and stare around the room. "Is that you? Where are you?"

A figure steps forward into the light, dragging a chair with him. He straddles the seat, one muscular, tattooed forearm resting along the back of the chair. When he smiles, his emerald eyes glimmer.

"How are you going to kill me, your highness?" he purrs in a voice like black velvet. He's wearing black boots and jeans, and a tank top that fits loosely across his muscular shoulders. The green eyes of the skull tattoo on his throat flame in the dim light.

A second figure strolls out of the darkness. Lean but broad through the shoulders with narrow hips, long legs, and careless black hair. There are silver rings decorating his fingers, fine silver chains around his neck, and cuffs on his ears. The shirt he's wearing is made from fine fabric, soft and expensive-looking, unbuttoned low on his smooth chest. Abstract tattoos decorate his skin, and the nails on one of his hands are painted black. Those dark eyes of his are soulless black holes in his face.

He hunkers down beside my chair and tugs on a few of the ropes that bind my arms and legs. Testing them.

"Struggle for me," he murmurs.

I stare at him, perplexed. "What?"

His gaze travels lovingly over the ropes. Blood red ropes. Beautiful, twisting knots and loops.

"Struggle for me. Try to get away." He wants to watch me pull against my bindings because he gets sick pleasure from seeing me at his mercy.

"Go smash your dick with a hammer," I snarl at him.

Acid bursts out laughing. "Nice try, Thane."

This is Thane? I've never met him, but he and Vinicius work together and I heard his voice once. He called Lorenzo the night a woman's body was found in the canal. He sounded unemotional as he relayed what he'd learned from the police scanner, but as I gaze into those dead eyes, I see his inhumanity is on a whole other level.

"You're supposed to be on our side," I tell him, then look at Acid. "So were you."

The smile drops from Acid's face. "Strife is on Strife's side. Always has been. Always will be."

My eyes are slowly adjusting to the darkness. I peer into the shadows, searching for the video camera and whatever they're going to use to kill me. Whatever they have planned, it will be lurid and violent.

"Why did you kill Salvatore, Vinicius, Cassius, and Lorenzo's sisters?"

Acid and Thane exchange glances, both of them smiling. All the hairs stand up on the back of my neck.

"Why do you think?" Acid asks, turning back to me.

"Because you're petty assholes. Nine years ago, you

thought that with Salvatore's father gone, you'd be able to take control of this area of Coldlake. Then the Coldlake Syndicate was formed and you discovered you'd be answering to Lorenzo. The four of them are too powerful for you to take on, and so you lashed out at their sisters instead."

"Ah, she's got us all figured out, Thane," Acid says with a smirk. Thane has moved back to prop his shoulders against the wall, his expression blank.

I'm talking about the vicious murder of four innocent women, and Acid's *smiling*. "Lorenzo nearly killed himself when Sienna's body was found. Cassius obliterated everything around him in grief and fury. Vinicius never got his lost twin sister back. Family is everything to Salvatore and you ripped his apart. You almost destroyed them over a few shitty square miles and a bar."

Acid rubs a hand over his jaw. "You really love those men, don't you?"

All four of them burn brightly in my heart. I want to scream and cry. I want to struggle, but I won't give them the satisfaction. There's probably a camera trained on me right now, and if one of my men ever sees this, I want them to know that I held it together as long as I could and I never, *ever* begged for mercy.

There's no point begging. Mercy has long fled this place. Only pain and death remain.

Thane speaks in a flat, cold voice. "Strife isn't just a bar. Strife is who we are."

"Pieces of shit is what you are," I snarl. If I'm going

down, I'm going down swinging. "So tell me, what kind of death do you have planned for the Princess of Coldlake? You had better make this good. I want to go down in history with the grisliest death this city has ever seen. How about tying me to a throne and electrocuting me slowly? Hammering a crown of nails into my head, one by one? What's it going to be?"

Acid gazes at me in disbelief. "Damn, girl. You've got a sick mind."

The Black Orchid Killer has a sick mind. I'm just riffing to hide my terror.

Acid and Thane exchange glances, like they're not sure what to say next, and the first trickle of doubt runs down my spine. The Black Orchid Killer would know exactly what he wanted to do next. He's had more than a year to plan my grisly death. I barely know Acid and I don't know Thane at all, but I do know they're from the streets. They're accustomed to the swift, messy justice of baseball bats and stolen guns.

So what's really going on here?

I close my eyes and think back to the night Acid was shot and Lorenzo and I saved his life. The moment Acid woke up, he was intent on finding out who I was and what I was doing with Lorenzo. He delights in irritating Lorenzo, but even though they piss each other off, I sensed grudging respect between the two of them. Acid is curious. Smart. Opportunistic. What will he get out of torturing me to death? It seems like a lot of bother without any material gain. Surely I'm much more useful to him alive.

Relief floods through me so fast that I start to laugh, and my eyes pop open. "Oh, thank God. You're not going to kill me. You really had me going there for a moment."

Thane's heavy brows lift. "You sure about that, baby?"

I stop laughing. That's Salvatore's pet name for me. That's what Mom called me. "Don't call me baby, asshole."

"Touchy, touchy, your highness," Acid mocks. "I guess that's how we'll start torturing you, by carving 'baby' into your pretty flesh."

How crude. Even that feels nothing like what the Black Orchid Killer would do. "Lorenzo told me about the—" I'm about to say *videos* but catch myself just in time. No one knows about the videos except for the five of us and the killer. "Lorenzo told me how their sisters were killed. If you wanted to do that stuff to me, you'd be getting on with it, not sitting here having a chat."

"We're getting there."

"Yeah? How are you going to do it?"

Acid shrugs. "Chop you up. Stick a flower in your mouth. Chuck you in the river."

"And then?"

He gives me a baffled look. "Then nothing. Job done."

I smile and shake my head. "You're not the Black Orchid Killer. Either of you."

They don't know anything about the Black Orchid Killer's MO. If they really were the killer, I'd be screaming and bleeding right now and they'd be gloating over the pain my men will be in when they find my body. We wouldn't be sitting here bantering.

Acid and Thane exchange glances and Thane shrugs.

"Fine, we're not the Black Orchid Killers," Acid admits. "But we weren't trying to make the syndicate think we were, anyway. I didn't drop a black flower on the street for anyone to find when we snatched you."

"So why pretend to me?"

He gives me a smile that I may have found charming if I didn't hate his guts. "You jumped to the conclusion. We've got time to kill so I thought I'd play along."

I glare from one man to the other. If they've got time to kill then they're waiting for something or someone. To ransom me to the syndicate? Like they'll give Acid a cent when they can storm in here and take me back. I can't wait. "You're so screwed, Acid. My boyfriends are crazy when it comes to me. Lorenzo's going to personally take you apart, piece by piece."

Acid leans forward and whispers. "Lorenzo's dead, your highness."

The relief I felt a moment ago is suddenly doused with ice-cold dread. "Shut your mouth. No, he's not." I start to struggle against the ropes out of sheer desperation. Thane's eyes light up.

Acid smiles wider. "Cross my heart and hope to...well. Just cross my heart. I don't want to go dying now that everything's turning out just how I want it."

"Just because something went down tonight, doesn't mean anyone's dead."

Acid spreads his hands. "You have your proof. We all do. Orchid Protocol."

I stop struggling. "How do you know about Orchid Protocol?"

"Lorenzo set it up a few weeks ago and told his best friends down here at Strife all about it. If something happened to him, it would trigger an alert: Lorenzo's dead, go save his princess."

I want to punch Acid right in his smiling mouth.

"With any luck," Acid continues, "one or more of the Coldlake Syndicate will be dead along with our dear boss, and then the Strife men and I will decide whether to exchange you for Lorenzo's territory and power, or..."

"Or what?"

Acid smiles wider. "Or hand you over to your father. A cool million in exchange for his baby girl sounds pretty great to me."

I killed a man recently, but I didn't *want* to do it. I was protecting Vinicius and myself from a dangerous gang leader. As I look into Acid's handsome, smirking face, I want to inflict serious bodily harm on him. "Your plan won't work because Lorenzo isn't dead."

Acid rubs a hand over his jaw. "If he were alive, do you really think you'd be sitting here with us right now?"

Despair washes over me. Lorenzo is too dangerous to die. The others wouldn't let it happen. *He* wouldn't let it happen.

Acid laughs softly. "Long live the Coldlake Syndicate."

2

Salvatore

N *inety minutes earlier*
The day Ophelia's body was found, I stopped believing in happiness.

There's no point in trying; there's only existing, and suffering. Existing isn't so bad. You get to make money. You get to drink good wine. You get to fuck. The syndicate and I had plans for Coldlake.

But there was no joy anymore. It was all sucked out of me when I laid eyes on Ophelia's broken body. Her mutilated face. The terror in her dead, staring eyes. I thought I'd seen everything, but who could do something so heinous to another human being?

Then Evelina's body was found. Then Sienna's, and

finally Amalia's. The whole of Coldlake should have been screaming for justice, but the city was silent.

That's when I realized.

Everyone hates us.

Chiara's eyes were filled with hatred and fear the night of her seventeenth birthday, and by then I was so twisted that I loved it. I wrapped my arms around her and kissed her until I could taste her revulsion.

How fun it was to play with Chiara those early months, toying with her the way a cat toys with a mouse. Mocking her with kisses. Tormenting her with my presence. Goading her into blushes and angry words. This girl was going to hate me more than anyone else in the world.

Only, she didn't hate me. Chiara's hatred was for her father and her father alone. Something shifted inside me, and for the first time in eight years, I didn't feel sorry for myself.

I was sorry for *her*. I wanted revenge for *her*.

Then, I just wanted her.

The first time she smiled at me, halfway drunk and sitting on the edge of the fountain where Ophelia had sat all those years earlier, I saw what I'd become. The person everyone believed me to be. A man my sister would have hated.

You're a criminal, Salvatore, Ophelia once said to me, *but that doesn't mean you have to be a monster like Dad.*

From my position behind a broken-down piece of wall, my gaze sweeps over the abandoned building. I flex my hands on the assault rifle I'm holding and notice that my palms are sweating.

I want to end this. I want this over once and for all and to return to the woman I love. My love for Chiara is pure, but if I never get justice for Ophelia, regret will slowly poison me from the inside out and I'll turn back into the monster I was for eight long years. A man who delights in hate.

I take a deep breath to settle my pounding heart. Vinicius, Cassius, and Lorenzo are all in position, dressed in black and holding guns of their own. We have all four corners of this property pinned down and no one's getting in or out alive without our say-so. Any minute now, I could be face to face with the man who brutally murdered Ophelia. I want to cut strips of flesh from his body and make him tell us why, but I think I want him dead more than I want to hear vile words spill from his mouth.

There's a skittering of stones, and adrenaline shoots through me. Someone lurches out of the shadows and toward the building and I take aim with my gun. Their footsteps are uneven and they're weaving like they're drunk or drugged. I can barely make them out in the darkness. Mr. De Luca? No, this person is too small to be a man and the wrong shape. It's a woman.

Someone is creeping along behind the figure, low and stealthy. A wisp of blond hair pokes from underneath his ski mask. Lorenzo. He's following closely but not attacking, seeming just as puzzled about this person as I am.

As Lorenzo passes a parked van, one of the many vehicles in the lot, the back doors burst open and several figures pounce on him.

A woman screams.

The flurry of movement is so unexpected that it takes me a moment to realize what's happening. I bring the barrel of my gun around to fire, struggling to make out who's who in the darkness. I can hear the dull thwack of a rifle butt on flesh and the blond man grunts in pain.

"*Lorenzo.*" I've yelled loudly enough that the other two will hear me, and I raise my weapon.

I'm about to peer down the sights to take aim at one of the figures, when a tall, lean man steps slowly out of the van. All the hairs stand up on the back of my neck. Whippet thin, he holds himself as still as a stone and radiates cold. I can't see his eyes as his face is covered, but somehow I know he's not blinking.

It's him.

It's fucking him.

I don't know how I know, but I feel it in my gut and my blood and my bones that I'm looking at the Black Orchid Killer.

Suddenly, the figure sprints forward, grabs Lorenzo along with the other men, and drags him toward the open doors of the van.

Shit, shit, shit.

Lorenzo's lost his weapon but he fights like he's possessed, snarling and swearing, punching and kicking when he can. I take aim at one of the figures on the left and shoot, but it's like the bullets don't hit. They're wearing body armor like a SWAT team.

"*Salvatore.* Trunk of my car, left-hand side," Lorenzo shouts. He keeps shouting but his voice becomes muffled. "It's him, Salvatore. Do it. *Fucking do—*"

The van doors slam closed on him, and the engine roars as it speeds out of the lot. Panic rolls through my body. He's taken Lorenzo. I heft the gun in my hands and shoot the tires, but I either miss or it doesn't work.

I run to Lorenzo's Mercedes and open the back. On the left-hand side is a khaki box, and I flip it open revealing a grenade launcher, a heavy weapon that shoots high-caliber explosive projectiles over long distances.

The van is racing down the road, growing smaller and smaller. I've only got a few seconds before it turns a corner and disappears.

My throat burns. Lorenzo's in that van, the most unexpected friend I ever made. The most unlikely, but also the most loyal. He came from nothing and clawed his way to where he is through sheer force of his titanium will. Coldlake wouldn't be the same without him. *I* wouldn't be the same without him.

But the four of us made a pact a long time ago. *If you've got the chance to take the killer out, you do it, no hesitating. No matter the consequences.*

And here I am, hesitating.

He'd want me to do it. For Sienna. For Ophelia, Amalia and Evelina. I have to do it for Lorenzo, for the torture that awaits him at the hands of this killer if I don't end this now.

I heft the heavy weapon in my grip, flick off the safety, and peer through the sights. Someone runs to my side. Vinicius. He gives a moan of anguish like an animal in pain, but he doesn't stop me.

I wish he'd fucking stop me.

I aim at the van's back doors, my chest so tight that my lungs are burning. I'm a monster again. I'm a fucking monster and I'm going to kill one of my best friends.

My last thought before I squeeze the trigger is... *How am I going to tell Chiara?*

3

Chiara

The heavy metal door creaks open and a muscular, bearded man with bright blue eyes appears. He glances at me, then looks at Acid and shakes his head.

"Are you sure?" Acid asks.

"One hundred percent."

I look from one man to the other, trying to discern whether they're happy about whatever's happened or not.

Acid gets to his feet. "Let's roll, your highness."

"What's going on?" I ask, wondering where we're rolling to. Is Acid going to ransom me to the syndicate or Dad? I could be face to face with my father within the hour. I wonder if he'll kill me or lock me up.

Thane comes forward and cuts through the rope that's holding me to the chair, though my arms are still lashed to my torso. Then he dips his shoulder and hauls me over it. I spit curses at him as he carries me through the door and up some dank steps.

I'm placed on my feet on some dingy patterned carpet. Music is playing on a flashing jukebox. Bottles of liquor line one wall.

Is this Strife?

Acid heads over to the bar. "What's your poison, your highness? You can have anything you want as long as it's whiskey or beer."

I stare straight ahead, my teeth gritted.

The bearded man is leaning against the bar, his arms folded as he glares at me.

"Who are you?" I ask.

"Zagreus."

I don't think I've heard of him. I'm about to ask him what he does, when someone dressed in black blows through the front door so fast that it slams against the wall. Blond hair flies around his face and his white-blue eyes sparkle with fury.

"I will fucking kill you, Acid!" Lorenzo roars at the top of his lungs. "I will rip off your balls and make you eat them. I will tear your flesh from your bones and feed you to the Coldlake fucking catfish."

I take a sharp, grateful breath at the sight of Lorenzo, angrier than I've ever seen him but all in one piece. I blink rapidly, tears of gratitude and relief swimming in my eyes.

He's alive.

He's alive.

Salvatore comes through the door behind him, also dressed in black. He's holding an assault rifle and his expression is murderous. The two of them both search me with their eyes, and I manage a smile for them.

I'm okay.

You're both okay, too.

This nightmare is finally over.

"Cassius and Vinicius—"

Salvatore speaks quickly. "They're fine, baby. They're looking after someone for us. Hold tight, we're going to get you out of here in just a moment."

I can't do much more than hold tight while I'm still tied up. Lorenzo stares at the ropes on my body and then turns to Thane. "Are you fucking kidding me?"

Thane folds his arms and shrugs. His catlike eyes almost seem amused.

Salvatore frowns at the ropes. "Is that shibari?"

"Yes," Lorenzo hisses.

"What's shibari?" I ask, and then immediately wish I hadn't. Acid starts to laugh and then smothers it with a hand over his mouth. I can tell he's still grinning, though.

Lorenzo reaches inside his jacket and then growls in frustration as he realizes he doesn't have his knife anymore. He threw it into the canal the night he first kissed me. "Someone give me a blade. *Now.*"

Thane produces his small knife again and steps toward me. "I'll do it."

"You're not going near her." Lorenzo snatches the blade from him. He turns his back to Acid and Thane and comes over to me. Instead of getting to work on the ropes, he wraps his arms around me and presses his forehead against mine, eyes closed. His breathing is harsh and uneven and his whole body is rigid.

"Are you all right, princess?" he asks in a tight whisper, not opening his eyes.

"I'm fine. Nothing happened to me. What happened to you? I was so afraid."

"I'll explain later." Lorenzo pulls back and stares at the ropes crisscrossing my body, rage filling his expression. He works quickly and carefully with the blade, cutting through the knots and loops.

"What's shibari?"

"Japanese rope bondage," he says through his teeth.

My face flames. Don't look at Thane. Don't look at Thane.

I can't help myself. I shoot a glare at him over Lorenzo's shoulder and there's a faint smirk on his lips as he watches his tattered ropes fall around my feet.

As soon as my arms are free, I throw them around Lorenzo. He holds me, his grip fierce as he murmurs in my ear, "Give Salvatore and me one minute, and then we're getting you out of this hellhole."

I feel Salvatore's hand on the nape of my neck as Lorenzo pulls away. I fling my arms around him and he squeezes me against his chest and kisses my mouth. When I pull away from him, his eyes are alarmingly hollow.

"Are you all right?" I ask, touching his cheek.

He takes a shaky breath. "There was a near miss tonight. I think it's taken ten years off my life."

"What—" I start to ask, but Salvatore shakes his head and turns back to Acid and Thane, gripping his assault rifle like he's a split second away from opening fire at them.

"Your crew is safe; your woman is safe." Acid toasts Lorenzo with a glass of whiskey. "Everything's come up roses for the Coldlake Syndicate, just like it always fucking does. You're welcome, by the way."

A vein bulges in Lorenzo's forehead. "You're the backup crew. *The fucking backup crew.* You're the last ones on the list I want touching my woman unless it's absolutely necessary. When Orchid Protocol is enabled, you're meant to report to my security detail for instructions, not run them off the road and pistol-whip them."

Acid shrugs and takes a mouthful of whiskey. "Shows how shit your detail is if Thane and I were able to disable them."

The jukebox in the corner switches to a pounding metal track. Salvatore points his assault rifle at it and empties half a clip into the machine. I wince at the blast of gunfire. The jukebox explodes in a shower of sparks and falls silent.

Acid sighs. "Ah, man, that jukebox has been here longer than I have. It's a classic."

"What's Orchid Protocol?" I ask. "When they grabbed me, I thought they were the Black Orchid Killers."

"No. Just a bunch of *fucking assholes*," Lorenzo seethes.

"I set up an emergency protocol. If two or more conditions are met, it's triggered automatically. In this case, my phone registered that someone else was accessing it and my life signs went dark." He holds up his wrist and I see he's wearing a smartwatch. The screen has been smashed. "I got jumped and my phone fell out of my pocket."

"Nicole. Was she the one using your phone? I swear it was her voice."

Salvatore puts a hand on my shoulder, but his eyes are still trained on Acid. "Yes, it was Nicole. She's alive. I'll tell you everything in just a moment."

I take a deep, grateful breath. Nicole's alive. She wasn't killed because of me.

"Why did you do it, Acid?" Lorenzo snarls. "If you say it's because you were bored, I'll torch this place with you in it."

Acid swirls the whiskey in his glass. "I had my reasons."

Lorenzo waits.

"I thought you were dead. If you're gone, I'm not answering to any of those fancy fucks you call friends." Acid jerks his chin at Salvatore. "They don't know the first thing about what it takes to stay alive in the west. Snatching the Princess of Coldlake seemed like a good insurance plan."

"What would you have asked for in exchange?" Lorenzo asks.

Acid runs his tongue thoughtfully over his teeth. "Your quadrant. And Lasher." He glances at me and smiles, but I don't understand. I don't know who Lasher is. "I think I could have got both in exchange for her."

Salvatore glances at Thane and Zagreus. "You two were both in on this?"

"Strife sticks together," Zagreus tells him.

"Sure you do," he sneers. "How's Lasher these days?"

Zagreus gives him the finger.

Lorenzo pulls out a gun and points it at Acid's head. "Any last words?"

Salvatore turns the barrel of the assault rifle on Thane.

Acid shrugs, nonchalant as always, but his eyes burn with anger. "Dunno. Go fuck yourself?"

I remember how Acid's body looked riddled with bullets, and how Lorenzo pulled them all out and stitched him up. My blood runs in his veins. This is how Acid repays the people who saved his life.

I step forward and put my hand on Lorenzo's arm. "Don't kill him."

"What they did is unforgivable," Lorenzo says tightly.

"I know. I don't want you to forgive them." But if Lorenzo kills the Strife men, this place will be overrun by enemy gangs in no time and soon they'll be on Lorenzo's doorstep. The four of them have the Black Orchid Killer, my father, and the rest of Coldlake to contend with. It's Strife's job to hold back the gangs.

Salvatore tilts his head and quirks a brow at me. "Oh? What do you have in mind, baby?"

I look from Acid to Thane to Zagreus. "They're so keen to have Strife all to themselves. Let's give it to them."

"Princess—" Lorenzo growls through his teeth.

"Not officially. This is your territory and it's staying that way. What I mean is that the next time the Geaks or the Blood Pack attack, these three can fend them off without Lorenzo's help." I look at Acid. "The gangs want Lorenzo dead and I'm sick with worry every time he comes down here to save your ungrateful asses."

There's a bandage around Lorenzo's shoulder beneath his clothes. He was shot the night I killed Jax, the leader of the Geaks. The Geaks tried to torch Strife in revenge for the killing. Lorenzo was right here at Acid's side, fighting them off, and all the while they were waiting for their chance to double-cross the syndicate.

I step in front of Lorenzo's and Salvatore's weapons and face the three Strife men. "Lorenzo takes bullets for you all, and this is how you repay him. I'd like to see more gratitude from you, Acid. Until then, you're on your own."

"Please," Acid sneers. "Your precious Lorenzo was barely clipped while I was shot to pieces making money for your boyfriends." He lifts his shirt, showing the scars on his muscled chest and stomach.

My eyes narrow at the way he sneers *boyfriends*.

Go on, call me a slut.

I dare you.

"Watch the way you speak to me, Acid, or I'll step aside and you'll look worse than that jukebox in three seconds flat. You were making money for yourself while the syndicate was taking its rightful cut. Lorenzo's put his life on the line for you again and again. He doesn't interfere with how you run this place. I know that because he's too busy holding the rest of Coldlake together, along with Salvatore, Vinicius, and Cassius. Grow the hell up and realize that you already have everything you need. If you don't like it, go and team up with the Geaks, and I'll personally come after you and put a bullet in your head. Just like I did Jax."

"Are you finished?" Acid asks tightly, his eyes shooting sparks.

I glance at Thane, who hasn't said a word this entire time but is following the conversation with cold, narrowed eyes. Zagreus is watching me with tightly folded arms. "No, I'm not finished. You fucked up tonight, and now you owe me. All three of you. Whatever I want in the future, you're going to do it for me. You three go on breathing thanks to the Princess of Coldlake, and don't you ever forget it."

Salvatore hefts his assault rifle onto his shoulder. "Yeah. What she said."

As I meet Salvatore's eyes, he smiles and winks at me. I remember what Lorenzo said a few weeks ago when I told him that Salvatore and Cassius only want me to do as I'm told.

They're old-fashioned, but they'll come around soon enough. Show 'em what you're made of, and their dicks will be so hard they'll forget about everything else.

Lorenzo isn't lowering his weapon. His fingers are flexing on the gun grip like murder is the only thing that will make him feel better.

I touch his arm and say softly, "Let them be for now, for the sake of your sisters. We need to focus on their killer."

Finally, Lorenzo drops his arm. "If you ever put Chiara in danger again, I won't hesitate. She could beg for your worthless fucking life and I won't hear it."

We turn to go, but Acid can't resist having the last word. "Off you go, your highness. Next time you need saving, I'll be there."

I glance over my shoulder. "Other way around, Acid. Of the two of us, you're the one who always needs saving." I look meaningfully at his tank top that conceals the bullet wounds that Lorenzo stitched closed. The flesh that would be riddled with bullets right this second if it weren't for me.

He slaps his hand to his chest as if he's been shot. "Ah, you got me." Then he smiles broadly, green eyes glittering.

And I thought my men had the biggest egos in Coldlake.

Outside, the moon has set and there's no one about except for a few distant cars and a stray cat slinking through the bushes. Or is it a rat? Probably a rat. The Strife men are fiendishly possessive of this corner of Coldlake, rats and all.

Lorenzo holsters his gun, his expression bitter as we walk toward his car. "You were right to say what you said, princess, and you put those fuckers in their place. Unfortunately, if the gangs attack Strife—*when* the gangs attack Strife—I'll be down here fighting alongside Acid. I can't afford to lose this territory to the southwest."

"But you were a millisecond away from shooting them all."

"Doesn't mean I don't need them, the ungrateful fucks."

A sour taste fills my mouth as we approach Lorenzo's Mercedes G-Class 4WD. "It gets on my nerves how they take your help for granted. There are three of them and their security staff, and they're all armed. It's been nine years since you took over this part of Coldlake from Salvatore's father. When are they going to accept you're in charge?"

Lorenzo gives me a hard grin. "Maybe in another nine years."

Salvatore throws his assault rifle in the back of Lorenzo's car. He braces his hands on the roof of the vehicle, bows his head, and growls, "Jesus fucking Christ. *Jesus fucking Christ*."

I put my hand on his back. "Salvatore?"

He turns suddenly and sweeps me into his arms, and to my surprise, he yanks Lorenzo to him as well and the two of us are clenched savagely against his chest. His breathing is rough and panicked. "That was too close. Too fucking close."

"With Acid?" I ask.

"No. What happened earlier. Lorenzo—"

Lorenzo extricates himself from Salvatore and turns away. "Nothing. Let's get moving. Tonight isn't over yet."

But Salvatore grabs him by the shoulders, turns him around, and shakes him. He's turned a sickly shade of gray and his brow is clammy with sweat. "It's not nothing! I nearly killed you. One more millisecond and I would have pulled the trigger."

"Yeah, but you didn't." Lorenzo narrows his eyes, darts a look at me then back at Salvatore. His meaning is clear. *Not in front of Chiara.*

Yes, in front of Chiara. "What do you mean, you nearly killed him?"

Salvatore thrusts his hands through his hair. "Do you ever feel that another terrifying reality is so close it's like it could reach out and drag you away? Tonight was a fucking nightmare."

Lorenzo puts his hands on Salvatore's shoulders. "I'm fine. Chiara's fine. The others are safe. This is reality, what we're standing in right now."

"It nearly wasn't."

"But it is," Lorenzo insists and then mutters, "not that this reality can't fucking suck sometimes, too."

Salvatore shakes his head. "Let's not go through that again, okay?"

"It's not at the top of my bucket list," Lorenzo says, heading around the car to the driver's side.

I go to Salvatore and wrap my arms around his waist. It seems like he's had an even worse night than I have. "What happened tonight? Why did you nearly shoot Lorenzo?"

"Tell her while we drive," Lorenzo says, getting into the Mercedes and slamming the door.

Salvatore and I climb into the back seat and I hold him tightly, afraid to let go in case he's ripped away from me again.

He kisses the top of my head. "It's been a crazy few hours. I'm sorry we left without telling you where we were going."

"Never mind that now. Tell me what happened."

"The Black Orchid Killer was meeting De Luca tonight, we assumed so he could give De Luca the video of Nicole's murder. The killer told De Luca not to involve the police, so he approached us for help. De Luca told us where the meeting was taking place, but a group of fucking armored guards and the killer himself were waiting to ambush us."

"You're kidding. He knew you'd be there?"

"He was counting on it," Lorenzo mutters. "The killer wouldn't have got the jump on us, only Nicole suddenly appeared, staggering around like she was on drugs. I was following her, wondering what the hell a dead girl was doing there, when they grabbed me."

"Everything went crazy, and then I saw him," Salvatore says, the blood draining from his face. "He was standing in the back of a van, seeming to suck all the light and warmth out of the air around him. I know that sounds stupid. He's not a vampire or demon. He's only human, but he gave me chills."

"Try having him breathing down your neck," Lorenzo says through his teeth. "Demon is about fucking right."

Salvatore's arm is covered in goosebumps. So is the back of Lorenzo's neck.

"He grabbed Lorenzo and drove off with him," Salvatore says. "Lorenzo managed to tell me that there was a grenade launcher in the back of his car first, and I got it out. I had it pointed at the van and I was about to fire. And then—"

"Then I ran the van off the road and crashed it."

I cover my mouth with my hands in horror. No wonder Salvatore looks like he's seen a ghost.

"How did you even manage to do that?" Salvatore asks.

"I threw them off me by slamming them against the sides of the van, and then I dove for the steering wheel and twisted it. When we crashed, they all ran off."

I wrap my arms around Lorenzo's shoulders from behind and hug him tight. "You nearly died."

Lorenzo doesn't look away from the road ahead, but the corner of his mouth tilts up. "Please. You'd have to nuke me from orbit."

I press my lips against his throat. My men are flesh and blood and they could be ripped from me without warning. I don't want to forget that because I never want to take them for granted.

I sit back and hold Salvatore as tight as I can. "What a crazy night you've had. Where are Cassius and Vinicius?"

"Still back at the abandoned building. Lorenzo's taking us there now."

"Why?"

"Because we need your help with a ghost."

4
_____

Cassius

Panicked breathing emanates from inside the kitchen cabinet. I crouch on the dusty floor, resisting the temptation to rip it open, drag the girl out, and demand to know why she's alive.

Why you, and not my sister?

"Nicole De Luca. What happened to you?" I exchange glances with Vinicius, who looks as confused as I feel. It shouldn't be possible. Nicole De Luca was killed. I saw the pictures. The sadistic, blood-soaked pictures that were the handiwork of the Black Orchid Killer.

"My name is Cassius Ferragamo. Can you come out and talk to me?"

Nothing.

"I'm going to search the area for Mr. De Luca," Vinicius says softly. "He hasn't appeared and I'm worried about him."

Good point. De Luca was supposedly meeting the Black Orchid Killer here tonight, and the four of us planned to kill him. Then his last victim, Nicole De Luca, suddenly appeared, staggering like she'd been drugged. "Who brought you here, Nicole? Did you see his face?"

Vinicius waits to see if she's going to answer, then checks his gun and heads outside.

I ease myself down on the floor and get comfortable, my back against another one of the cabinet doors. Salvatore and Scava heard from Scava's men and they've gone to collect Chiara from Strife. They'll be at least another hour or two as they deal with Acid and the others. Anger burns through me at the thought of their filthy fucking hands all over our woman. I've met Acid a handful of times and I've always hated his swagger. His arrogance. His constant smirking. I hope they kill him slowly.

The floor beneath me is gritty. The pants I'm wearing are Italian wool and my sweater is black cashmere. I'm sitting in an abandoned kitchen in gang territory, trying to coax a frightened girl into talking to me. I could just rip the cabinet door open and drag her out. Scava suggested doing just that when we realized she'd crawled inside to hide, but even his heart wasn't in it. Nicole's been in the Black Orchid Killer's hands. Who knows how much he's already traumatized her.

I turn my head and ask her, "You went to St. Osanna Catholic Girls' School, didn't you?"

Silence.

"Chiara's missed you. She's talked about you often."

More silence. Maybe she's passed out.

"I'm from Naples. Do you speak Italian like Chiara? *Come è il tuo Italiano?*" *How is your Italian?*

Finally, she speaks in a frightened whisper, "*Bene.*" *Good.*

I continue softly in Italian, "I'm pleased to hear it. When you visit Italy, people will be impressed by the American girl who speaks our language so well."

"*Sì,*" she replies, and then whimpers, "Are you going to kill me?"

"No one is going to hurt you. I'm here to protect you. Vinicius is just outside and we're both armed. Whoever took you prisoner can't get to you now."

"But you can."

"You know who I am?"

"Everyone knows who you are. You're Cassius Ferragamo of the Coldlake Syndicate."

The drugs seem to have worn off and she's no longer slurring, but she is shivering in fear.

"Then you'll know I'm not a gangster. I'm a businessman. A lot of people who work for me are women and I treat them well."

Scared, injured women aren't good for business. Happy women smile. They dance better. They fuck better. They earn better money in my strip bars and sex clubs.

"Do you make Chiara work for you?"

"Of course I fucking don't," I growl. Let other men fuck my woman for money? I've endured rumors about myself since I became one of Francesco Fiore's captains at the age of twenty-four, but people saying that I'm whoring Chiara out is on another fucking level.

"Do you know what makes me happy, Nicole?"

"What?"

"Chiara."

Nicole takes a shaky breath. "What does happiness even mean to someone like you?"

"The same thing that it means to everyone. That the people I love are safe and taken care of."

"Chiara isn't happy. She never wanted to marry Salvatore, and then you kidnapped her. You've all been horrible to her. You're *monsters*."

Only the five of us know what the past few months have meant to all of us. It's been bloody, it's been brutal, and it's been beautiful.

"Even villains have hearts." Big hearts, to go with our ambitious plans and desires.

"Where was your heart when Chiara was being forced to marry Salvatore Fiore, and you kidnapped her from her wedding?"

I gaze across the darkened, decrepit kitchen, picturing Chiara in her beautiful white wedding gown, the veil in her golden hair that tumbled down her back. She clutched her bouquet of flowers and turned to me in a rustle of silk, her eyes wide and her lips parted. A beautiful bride, just eighteen years old and mine for the taking.

I scooped her up in my arms and walked out of that church with her, and I never looked back.

"My heart was lost, but Chiara found it. She found all our hearts."

Nicole is silent and I think that she's not going to reply, but she says in a tear-filled voice, "She did? That's... If anyone could find your hearts, she could. Chiara always saw the best in everyone."

Nicole dissolves into pitiful sobbing. I put my palm against the cabinet door, wondering if I should open it. "Nicole?"

Vinicius appears in the doorway and hisses, "Why is she crying? What did you do?"

I gesticulate angrily and whisper, "I don't know! She just started crying."

"Chiara is the best friend I ever had and I turned my back on her when she needed me," Nicole sobs. "I didn't want to, but Dad made me. She's never going to forgive me."

Vinicius comes over and crouches next to the cabinet door. "Nicole, it's Vinicius. I promise you that when Chiara gets here, all she's going to be is grateful that you're alive. Please tell us what happened here tonight and where you've been."

But Nicole goes on crying quietly, brokenly, and doesn't reply. We'll just have to wait for Chiara.

I send a text to the group chat. *We're still at the aban-*

doned building. Nicole's hiding in a cupboard and she won't come out. We need Chiara. Have you killed everyone at Strife yet?

I hope they have. Fucking Acid. Fucking Thane. Fucking Zagreus. I said all along that Lasher is the only one of the Strife men who's worth anything. The other three are slippery bastards who don't give a fuck about Coldlake and anyone in it except for themselves.

A message comes through from Salvatore. *Not yet.*

Then hurry up, I send.

A moment later Salvatore replies, *Be there in ten.*

I sigh and shove my phone in my pocket. Why do I get the feeling that Acid and the others aren't going to pay for this with their lives? After what they did tonight and the danger they put Chiara in, their blood and entrails should be painting the broken concrete outside their shitty bar.

Scava, I'm disappointed in you.

A few minutes later, we hear the purr of an engine. It cuts out and car doors slam. There are quick footsteps and Chiara hurries through the door as I get to my feet. Her eyes are wide and bewildered and she grasps my shoulder and touches my cheek as I pull her into my arms.

"*Bambina*, are you all right? Did they hurt you?"

"I'm absolutely fine. Where's Nicole?"

I step aside and point to the kitchen cabinet, and Chiara drops to her knees and calls softly through the wood.

"Nicole? It's me. Nicole, please come out."

I turn to Scava and say under my breath, "What happened at Strife?"

"I'll explain later," he says through clenched teeth. Salvatore is standing in the doorway and gazing at Chiara. The only person who could stop these men from doing what they set out to do is the small blonde woman who's currently sitting on the floor with her hands pressed against a cabinet door.

"Nicole? Please talk to me."

A hesitant voice carries through the wood. "Chiara?"

Chiara's eyes widen and fill with tears. "It *is* you. You're alive. Oh, my God, you're alive. Please come out. I promise no one is going to hurt you."

Slowly, the cabinet door creaks open. A head with dark hair appears, and a tear-streaked face. Nicole's eyes lock with Chiara's, and both girls throw their arms around each other, shoulders shaking with sobs.

"You're *alive.*"

Nicole buries her face in Chiara's shoulder and cries, "I'm sorry, I'm so sorry."

The four of us stand over the girls and exchange glances. The *I'm sorries* bother me. What does Nicole have to be sorry about?

"I tried to stop them, but they wouldn't listen to me." Nicole pulls away from Chiara and her petrified gaze darts from one of us to the next. "I never wanted to do it. Please don't kill me."

5

Chiara

"No one's going to hurt you," I assure my friend. "You're safe now. Come on, we've got to get you out of here. We'll take you somewhere safe. Lorenzo?"

I look to the blond man for permission to bring her to the compound. His jaw is tight, and it looks like he's tempted to put his gun to Nicole's head and demand she tell us what the fuck is going on right this second, but he nods.

Cassius steps forward and helps me to my feet. "Chiara, you and Nicole come with me. Scava, lead the way, and the two of you follow behind. Keep your weapons handy. He's still out there, somewhere."

A shiver goes down my spine. The Black Orchid Killer. He was here tonight. He nearly took Lorenzo prisoner, and Salvatore was going to kill his friend rather than let him be tortured to death like his sister. If Nicole had a part in this plan then I don't know what I'm going to do.

We have to know what she knows. It could be the answer to everything.

The men walk in lockstep around Nicole and me as we head for the cars. I sit with Nicole in the back of Cassius' white SUV, my arm around her shaking body. Her skin feels frozen and her face is sickly and washed out.

As soon as we pull into the garage at the compound and get out of the cars, I turn to Lorenzo. "Can you please check Nicole over to make sure she's okay? I think she's been drugged."

Irritation suffuses his handsome face. He looks ready to interrogate her rather than examine her, but he nods. "Bring her through."

I take Nicole's hand and lead her down the concrete hallway. At the door to Lorenzo's operating-room-slash-doctor's-office-slash-morgue, she freezes in her tracks, her eyes wide.

"I know it looks scary. I hated this room the first time I saw it, too, but I promise that you're safe here. Lorenzo is a doctor."

"I'm not a doctor," he replies, and I shoot him a look as Nicole turns even paler. Now is not the time to split hairs.

He pats one of the metal tables. "Come on. Up here." Then he stands back and folds his arms. I can practically hear him counting to ten. If she doesn't do as he orders, quickly, he's going to walk out.

"I'm right here, Nicole. I won't leave you alone. Lorenzo has examined me plenty of times and I promise you're in good hands."

Lorenzo darts a sly look at me, as if recalling the "examinations" he's given me. Bites. Needles. Scalpels. Bloodletting. All kinds of fun.

Nicole seems like she wants to run far, far away, but I slowly convince her to sit on the table. Lorenzo gets to work, taking her pulse and blood pressure and listening to her heart. He shines a light in and out of her eyes, just like he did the night Vinicius was beaten over the head with a baseball bat. He examines her nails, and then pushes back her sleeves and checks her forearms.

"What are you looking for?" I ask him.

"Defensive wounds. Broken nails." To Nicole, he says, "Did anyone hurt you? Attack you?"

She shakes her head.

"Were you given any drugs?"

"Pills."

"How long ago?"

"Tonight. Earlier. I don't know."

"Do you know what kind?"

She shakes her head again.

"Probably tranqs," he mutters and turns to me. "She'll sleep off the drugs and she'll probably feel sick tomorrow, but other than that, she's fine. She can stay here, and you can talk to her, but I'm locking her in one of the upstairs rooms."

My mouth falls open. "She was taken prisoner by the Black Orchid Killer. Try and find some compassion."

Lorenzo's expression turns glacial. "Was she?"

He steps back and leans against the counter, arms folded.

I stare between the two of them. Wasn't she? I look at Nicole's arms and her face. There's not a mark on her. She hasn't been restrained or handled roughly. She hasn't fought for her life. It's strange, but I'm not going to draw any conclusions until Nicole's had the chance to speak for herself. "I'm going to take Nicole upstairs, help her change into some of my pajamas and put her to bed."

Lorenzo shakes his head, mistrust filling his expression. "Not by yourself, you're not. Not until she's been strip-searched. Actually, not even then."

"Nicole's not going to hurt me."

"Maybe. Maybe not. Do you think I'm going to take that risk when it's your life on the line?"

I take a deep breath and let it out slowly. "I'm going to put Nicole to bed. You can stand outside the door if you feel it's necessary, but that's *it*."

His eyes flare with anger. I haven't forgotten his expression as he burst into Strife. He was beyond furious, but he was terrified as well. I go to him and put my hands on his chest, gazing up at him.

"I'm fine," I whisper. "You're fine. Everyone's in one piece."

Lorenzo's scowl deepens. He's furious, but not with me. With himself. "Orchid Protocol was meant to keep you safe, not put you in more fucking danger."

"It was a good idea, but it would have been nice to know about before it happened. Have you got any more tricks like that up your sleeve?"

He shakes his head.

"Good. I didn't enjoy that. I'll listen to whatever plans you have to keep me safe, but you have to tell me about them first."

I go up on my tiptoes and press my mouth against his. A promise for later.

"You need to de-stress," I say softly.

"You're fucking right about that," he growls, kissing me back even harder.

I glance over my shoulder at Nicole, whose eyes are blank like she's retreated into her mind. I whisper furtively, "As soon as we have time, we can go to your room and you can take all your frustrations out on my body. And I'll say thank you and come all over your dick."

Lorenzo's hands clench on my waist and his gaze becomes feral. "I'll hold you to that, princess."

"You can. But I'll take Nicole upstairs now."

He takes a deep breath and growls, "Fine. But I'm waiting outside that door, and we're locking her in until I can track down De Luca. He's got some explaining to do."

Together, we walk an unresponsive Nicole up to one of the spare bedrooms. I grab some joggers and one of my favorite big T-shirts. It's not until I pass Lorenzo that I realize it's one of his T-shirts, and he snatches it out of my hands.

"That's not for other girls. Get her a different one."

Instead, I get one of the T-shirts Cassius bought me when I was a prisoner at his penthouse and go into the spare bedroom and close the door. Nicole is sitting on the edge of the mattress.

"You all right in there, princess?" Lorenzo calls through the door almost immediately.

"Just unstrapping all the guns and knives from Nicole's body."

"*What?*"

"I'm kidding."

"Now is not the time for jokes," he mutters.

I put the clothes on the bed next to Nicole and sit down next to her. Wordlessly, I put my arm around her shoulders and hold her. "You tried to warn us there was danger. Thank you."

Nicole stares at her hands in her lap.

"I'm so happy you're alive. I thought you were dead."

She looks away, her face creasing. "I never wanted to do it. They made me."

"Do what? Who is they?"

But Nicole pulls away and lays down, covering her head with the blanket and sobbing harder than ever. "It was a trap for those four men. I'm sorry. I'm so sorry."

I stroke her shoulder for a few minutes, my touch soft but confusion rolling through me. I want to demand she sit up and tell me what's going on, but she's been through enough already tonight.

When I leave the bedroom, Lorenzo is gone and Cassius is waiting outside for me. He's still dressed in a black sweater that's tight across his muscles and his brown eyes are almost black in the dim light. I reach up and touch his curls, going up on tiptoe so I can be closer to him. My big bear of a man.

Before I can say a word, he sweeps me into his arms and squeezes me tight. There's a lot of Italian growling in my ear, and I catch the words *Strife, Acid,* and *fucking kill that motherfucker.*

He pulls away and takes my face in his hands. "*Bambina*, I thought we were all going to die. Us, and you. I have not endured such a night in nine years."

Cassius' mouth descends on mine. His hot tongue parts my lips and I'm pressed back against the wall, his hard body searing my own as he presses into me.

"Where are the others?" I ask between feverish kisses.

"Lorenzo and Salvatore have gone out to look for De Luca. Vinicius is searching the crashed van." He slides his hands down to my ass and squeezes me, all of his fingers digging into my flesh. "I need you, *bambina*. Now."

I need him, too. I look up and down the hall. My room is right next door, but I don't like the idea of Nicole over-hearing me taking a pounding from one of the Coldlake Syndicate. Lorenzo's is farther down the hall but it would be inconsiderate leaving his sheets smelling like sex while he's out there working. Lorenzo's wound up enough as it is.

I take Cassius' hand and head downstairs to the living room. With the lights off, the sofa looks private and inviting.

Between hungry kisses, Cassius strips my clothes from my body and then lays down on the sofa on his back.

"Come on. Come and sit on my face. I want to eat you up."

He coaxes me up his body until I'm straddling his face. "Are you sure? Can you breathe?"

The first swipe of his tongue shuts me up. *Oh, God.*

Cassius holds me by the hips with his big hands, moving his mouth and tongue slowly against me. Savoring me. His chest with its sprinkling of dark hair is hot against the backs of my thighs. I close my eyes and enjoy it. He can worry about whether he can breathe.

While he licks me, Cassius unfastens his pants and his cock stands up proudly. I reach behind me to stroke him up and down, caressing the ridges and veins of his length. I wriggle back down his body and get rid of the rest of his clothes. His burning hot skin feels intense against my inner thighs. The sight of the swollen head of his cock makes my mouth water, and I wrap my hand around the base and sink down his length with a sigh.

He holds up his hands and I thread my fingers through his. We hold each other, palm to palm, while I rock back and forth on his cock. Every movement of my hips feels like heaven as I drive him deep into me and then out again.

"Don't ever leave without telling me," I whimper,

working out all my frustration on his length. "Don't do anything like that again."

"You're magnificent," Cassius murmurs, gazing at my breasts, my hips, my sex.

"Promise me," I gasp.

"We promise, *bambina*. We won't do that again. I'm right here with you."

I give myself exactly what I want. The pace I need. The depth of the thrusts. The delicious stroke and slide of his thick length. I lose myself in it, letting his strength support me and feeling embraced by his hungry gaze. When I come, I want to cry out long and loud but I remember just in time to bite my lip and moan his name in a whisper.

"Isn't that perfect?" Cassius murmurs, and then suddenly grasps my hips and thrusts up into me.

My eyes fly open and my hands land on his chest. His brows draw together and he's laser-focused on pounding me from below. Urgent, delicious thrusts that have me wanting to shout even louder than before.

He pulls me up and off him, his muscular chest heaving as he finishes in his hand. When he opens his brown eyes, he blinks slowly and his whole body relaxes.

"What a fucking night it's been. That's so much better."

Cassius is not wrong there.

He tucks one hand behind his head and gazes up at me, a finger playing around my nipple. "Those Strife assholes better not have touched you."

I shake my head, resolving not to tell Cassius about the rope bondage when he's finally relaxed. He looks so handsome, lying beneath me with a smile playing around his lips. My bear of a man who shows a ferocious face to the world but loves to hold and cuddle me in secret.

I stroke my fingers down the black hairs on his chest. "Can I tell you something?"

"Of course."

"I love you, Cassius."

His eyes widen—and then he smiles. "What made you say that now?"

"Because it's true, and I wanted to."

He goes on smiling, stroking his fingers through my hair and saying nothing.

I sit up. "Why aren't you saying it back? Do you not love me?"

Cassius cradles me against his chest. "So impatient. I was enjoying the moment. The first time my beautiful girl says *I love you. Ti amo, bambina.* Of course I love you."

"I haven't said this to the others—"

A triumphant smile flashes over his face. "I'm the first?"

I press a finger to his lips. "So you can't say anything. And no crowing about being first. It doesn't mean I love them any less than I love you."

"I know." *But I'm still first* is written all over his face.

"You don't doubt that I love the others as well?"

He cups my cheek, his expression gentle. "Of course you love them. There was never any doubt in my heart that when you fell for one of us, you would fall for all of us. I see the way you look at the others. How you touch them and care about them. It's fucking beautiful."

There's not one trace of jealousy or envy in his face. What big hearts these men have, for each other and for me. "You like the way I look at them and touch them?"

He kisses me. "I do. It's so sexy, *bambina*."

"Cassius loves to watch."

"Cassius does," he agrees with a heated smile.

His pants start to ring, and he reaches down and pulls out his phone. There's a video call coming through from Lorenzo, and he answers it. "Scava."

"Hey, I—" Lorenzo begins and then notices me cuddled on Cassius' chest. A smile flashes over his face. "Hey, princess. Did you get railed?"

"She did," Cassius replies, pressing a kiss to my temple.

"Fuck you getting sex while I'm out here working," Lorenzo says, but I can tell he's not really angry.

"I have to make sure my *bambina* is happy," Cassius purrs.

"More like make your dick happy. How was the sex?"

"Wonderful, thank you. Did you find De Luca?"

Lorenzo sighs and pushes his hand through his hair. "Not at his house. Not anywhere. His wife couldn't tell me much, though I think they're getting a divorce. It doesn't sound like she wanted to go along with her daughter's fake-death plan. Mostly she screamed at me to give Nicole back."

Poor Mrs. De Luca. She's put up with so much from her

husband over the years and this must be the final straw. "Did you tell her that Nicole's safe here for now?"

"I tried, princess. She wasn't in the mood to listen and said she would call the cops if I didn't—" Suddenly he breaks off and growls, "Cassius, is that my sofa? Is your bare fucking ass on my sofa?"

Cassius grins. "And my balls. My balls are all over your sofa, Scava."

"I'm going to throw up."

"Chiara's beautiful ass is all over your sofa, too."

"Chiara's beautiful ass should be all over my face. Home in ten." He hangs up.

"And I was just thinking how the four of you love each other so much, and that's why this works so well."

Cassius reaches for his underwear and pants and puts them on. "I love that man like a brother, but I will never miss a chance to wind him up, and neither will he."

I drag my underwear up my legs and put on Cassius' shirt. I'm cuddled against him with my legs tucked beneath me when we hear the front gates grind open and a car drives down into the underground garage.

"I see you've put some fucking pants on," Lorenzo mutters a few minutes later as he strides in. He leans over and presses his mouth against mine in a hungry kiss. "Not you, princess. Never put pants on. In fact..." He reaches beneath Cassius' shirt for my underwear and drags them down my legs. "Panties off. I'm fucking you now."

He pulls me down the couch toward him and unbuttons his jeans, shoving them down a few inches and taking out his cock.

"I can see you're still wet from being fucked, princess. How much would it take for you to..." He shoves two fingers inside me, and I gasp. "Come again?"

I reach back and grasp the back of the sofa. Very little, by the feel of it. The slow screwing by Cassius will be perfectly topped off by a fast fuck from Lorenzo.

Lorenzo pulls his fingers out of me, leans over, and spits on my pussy. My body twitches and I gasp at the sensation.

He glances at Cassius with a wicked smile. "Spit on her, too?"

Cassius leans forward and rubs his middle finger over my clit, and then spits on it, so I'm glistening wet. My mouth opens in shock. That shouldn't be so arousing.

"Perfect," Lorenzo purrs as he grasps his cock and sinks into me. He groans as he thrusts deep. "I've been aching for this for hours."

Cassius props his temple on his fist and watches us, his dark eyes glittering.

"How did Cassius fuck you, princess?" Lorenzo asks, clearly enjoying having an audience. His speed picks up until he's fucking me with hard, greedy thrusts.

My breathing becomes uneven and I can't tear my eyes away from the sight of Lorenzo's cock pumping in and out of me. "He sat me on his face and told me I was pretty."

"Of course he did. Cassius' sweet angel. Now you're

Lorenzo's dirty bitch, aren't you?" He moves his hips back and forth in a hard, relentless rhythm.

"Yes, oh God, I am."

Cassius reaches between us and swirls his fingers lazily over my clit. "*Bambina*, are you going to be a good girl and come on Scava's cock?"

"Do as Cassius says, princess."

I look from one man's face to the next as they devour me with their eyes and hands, intent on making me burst apart in pleasure. My cries become panting wails until my head tips back and my body arches in climax.

"Fuck, yes," Lorenzo says through clenched teeth. "Milk my cock with that pussy of yours, princess."

He groans suddenly and pulls out, hovering over me and pumping his cock up and down in his fist. A moment later he spurts ribbons of cum all over Cassius' shirt that's half open on my breasts.

"Oh, shit. I got cum all over your shirt, Cassius." Lorenzo laughs softly, not sounding sorry at all.

Cassius shoots him a dark look but holds his tongue, probably because we defiled his sofa together not long ago.

I take off the shirt and ball it up, and Lorenzo gives me his T-shirt to wear instead as he pulls me into his arms.

"Kiss me, princess. I was nearly a dead man tonight."

His mouth descends on mine and he kisses me like we've been separated for a hundred years. I wrap my arms around his neck, my expression anguished. "I don't even want to think about that. Promise me you won't be careless with your life. I need you. We all do."

Lorenzo sinks his teeth into my lower lip, and then murmurs, "I promise I won't be reckless, but some things are worth dying for. Salvatore would have been right to pull the trigger if I hadn't crashed the van."

I trace the patterns of the tattoos on his muscled chest as he kisses me again. Better to die quickly at the hands of a friend than slowly in the clutches of an enemy, he means.

There's the sound of the gates opening, and a few minutes later Vinicius and Salvatore walk in. Both men look exhausted, but Salvatore smiles as he sees Lorenzo lift his mouth from mine.

"Well, well, well, look who's learned to kiss after all these years. I always knew you were a big fucking softie."

Lorenzo reaches for Salvatore. "You want one, too?"

Salvatore grins and shoves him away. "Fuck off. Did you enjoy yourself, baby?" he asks, turning to me, eyeing my rumpled hair and Lorenzo's T-shirt covering me, and Cassius sitting on the sofa without his shirt. "Looks like you did."

I look around at the four men, my heart feeling very full at the sight of them all in one room and in one piece. If I were in danger of taking any of this for granted, I'm definitely not now. "Always. And I'm even happier now I'm with you all."

Salvatore leans down to kiss me. "And I'm always happy when I get to come back to you."

"Me, too, kitten," Vinicius says, taking Salvatore's place a moment later and giving me one of his heavenly kisses.

He buries his face in my hair and breathes in deeply. "Mm, you smell like sex."

Now that we're all together, I look closely from one man to the next. "Is there anything you'd like to say to me about what happened tonight?"

I'm not angry that they crept off to confront the Black Orchid Killer without telling me, but I'm hoping that this can be a turning point for all of us.

Lorenzo and Vinicius exchange glances.

"I'm sorry you suddenly found yourself on your own," Vinicius says. "That was my fault, kitten. I wanted to wake you up with the good news that the killer was dead and it was all over."

"He wanted to protect you from worrying about us," Salvatore adds. "We all did."

Not worry about my men? Fat chance of that. "I worry about you even more if you suddenly all disappear."

"We won't do that again, *bambina*."

The others nod, and I can tell from their exhausted, shell-shocked expressions that they mean it. No one wants a do-over of tonight ever again.

"Good. Thank you." I settle back in Cassius' arms and rest against his bare chest.

"What did you all find out tonight?" he asks the others as they collapse onto the sofas around us.

"Fuck all," Salvatore tells us. "De Luca must be scared of us and he's gone to ground."

"There was nothing in that van," Vinicius adds. "It's probably stolen and won't tell us anything."

Salvatore shakes his head with troubled eyes. "There were men working with the Black Orchid Killer. He had a team and they grabbed Lorenzo. Doesn't that seem crazy to anyone else?"

Lorenzo's expression darkens. "Crazy, but we've seen this before. Sienna was dragged into a black car. There needed to be at least a driver and a kidnapper working together."

I feel Cassius tense against my side. "It was the same when Evelina was taken."

Salvatore stares across the room as if trying to make sense of this. "It makes me wonder if the killer is involved in organized crime somehow, or if he's in some position of power."

Vinicius darts an apologetic glance at me. "I've wondered once or twice if the killer is the mayor."

Salvatore shakes his head. "The man I saw wasn't Romano. The mayor is stocky. This man was lean."

I can understand why Vinicius would wonder about that. Dad is obsessed with power, and he's a killer, but he's also the most pragmatic man I know. He wouldn't waste time dropping flowers on sidewalks and setting up recording equipment.

"It doesn't seem like something Dad would do. When he killed Mom, he was quick, like a butcher. This psycho thinks he's some kind of artist." There's an unpleasant silence as we all remember the sadistic and grandiose ways their sisters were murdered.

Vinicius sighs. "You're probably right. I can't believe we

were all so close to him and then he escaped. But we'll keep looking. There are a few things I plan on asking Thane."

Salvatore's expression turns murderous, and I can tell he's remembering the red ropes.

"What can Thane help you with?" I ask, trying to muffle a yawn, but failing. Outside the window, the sky is just beginning to lighten.

Vinicius smiles at me fighting to stay awake. "That's for later. You can barely keep your eyes open, kitten, and neither can I. Let's all get some sleep."

"Is everyone staying here at the compound?" I ask.

They all exchange glances and Vinicius nods. "We'll sleep here and talk more when we wake up."

I reach up and cup Cassius' cheek. I haven't had my fill of his body against mine, yet. "Will you come and sleep in my room?"

He kisses my forehead. "Of course, *bambina.*"

We head upstairs and I strip off my clothes and get into bed naked. So does Cassius, and he wraps his big, warm body around me. I run my finger down the black bristles on his cheek. He's so handsome, and I imagine what he'll look like in five, maybe ten years' time when there will be silver bristles among the black. He'll be even more handsome, and sexy as hell.

"I haven't dared to think about the future too much," I whisper. "Do you think that one day this will all be over and we'll be free to be completely happy?"

"After what you told me tonight, that you love me? I know we will. All of us."

I'm bathed in the warmth from his chest. His love for me burns even hotter, and I feel it surrounding us. "Suddenly finding that you were all gone was awful. I never want to feel that way again."

Cassius has his eyes closed and he holds me tighter. "Nothing like that will ever happen again."

I wrap my arm around him and snuggle closer. As exhaustion sweeps over me and I melt into his arms, I whisper, "Good. I don't think I can handle any more surprises."

6

Vinicius

I open Chiara's door just after midday and she's fast asleep in Cassius' arms. Cassius opens his eyes, but he stays still apart from raising one questioning black brow at me.

Nicole, I mouth, and indicate the room next door with my head, and he nods, closing his eyes again.

Someone needs to have a private word with Chiara's former best friend, and I'm the best man to do it. The others are too short-tempered and intimidating to get one word out of the girl.

Lorenzo's given me the key and I unlock the door and go inside. Nicole is beneath the blankets, sleeping the deep sleep of the recently drugged. I watch her for a while, hands in my pockets, wondering what the best way is to handle this. Whatever I tell her and no matter what I do, she's going to assume I'm dangerous.

I sit down on the mattress, hard enough to jostle her body. Nicole's eyelashes flutter, and she mumbles before blinking and opening her eyes. Bleary, bewildered eyes. I swear that for a moment, she thinks I'm a hallucination.

I smile at her. "Hello."

She sucks in a frightened breath and sits up, crawling back up the bed. "Where am I? Who are you? What do you want?"

"This is Lorenzo Scava's compound, one of the most secure buildings in Coldlake. You're safe here. I'm Vinicius Angeli, and I want to talk to you."

Nicole stares at me and then at the closed door. "I don't feel safe. I'm locked in here with you."

I smile at her. "True. But I promise I mean you no harm."

Nicole turns pale and looks like she wants to throw up. I can't tell if it's the drugs or if she's terrified of me.

"Who asked you to pretend to be dead?"

She presses her face into her knees and moans. "I want to go home. I want my mom."

Tough. I don't doubt that she's been through an ordeal, but she's not leaving until I find out what the hell is going on. "Was it your father? Did he set a trap for us?" Her body shakes in fear and I sense I'm on the right track. I make my tone gentle. "Did you believe you were helping to save Chiara? I'm not going to hurt you or be angry with you about something you thought was the right thing for your friend."

Nicole refuses to lift her head, and I know she doesn't believe me.

I watch her thoughtfully with narrowed eyes. We could go around in circles like this for hours. "Let me start by telling you what we know, and then you can fill in the rest. How does that sound?"

"Where's Chiara?"

"She's asleep in the next room. She went through hell last night. You see, Nicole, people are always screwing with us. Chiara's father. My associates. It's so difficult to know who to trust and believe." For a moment I let my tone harden, and then smile again. "But between the two of us, I'm sure we can straighten out the truth from the lies. You and Chiara have been friends since you were children. Is that right?"

"Yes," she whispers. "She was my best friend."

"All right, then. So here's what I know about you and your father, and you can tell me if I get anything wrong. When Chiara became engaged to Salvatore last year, your father told you that you couldn't be her friend anymore. He didn't want to be friends with the mayor either, did he? But in the past few months, I'm guessing that Mr. De Luca and Mayor Romano made up. Perhaps around the time of the mayor's press conference when he claimed that we'd all kidnapped Chiara and there was a price on our heads?"

Nicole stifles a sob, and she nods again.

I thought as much. De Luca hasn't got any reason to entrap us, but his dear old friend the mayor has plenty.

"How scared you must have been for Chiara. I'm guessing that the mayor came to your house and spoke with your father, and then they spoke to you. They asked if you would help them draw the Coldlake Syndicate into the open so they could save Chiara and bring her home. Am I right?"

Nicole lifts her head slowly, her eyes huge and shining. "How do you know that?"

I smile at her. "Just a lucky guess. I'm a lucky man, Nicole."

"The mayor promised that he wouldn't hurt any of you. He just said that he wanted Chiara back."

Naïve fucking girl. What did she think was going to happen? That she and Chiara would go home and be best friends again, and the mayor would forget how much the syndicate had humiliated him?

Nicole must see the flash of anger in my eyes, as she flinches. "I just wanted to help Chiara. I wish I'd never posed for those horrible photos."

I wince as I remember the photos supposedly showing Nicole's dead and mutilated body. Not only were they graphic, but Nicole was posted in the Black Orchid Killer's gory style. "How did the mayor know what the photos should look like?"

"Mayor Romano had some of the crime scene photos from..." She trails off with a shudder. "From the other murders. I was spattered with fake blood and just had to lie there, and then someone working for the mayor touched them up to make them look worse. The whole thing was horrible and I didn't want to see the pictures."

No, I imagine she didn't. How grotesque, asking a young woman to fake being a murder victim.

"That's everything I've figured out for myself, Nicole. What I don't understand is what you were doing there last night."

Nicole twists her fingers together. "They lied to me, Dad and the mayor. I overheard the mayor telling Dad he was going to kill you all. You were supposed to go into the building, and there was someone standing by with a weapon to blow you all up. I lost it when I heard that. Dad made me take pills and tried to lock me in my room. I threw the pills up, but I don't think I got all of them." She rubs a hand over her eyes. "Everything's blurry after that. I hid in Dad's car and I intended to warn you all that it was a trap."

"You're lucky you're alive. You realize you could have been killed along with the rest of us?" I suppose the mayor or De Luca were watching the building, and they called off the plan when they saw Nicole.

"I wasn't thinking straight. The next thing I remember, I was talking to Chiara on the phone. I tried to warn her. You have to believe me that I didn't want any of you to die." Nicole implores me with huge, scared eyes.

"Did you remember what happened to your father? We didn't see him there. It seems he ran and left you behind. Your father is a weak and stupid man."

Nicole nods sadly. "That's what Mom says. I think she's really going to leave him this time." Her face crumples. "But he's still my dad. Please don't kill him. He was only doing what he thought was right. You shouldn't have taken Chiara and you have to let her go!"

"Chiara wants to be with us."

Nicole wipes the tears from her face and raises her chin. "If she does, it's only because she's confused or you've tricked her. Her mother was murdered by one of you."

I sigh and shake my head. "Nicole, the mayor murdered his wife. He slit her throat in front of all of us, including Chiara."

Her face transforms in horror. "That's not true!"

"You can ask her yourself."

"You'll let her talk to me? Even though we're both prisoners here?"

"Chiara doesn't need permission from us. She's in this house willingly, and she's our lover willingly. Our woman."

Nicole's expression is equal parts confusion and disgust. It stays that way as I stand up.

"When you do talk to Chiara, please be tactful about how you bring up her mother. Mayoress Romano was murdered right in front of her, and Chiara's never got justice. It's likely that she never will."

"When can I go home?" she calls after me.

I hesitate by the door and turn back to her. "I don't know. When it's safe."

"Why wouldn't I be safe?" she asks. "Are you going to hurt me?"

I shake my head. "Your father made you pose as a victim of the Black Orchid Killer. Your fake death was in all the papers and the killer will know that someone's copied him. If I were him, that would make me angry and I might want to finish you off for real."

Nicole's face goes slack with horror as I head out of the room and close the door behind me.

Downstairs in the silent kitchen, I make myself coffee and call Thane.

"Yes?" he says in his flat monotone when he picks up.

"The photos of Nicole De Luca's dead body. The ones you downloaded from the police server the morning Nicole's body was found. Did you notice anything strange about them?"

"Why?"

"They're fake."

"They didn't look fake."

"Why don't you check?"

"Why should I?"

My teeth clench. There's not one trace of shame in his voice after what he and the Strife men did last night. "Because I've just been having a chat with the girl in the fucking pictures."

I hear rapid typing, then a hiss of anger.

"Well?" I ask.

Thane's voice is tight with fury. "The photos were created three days before they were uploaded to the cloud."

Three days before Nicole was supposedly killed.

Chiara sobbed her heart out over her dead friend. We could have spared her that if Thane had been paying attention to his goddamn job.

"Vinicius—"

"Shut up and listen to me. That girl was Chiara's best friend and we told her she was dead because of you. You have no idea the suffering you've caused that girl. I pay you to work for me, not set up mutinies behind my fucking back. If it wasn't for Chiara and what she wants, I'd kill you myself."

Dead silence on the line.

"I know," he says without inflection.

"If anything happens to Lorenzo or anyone else in the Coldlake Syndicate, I'll make sure that Strife is razed to the ground and you three are driven off those streets out of pure spite."

I wish it hadn't come to this. Thane and I always had a good relationship. He's always been happy—in his peculiar way—to work for me because the work I give him is challenging and interesting. I used to respect him.

"That's fair."

"Yes, I know it's fair. If Chiara ever needs anything from you, I expect you to do whatever she wants without complaint."

"Can I ask you a question?"

"About what?"

"What's it like sharing a woman?"

"You piece of shit." I hang up and throw my phone onto the counter, cursing Thane to hell.

Lorenzo is standing in the doorway, his arms folded. Behind him, I can see Chiara and Cassius coming down the stairs.

"Thane?" Lorenzo asks.

"Yes."

"Why is he a piece of shit?"

I consider telling Lorenzo purely for the pleasure of watching him pick up a gun and load it with a bullet with Thane's name on it. "You don't want to know."

We head to the lounge and sit down on the sofas. Salvatore must have gone out early this morning, but he's back now and he kisses Chiara.

"I was talking to my security team and briefing them about De Luca," Salvatore says. "They're going to keep searching for him."

Lorenzo has a pen and he's twisting it between his fingers and over his knuckles, and one of his heels is bouncing on the carpet. I can tell he's wishing that the pen were his knife.

"I spoke to Nicole," I tell everyone. "De Luca made her pose for those pictures. De Luca, and one special friend of ours."

Chiara drops her eyes, and she says in a flat voice, "Dad."

"Yeah. The mayor. I'm sorry, kitten."

Chiara sighs. "At least Nicole is okay. We should let her go home to her mom."

Lorenzo and I exchange glances and I know he's been thinking the same thing I am. He rubs his hand over his jaw and shakes his head. "I want to hold on to her a little longer."

Chiara lifts her eyes to his. "She's my friend, not a hostage."

Salvatore sits forward. "Baby, the real killer was there last night. He's seen Nicole. He's probably furious that De Luca and the mayor pretended to be him and turned Nicole into one of his victims. What if he takes Nicole out of revenge and really does kill her?"

Her teeth sink into her lower lip. "Oh, you're right. How could Dad be so careless? He really cares about no one but himself."

"What I want to know is, how did the real killer know that we were going to be there last night?" Cassius asks.

I'm not particularly technical, but hanging around with Thane has given me some insight into how these things work. "If I had to guess, I'd say that after Nicole was reported as missing and a potential Black Orchid victim, the killer infected De Luca's devices with spyware. He would have been able to listen to all his calls and read all his emails and text messages. It's not hard to do. Thane does it all the time."

Once the killer had access to De Luca's devices, he'd find out the plan to have us all murdered in that abandoned building. I guess he couldn't resist trying to snatch one of us for himself, to torture and torment.

Chiara glances around at all the men and then at me. "I know I'm pushing my luck here after asking you not to murder the Strife men, but please don't hurt Mr. De Luca when you find him. This is Dad's fault, not his."

"We won't hurt him," I tell her, and Lorenzo scowls.

"Then why do you want to find him?"

"I want his phone. If I give it to Thane, he might be able to learn something about the killer from the spyware that was installed." It's a long shot, but it's something.

The five of us sit in silence, and I know that the others are remembering what went down at the abandoned building.

Cassius suddenly sits forward and glances between Salvatore and Lorenzo. "Describe what the two of you saw again. What he looked like. How he held himself. Everything."

"I didn't see much," Salvatore replies. "A man, lean like Vinicius and about his height. He was dressed in black and his face was completely covered. There was something sinister about him. He only focused on me, and on Lorenzo. That's what he was there for. Us."

"Did anything about him seem familiar?" I ask.

Salvatore shakes his head. "I don't know him. I didn't recognize him, anyway, but it would have been hard to recognize him when we couldn't see his face or hear his voice."

"I saw fuck all," Lorenzo mutters. "Half a dozen men grabbed me and were punching and kicking me. I knew Salvatore was in earshot. That fucking..." He searches for a word strong enough, "*fiend* grabbed hold of me and they all dragged me into the van. His hands were like ice. I've never felt a grip like it, like frozen metal digging into my flesh. I didn't even try to fight him. I just pushed everyone off, dove straight at the driver of the van, and wrenched the wheel to the side so we would crash."

"And I nearly passed out because I was a split second from firing a grenade at you." Salvatore turns pale at the memory.

Lorenzo clenches the pen so hard that it snaps, and he glares at Salvatore. "You would have avenged our sisters. I would have been raising a glass to you in hell."

Chiara reaches out to gently tug the broken pen from Lorenzo's grip and then twines her fingers through his. "But you found a way out of it because you're Lorenzo Scava."

Lorenzo stares at their joined hands. "I just wish I knew who that asshole was. By the time I pulled myself out of that wreck, the killer and all the other men had run off. Maybe it would have been better—"

My heart slams against my chest as I realize what he's going to say. "*No.* Your sacrifice isn't what any of us want. We get our vengeance together, or we won't get it at all."

Lorenzo lifts his blue eyes to mine and they burn savagely.

"No more death wishes, Lorenzo," I remind him. "You're staying. You're stuck with us."

The corner of his mouth tilts up. "More like you're all stuck with me." He hooks his arm around Chiara's waist, pulls her against his side and kisses her. She smiles against his mouth and threads her fingers through his hair.

The tightness in my chest eases up. If I lose him or Chiara or any of the syndicate in pursuit of this killer, the price of vengeance will be too high, and I don't want it.

"I can't believe we were within feet of this *bastardo*," Cassius mutters. "So close, and he slipped through our fingers."

Salvatore goes to the window and stares out onto the flat, green lawn. "We'll keep looking, for him and for De Luca. They can't have gone far."

7

Chiara

"This place is like a prison."

I look around at the steep, gray concrete walls and the security cameras. Nicole and I are sitting on the grass in Lorenzo's backyard. The sun is shining but the high walls are casting long shadows over us.

"Really? I like it here. It's safe. It's quiet." And it's honest. The world is a dangerous place and Lorenzo's tight security reflects that. I'd rather live here than in luxury surrounded by lies.

Nicole lifts her chin and gazes around us. Her long, dark hair falls limply over her shoulders. She's not as pale as she was the night we brought her here, but there's unhappiness etched into her features, something I never used to see before. "We shouldn't need to be this safe in Coldlake. It was never this dangerous when we were growing up."

"But it was, Nicole," I say gently. "We just weren't told about the danger. How much did you and I hear about the Black Orchid Killer when we were nine? Almost nothing because our parents protected us from that."

They were right to protect us from that horror then, but we can't be willfully ignorant about it now. I feel like Nicole is drawing a direct line from my men to the danger she's in like it's all their fault. Which is ironic, considering they're the ones who are keeping her safe.

"Being here with these men and their guns and knowing their enemies wish you harm," she shudders. "I don't know how you can bear it."

I gaze at her sadly. We used to be such good friends and understand each other so well, or at least *try* to understand each other. "They don't enjoy danger. They like hard work, and when they're not working, they relax with each other. Our favorite thing to do is eat Chinese food together. Cassius is ambitious and kind. Vinicius is a great talker and teacher. Salvatore loves his family and friends. Lorenzo keeps us safe and healthy. What we have together makes me happy."

Nicole's eyes widen as she listens to me recite their best qualities. "Can I ask you a question? That hazel-eyed one, he said some things about the five of you."

I can guess what the question is. All week, she's seen

how four men have been affectionate with me. "You mean Vinicius. Yes, they're all my lovers."

Her expression is more baffled than ever. "But...how? Why?"

I hold up my hand with its dazzling diamond engagement ring. "They asked, and I said yes. They're a package deal, those four. I wasn't sure if I liked all of them at first, but they grew on me. Now, I couldn't imagine being with just one of them."

"But how can you *like* them? They're horrible, violent men."

"For heaven's sake, Nicole. They're not *Batman* villains. They run this city how they want it to run and they look out for their own. What my father did, killing my mother in front of me? They would never do anything like that. They wouldn't use me to take revenge on my father because that's not part of their code."

I think back to the night we all played poker together. I was upset that I couldn't help them take revenge on my father. At the time it broke my heart, but it showed me how much I mean to them. I'm not a pawn, I'm part of them.

"They're extraordinarily good at looking out for themselves and each other, and extraordinarily handsome." I pluck at blades of grass and let them fall through my fingers. "It's okay, you don't have to like them. But I would like you to try and understand why *I* like them."

Nicole wrinkles her nose. "Don't they want their own girlfriends?"

I laugh. "They hate the idea, actually. They're very

protective and they'd go insane with worry if they had to keep me safe on their own. They share Coldlake, and they share me. We've got each other's backs."

Nicole's expression softens when I say *protective*. Lately, I don't think she's felt very protected by the people who are supposed to love her. "Do they get jealous? Are there fights?"

"They banter and wind each other up like old friends do. They all have very different personalities and backgrounds. It shouldn't work, but it does because they all have respect for each other."

Nicole glances around at the high walls. "You mean that? They won't use you like your father used you when he promised you in marriage? Like..." She takes a deep breath. "Like my father used me?"

I shake my head. "Not in a million years."

Her lower lip trembles, and she whispers, "You're lucky."

"I am lucky, but not only for that reason. I'm lucky every time they touch me. Every small thing they do for me and the sweet things they say. Most of all, I'm lucky for all the ways they've grown and helped me grow and how they've opened their hearts to me."

Nicole takes a deep breath. "All right, I believe you're safe here, but I don't belong. I've decided to go home."

My gaze snaps back to her. We explained to her last week that the Black Orchid Killer could be after her. "What? Are you sure?"

She sits up straighter and her lower lip firms.

Suddenly, she looks more like the Nicole I know and love. "It's dangerous, but Mom needs me. Dad's put her through hell, yet again, and I should be with her."

I've always loved Mrs. De Luca and I know how much Nicole adores her mom. If it were me, I wouldn't want Mom to be alone and worrying about me, either. "I don't know if the others will agree, but let's talk to Lorenzo about it."

We find Lorenzo in the lounge, a notebook open on his knees while he writes, his tattooed hand moving across the page.

"Lorenzo?"

"Princess," he murmurs, without looking up.

"Nicole wants to go home."

Lorenzo closes the notebook and stares at Nicole. She gazes back, her expression determined and her gaze unwavering. It's the first time she's been near him without shaking in fear.

He gets to his feet. "Fine. Let's go."

"Really? I thought you were going to argue with me."

His gaze flickers to Nicole. "She's not doing us any good and it's pissing me off to have her in my house. Nothing personal, Nicole. Those pictures of you brought back a lot of bad memories."

She gives him a tight smile. "I just want to put everything behind me."

Lorenzo gives her a dark look. He doesn't get the luxury of putting everything behind him while he's still living in it. "Meet me in the garage. I'll be there in two minutes."

"That man doesn't sugarcoat anything, does he?" Nicole whispers as we head downstairs.

"Not a thing."

We're waiting by Lorenzo's Mercedes when he strides toward us, something in his hand and his gaze fixed on Nicole.

"This is a silent panic button," he says, holding up a small object. "It's got a tracker. If you're abducted, hit it, and keep it on you. Stick it in your bra or something. He probably won't kill you right away which will give us a chance to find you. We'll be coming as fast as we can. Us, and everyone who works for us." Lorenzo stares at the device in his palm for a moment. "Screaming and crying won't do you much good. If you talk a lot and ask questions, he'll, uh," Lorenzo trails off and swallows. "Slow down."

He thrusts the tracker at Nicole and she takes it from him. "Who's tracking it?"

"Me." He holds up his phone. "With this." He shows her the new smartwatch that's replaced his broken one. "And this. If it goes off at any time, I'll know."

She gives him a tentative smile. "Thank you."

He frowns at her and darts a look at me, like he's not sure what to do with her gratitude. "Yeah, okay."

"You really think he'll try and kill me?" Nicole asks.

"Maybe. I don't know how that asshole's mind works,

but it would piss me off if someone tried to copycat me and didn't even finish the job."

"Lorenzo..." I say softly, seeing Nicole turn pale.

"Just being honest," he mutters.

Nicole closes her hand around the tracker and nods. "I'll remember your instructions."

He jabs a finger in her face. "I'm not doing this for free. I want something in return. If you find out where your father is, call a bar in the west called Strife and leave a message for me. De Luca doesn't know it, but he could help us catch this killer."

"You won't hurt Dad, will you?"

"No one's going to hurt Mr. De Luca," I assure her.

"Depends how long he takes to show up. I'm losing my fucking patience," Lorenzo says as he turns away and gets in his Mercedes 4WD.

I sit in the back with Nicole as we drive through the streets. Twenty-five minutes later, we pull up outside her house.

She sits forward to talk to Lorenzo. "Thank you for protecting me this past week. I'm grateful for what you've done. You and Chiara."

"Yeah, well. It's good you're in one piece. Try and stay that way."

She squeezes my hand and smiles before getting out of the car. At her front door, she reaches for her keys, realizes she hasn't got them, and knocks. Mrs. De Luca opens the door and bursts into tears when she sees her daughter.

I get out of the back seat and open the front passenger

door, giving Mrs. De Luca a wave as she hugs her daughter, but she doesn't even notice I'm there.

As I get into the car, Lorenzo has both forearms resting on the steering wheel and he's gazing at mother and daughter. Before she disappears inside, Nicole glances over her shoulder and gives Lorenzo an uncertain wave and a smile. As if without thinking, Lorenzo lifts his fingers in a salute. Then he starts the engine and we peel away from the curb.

"I'm glad she's home with her mom," he mutters at the road ahead.

"I know you are. That's why I love you."

Lorenzo whips his head around and stares at me. "What?"

We sail through a stop sign and a car horn blares.

Lorenzo swears and swerves around the truck he's about to T-bone. "Why did you say that? Has Vinicius been blabbing to you or some shit?"

"What do you mean?"

He keeps shooting glances at me as we drive. It's not until we get on the freeway and merge into traffic that he asks, "You're saying that why?"

I smile at him. "Lorenzo, did you tell Vinicius that you love me?"

He adjusts the rearview mirror and scowls at the road ahead. We drive in silence, and then I feel Lorenzo's hand creep into my lap and take hold of mine.

"No one's ever said that to me before. I didn't grow up in a house where people just said that shit to each other."

"Well, I mean it. I love you, Lorenzo."

He squeezes my hand tighter but his throat seems locked up tight. I don't need him to say anything back. I just need him to believe me.

"Do you think you might get a taste for hearing me say that?" I ask.

"Don't know. I would chuck away another knife for you, but I haven't got any more knives."

I draw his hand up to my mouth and kiss his fingers. "I felt it when you did that. Love. You don't need to say it."

"Have any of the others said that they love you?"

"Why?"

"A man likes to know."

I laugh and squeeze his fingers. "It doesn't matter what I've said to the others or what they've said to me. What's happening in this car is about you and me."

A smile drifts over his lips. "Just you and me, huh? Thank you, princess."

As we're about to pull into the compound, my phone rings. It's Salvatore and I put him on speakerphone. "Hey, I'm with Lorenzo and we're nearly back at his place. What's up?"

Salvatore doesn't bother to say hello and he speaks quickly. "I'm on my way to East Coldlake Hospital."

Fear shoots through me. "Why? What's happened?"

"Ginevra's having the baby."

Lorenzo and I exchange glances. I don't know about him, but I'd completely forgotten that Ginevra was due soon. I haven't seen her since she was helping me organize my wedding to her brother. Salvatore tried to make her leave Coldlake when Nicole went missing, but she refused to travel while she was pregnant.

Lorenzo frowns. "Now? Isn't it too soon?"

"Nearly four weeks too soon."

"Four weeks is nothing these days," Lorenzo assures him. "Chiara and I are on our way. Meet you there." He puts the car into reverse and turns around, his hand cupping my headrest as he checks over his shoulder.

"Thank you, Lorenzo. Baby, can you call Vinicius and Cassius for me?"

"Of course. I'll do that right now. See you soon, Salvatore."

I hang up, and then call both men at the same time and tell them where to meet us. A wave of anxiety passes over me as I finish the call, and I turn to Lorenzo. "Will the baby really be all right?"

Lorenzo frowns at the road ahead. "Babies aren't really my area of expertise, but Ginevra's healthy. Salvatore's never mentioned any problems with her pregnancy. We'll know more when the baby arrives."

I tuck my hands between my knees and squeeze them tightly, whispering automatically under my breath.

Lorenzo glances at me. "You praying, princess?"

"Catholic school habit. Who knows? Maybe it will help." Just saying the words are calming, and I know Ginevra would appreciate it. She goes to church even if her brother doesn't.

He reaches out and squeezes my shoulder. "There's never a dull moment lately, is there?"

I can't help but laugh. "And I thought having the Cold-lake Syndicate as my boyfriends would be a life of peace and tranquility."

"Oh, yeah. Like a fucking beach holiday."

We park near the main entrance of the hospital just as Cassius is pulling in. Vinicius isn't far away, and so we wait for his red Ferrari to arrive before we all head inside together. We're not allowed to see Ginevra, but we sit in the waiting room and I text Salvatore to say we're here.

A few minutes later, he pushes through the double doors from the maternity ward, his expression tense and his hair rumpled like he's been pushing his fingers through it.

"Hey. She's still in labor. No news yet."

Cassius grips his shoulder. "I was born four weeks early and it didn't do me any harm. I'm bigger than both my parents and as strong as an ox."

"Ginevra's strong and healthy," Lorenzo tells him. "She and the baby will be fine."

Cassius watches Salvatore, his brow wrinkled in concern. "You can go back to Ginevra if you like. We'll wait here."

Salvatore shakes his head. "I'll stay with you. They won't let me into the room, anyway. I'm just pacing up and down outside the door."

I go over to him and take his hand, and he gives me a tight smile. "Baby, I'm so glad you're here. Distract me?"

"Nicole has gone home," I tell him. "Lorenzo gave her a tracking device. Her mom was so happy to see her."

"I bet she was. How are you? Are you worried about her?"

"I am, but I think she's better off where she is. She didn't enjoy being at the compound and she and her mom will look out for each other. I'd feel better if her father were home, though."

"Cowardly asshole," Vinicius mutters on my other side.

We sit in restless conversation for nearly two hours. Salvatore turns expectantly toward the maternity ward doors every time they open, but it's never news for us.

Finally, a tiny, gray-haired woman appears. It takes me a moment to recognize her. Guilia, Antonio's mother and Ginevra's mother-in-law, dressed in a rose-colored skirt suit with gold earrings. She scans the waiting room with intense eyes.

"Salvatore, *ha avuto il bambino.*"

I jump to my feet with a delighted gasp. "She's had the baby? It's a boy?"

Salvatore squeezes my hand even harder. "Is Ginevra all right?"

She beckons him over. "*Sì, sì,* the mother is fine. You have a beautiful nephew." Then she adds, with pride in her voice, "My grandson is seven pounds, three ounces."

I look between her and the doors, suddenly desperate to see Ginevra and the baby.

"Can I see my sister?" Salvatore asks, and Guilia holds

the door open for him. Reluctantly, I let go of Salvatore's hand.

"Do you want to come?" he asks.

"Well, yes, but I'm not family."

Salvatore looks around at us. "Of course you are. All of you, come on."

Guilia's eyes open in surprise. "But—"

I shoot her an apologetic look as we walk past her in a pack. There won't be much space with the five of us crowded into the room, but Ginevra has enough backbone to tell us all to get lost if we're too many.

Salvatore opens the door to Ginevra's hospital room as Vinicius says, "The three of us will wait here. You and Chiara go in."

Inside, Ginevra is sitting up against the pillows, her face flushed and tired but with a smile on her lips. Her arms are cradled around a tiny, sleeping baby. She glances between me and Salvatore, and past us to the other three men. I wonder how much she knows about the five of us. We haven't had the chance to talk lately, but Salvatore must have said something to her about our relationship.

She gives us an exhausted smile. "All of you, come in and meet him."

I hurry forward, reaching the bed before Salvatore does. The baby is tiny, pink-faced, and perfect, his eyes closed as he sleeps. Ginevra is cupping his head and gazing at him in wonder. On the other side of the bed, Antonio stands with his back against the wall, looking bewildered, but proud.

Salvatore puts his hands on my shoulders, gazing at the baby with a lopsided smile on his face. "Well done, Ginny. He's perfect."

"He is, isn't he? Would you like to hold him?"

He laughs. "I think Chiara's dying for a cuddle. She can go first."

I accept the warm little bundle from Ginevra and he stirs in my arms. "Hi, baby," I whisper, a huge smile on my face. "We're so happy you're here."

I look around for Salvatore and notice that he's moved back to stand by the window. I take his nephew over to him and we stand close, our heads bent over the sleeping child.

"Isn't he perfect?"

"He's the most precious thing I've ever seen," Salvatore murmurs, brushing the baby's cheek with his forefinger. How wonderful it would be if it were our baby in my arms. I shouldn't want this, not when our lives are in so much turmoil, but I do. I want this so badly.

I look up at Salvatore, my heart so full that it's hard to breathe. "I want to tell you something but we have to be really quiet. This is just for you and me."

"What is it, baby?"

I go up on tiptoe and kiss Salvatore's cheek, and he holds me and the baby steady in his arms. "I love you, Salvatore."

A smile breaks over his face and he closes his eyes. My beautiful, strong, clever man. He presses his forehead against mine and whispers, "You do?"

I nod.

"I love you, too."

"What are you two whispering about?" Ginevra calls from the bed.

Salvatore kisses me, and then says, "Chiara says I'm not allowed to order you to call him Francesco."

"Good, because we're not calling him Francesco. Dad's name was lovely but it's horribly dated. We're calling him Camillo."

Salvatore laughs and we walk back over to the bed. "But that's Grandpa's name. Even more dated."

"Camillo has come back into fashion, and Antonio has a favorite uncle called Camillo, so it's perfect."

"Hello, Camillo," I whisper, kissing the baby's head. "It's lovely to meet you."

Vinicius, Cassius, and Lorenzo were all out in the hall, but when I look up, all four of my men are clustered around and staring at me. Salvatore with pride and love. Vinicius with affection. Cassius like he's imagining me pregnant, and Lorenzo with complete blankness, which I know by now means he's feeling too much, not nothing. I haven't thought about children since I was engaged to Salvatore, but suddenly my heart aches with the need to hold one of my own babies like this.

"Come on, Uncle Sal. Your turn," I say, depositing the baby carefully into Salvatore's arms. The *I love you*s we just spoke to each other are hidden in our smiles.

"You just couldn't wait to get here, could you? So impatient," Salvatore murmurs, rocking the baby back and forth. "Just like your uncle Salvatore."

There's something that makes me feel warm and fuzzy at the sight of a man gently holding a baby. The sight of Salvatore and Camillo gets me right in the heart.

Vinicius comes forward with a smile. "I love babies. May I?" He takes Camillo from Salvatore and promises him that when he's old enough, he'll teach him everything that a boy should know.

"How to fly a kite and change a tire?" I ask with an amused smile. More like picking locks and cheating at cards.

Vinicius gives me a sly smile. "What else, kitten?"

He passes Camillo over to Cassius, who gives the baby a stern look. "*Bambino*, you be good and respectful to your mother and grow up big and strong like your uncle Cassius." Then he smiles and kisses the baby's head. "*Bravo ragazzo.*" *Good boy.*

Lorenzo has come up beside him and reaches for the baby. From the bed, Ginevra makes a strangled noise.

A wall slams down behind Lorenzo's eyes and he drops his arms and steps back.

I glance between the two of them. "Ginevra? Can Lorenzo hold the baby?"

"Don't worry about it, princess," Lorenzo mutters.

An awkward silence stretches while everyone exchanges glances and doesn't know what to say. Ginevra is looking between Lorenzo and me, her brow wrinkled in confusion.

"You call her princess?" she asks.

"Yeah. What about it?"

She plays with the blanket covering her legs. "It just doesn't seem like something you'd do."

"Ginevra, you don't know me."

I wish Ginevra could see the Lorenzo I see. He's not a dangerous tattooed gangster who enjoys hurting people. The tattoos covering his body are a tribute to his sister, and he saves just as many lives as he takes.

"I guess, but we're not strangers, either," Ginevra points out. "Do you remember the last time we were in the same room?"

Lorenzo glances at Salvatore and back at his sister, his jaw tight. "Yeah. You just got back from Naples. You were twelve or something."

"Thirteen. You came to our house smelling of blood and wearing ripped jeans. You looked...crazy. I think you were drunk."

That must have been when Ginevra returned to Coldlake just after the Black Orchid Murders.

"Sounds about right. I was drunk for months on end back then."

"You and Salvatore were talking business and I was hanging around him because I was lonely and scared. You roared at me to get the eff out of your sight. I was just a child. I don't think you like children very much."

Lorenzo shoves his hands into his pockets and shrugs, his eyes turning cold and avoiding her gaze. He's a fraction of a second away from storming out.

I go over and put a hand on his arm. "I know that's not true. Were you upset about something that day?"

"She reminded me of someone I didn't want to remember."

Salvatore gazes at his sister, and says softly, "She does look a lot like Ophelia."

"You were wearing yellow that day, just like she was. In the video," he finishes.

Ginevra's mistrustful expression changes to shock, and then finally to sadness. "Oh, I never..." She swallows. "Knew. The details, I mean. Salvatore told me what you did for her."

The tension goes out of Lorenzo's shoulders as he realizes Ginevra understands. He didn't watch those videos to be a hero or for the sake of the syndicate. He watched them for their sisters, hunting for clues that might tell him their killer's identity.

But it didn't work. All Lorenzo got was a head full of horror that's been with him ever since.

"How did you get past everything you saw? You're not drunk now, I'm guessing."

Lorenzo finally meets her eyes. "That's my business."

Ginevra gives him a tentative smile. "Of course, I'm sorry. Please hold the baby, Lorenzo. You're going to be like an uncle to him, too."

Cassius walks over to Lorenzo, who gazes at the baby, the anger melting from his face. He takes Camillo from Cassius and cradles him in his tattooed forearms. When he touches the baby's hand with a forefinger, Camillo wraps his tiny hand around Lorenzo's finger.

"Strong little fucker," he murmurs, blond hair falling

into his eyes. A smile turns up the corner of his mouth. "Here. You better have him back, Uncle Sal."

Salvatore accepts the baby, and I take Lorenzo's hand and turn to Ginevra. "The four of us will be in the waiting room. Salvatore, come and find us when you've had your fill of your nephew."

As we walk down the hall, Vinicius takes my other hand. "I have to say, you looked beautiful holding that baby."

"And you all looked ridiculously sexy." Is that the right word? Can men look sexy holding babies? Apparently, my men can because suddenly I'm dying to touch them all.

Lorenzo heads off to find the cafeteria to buy us all coffee as Vinicius, Cassius, and I sit on the hard plastic seats. A television is mounted on the wall, set to a local news channel. I wince as I realize the two hosts are discussing the upcoming election. Dad and Christian Galloway's pictures appear on the screen.

My attention is snared by the headline plastered across the bottom of the screen. CHRISTIAN GALLOWAY IN CORPSE SEX SCANDAL.

Cassius is watching the news with me and I grasp his arm. "Am I reading that right?"

He nods slowly, seeming like he's as confused as I am. We both get up and move closer to the screen so we can hear what's being said.

"...online claims that Christian Galloway engaged in sexual acts with a corpse while he worked as a pathologist.

We spoke with a member of staff who worked as a pathologist alongside Galloway."

A piece of video footage is spliced into the broadcast, showing a woman in her late forties wearing a troubled expression. "Mr. Galloway gave me the creeps and would work late all the time. He definitely had access to bodies while there was no one else around."

The broadcast cuts back to the hosts. "A further witness who wishes to remain anonymous has recalled an incident from Galloway's medical student days in which he used a body as a crude puppet for an April Fool's prank."

The second host replies, "Early polls have the incumbent mayor leading by a comfortable margin. This scandal could end Christian Galloway's mayoral hopes for good."

Vinicius whistles low and shakes his head. "I hope Galloway hasn't ordered any furniture for the mayor's office. He was a pathologist before he ran for mayor?"

I nod. "Years ago. Then he went into law and became a coroner, and lately, he's been running for mayor."

Now that I think of it, he would have been the coroner the year the syndicate's sisters were murdered. Bitterness washes over me. I suppose he did as little as possible to obtain justice for the women like every other official in Coldlake.

As I go back to my chair, I see that Lorenzo has returned with coffee and he's seen the tail end of the broadcast. I try to imagine Christian Galloway playing with a corpse, and worse, having sex with a corpse, but the mental images are just too awful.

"Lorenzo, you must have worked on bodies in university labs. Did you see students playing pranks?"

He passes coffee to the other two and hands me a latte. "Oh, yeah. Being around corpses is fucking weird. Students find ways of blowing off steam."

"Did you play pranks with the corpses?"

He gives a humorless laugh. "Me, princess? Monday to Friday I was cutting up corpses. On the weekend I was making them. I didn't need pranks to blow off steam." He gestures at the television with his coffee. "Why anyone goes into politics is beyond me. It's a thankless fucking task and all your private shit gets spread out for everyone to see."

"People want power," I reply, taking a sip of my coffee. The news seems to be drawing a direct line from Galloway playing pranks with bodies to necrophilia. Lorenzo makes it sound like a medical student messing around with corpses isn't the smoking gun the news hosts make it out to be, but then Lorenzo's idea of what's normal isn't necessarily other people's idea of what's normal.

Vinicius nudges me with his elbow. "Look. Coroner Weirdo is being interviewed."

"I will not answer degrading questions about fallacious rumors. There are real criminals in this city who have never answered for their crimes." Spittle is flying from Christian Galloway's lips and there's a crazed expression in his eyes. "Four men in particular who need to be rooted out and punished."

Lorenzo gives the television the finger.

"He needs to get a fucking grip," Cassius mutters and then turns to me. "Is he always unhinged like this?"

Together, we watch more of Galloway's ranting and raving. Is it the rumors that have pushed him over the edge, or is it because the truth about him is finally out?

"Not that I've seen. I think he's losing it."

"With an opponent like him, Mayor Romano will have an easy victory," Vinicius says.

My heart sinks. Another term for Dad. More power for a murderer, and the adoration of everyone in Coldlake.

8

Chiara

Salvatore is grinning as we leave the hospital and head for the cars. Becoming Uncle Salvatore has put a bounce in his step, and I try to focus on the happiness that a new baby brings rather than dismal thoughts about Dad.

"Baby," Salvatore murmurs, pulling me into his arms as we stand next to his Maserati. "I'll be thinking about you holding that baby for the rest of the day." He tucks his lips against my ear and kisses me there. "And I'll remember what you said."

I love you.

My heart fills with happiness. These are the moments I

cherish, safe in the arms of my men in the midst of the storm that rages around us.

"Get your raging baby hormones in check and get in the fucking car," Lorenzo says as he heads for his Mercedes. "We've got work to do."

"Me?" I squeak.

"Not you. Uncle Sal."

Salvatore grins and gives me a final kiss. "Lorenzo and I have a lead to follow up. It probably won't be De Luca, but we'll check it out. See you later, baby."

The two of them drive off first and then I ride with Cassius, and we head back to the compound, following Vinicius' car. Cassius is in an intense, silent mood as we drive, occasionally reaching over to squeeze my thigh with his enormous hand.

As we get out of the cars in the underground garage, Vinicius calls, "I'm going to sort out the armory and see what needs to be restocked."

"Sure," Cassius calls after him, his eyes never leaving my face. He moves slowly toward me.

"Cassius, are you all right? Are you worried about something?"

His arms slide around me and he pulls me sharply against him. The thick rod of his erection pushes against my belly. Oh, he's not worried.

He's horny as hell.

After an hour of watching my men coo over a baby cradled in their muscular arms, I'm feeling aroused as well. Cassius kisses me hard, parting my lips with his.

Vinicius' obnoxious red Ferrari is parked next to Cassius' SUV. Cassius spins me around and pushes me over the hood, my ass in the air. I land on the metal with a soft thump.

"If we dent this, Vinicius will be so mad."

"I'll buy him a new one," Cassius says, more interested in getting my jeans off, pulling my underwear down and spreading my legs just right. He hunkers low on his heels and licks me all the way from my clit up to my ass in one long sweep.

"*Cassius*." My fingers curl on the warm car hood, and my eyes close in bliss.

His insistent tongue swipes me again and his fingers spread me open. I feel him push his tongue deep inside me, before standing up and pulling the rest of my clothes off.

Butt naked in Lorenzo's concrete basement isn't the coziest place to be, but with Cassius' hands on me, I don't feel cold in the slightest. I feel him unzipping and he notches his thick cock up at my entrance, before driving himself home inside me. I yelp at the sudden shock of his intrusion.

Cassius groans in pleasure and thrusts in a slow, powerful rhythm. "This is all I've been able to think about for the past hour. Your pussy is heaven."

I'm lost in what he's doing to me. So lost that when I feel a hand on my ankle my eyes open in surprise.

Vinicius is kneeling down beside me and is slipping my bare feet into red high heels.

"Perfect, Vinicius," Cassius says appreciatively.

Vinicius leans over and gives me a kiss. "If you're going to be fucked on the hood of my car, kitten, let's make this as lurid as we can." His gleaming gaze wanders over me. "That's so hot. Everyone has to see this."

He digs out his phone. I hear the sound of a call going through and then Lorenzo asks, "What's up? I'm driving."

"Nothing. Just saying hi," Vinicius says, positioning himself so that Cassius and I are in the background of his video call. Cassius has his hands holding my waist and he's intent on fucking me.

Salvatore has answered as well, and he sounds distracted as he says, "Vinicius, what do you—wait, what's happening behind you?"

"Holy shit," Lorenzo says, in a very different tone.

"Is everyone watching?" Cassius asks, not letting up on his pounding rhythm.

"Oh, they can see," Vinicius tells him, pointing the camera so it travels down my body.

"I'm going to crash my fucking car," Lorenzo says.

Remembering how he drove through a stop sign when I said *I love you*, I call out, "Please be careful, Lorenzo."

"I'm pulling over," Salvatore says.

"Listen up, everyone. I've got something to say," growls Cassius.

I moan as he hits that sweet spot inside me. Now isn't the best time for a group meeting when all I want is to come.

"Remember how we agreed we would pull out?" Cassius asks. "I'm done with that."

My eyes snap open. Wait, what?

"I never liked it. A Ferragamo does not pull out." His big hand squeezes my ass. "*Bambina*, you're ours, I want you pregnant and we're starting now. I don't even remember why we decided on that bullshit."

Vinicius' smile is devilish. "We were pulling out because there was a chance Salvatore was going to marry Chiara. It's only polite not to nut in another man's fiancé."

"She's not my fiancé now," Salvatore says, in a sly voice. "She belongs to all of us."

Cassius is pounding me with determined thrusts of his cock. I want to tell them that we should all talk about this like grown-ups. Make a proper, thoughtful decision. But the primal, lizard part of my brain that can't speak, can't reason, *loves* Cassius' idea, and all I want is the enormous man thrusting into me to show me what a man he is.

"Cassius," I moan, high heels braced against concrete, turning my head to look into the camera that Vinicius is holding up. I can't help but smile into the camera as the others watch.

"Fuck, yes." Lorenzo's voice is tight and urgent. "Blow your load in her sweet pussy."

Cassius takes a tighter grip on me and doesn't let up. "You're going to stay right there, *bambina*, while I fill you up like I've been aching to do from the start."

Vinicius keeps broadcasting our sex while Cassius groans deeply, his rhythm stuttering as he thrusts deeper and shouts with his climax. I brace my feet against the ground and arch my head back. This is what I've been missing. The satisfaction of feeling them finish inside me.

There's a moment of stunned silence. Then Salvatore breathes, "Fuck yes, we're making babies."

"Got to go," Vinicius says and hangs up.

I push myself up on my elbows and look around. Vinicius is pulling off his shirt as he moves behind me. His cheeks are flushed red as he takes hold of my hips.

"My turn, kitten."

"Wha—" My question is lost in a gasp of pleasure as Vinicius grasps his cock and thrusts his length home. The orgasm that was pent up inside me as Cassius screwed me suddenly coalesces and bursts forth.

"You're full of Cassius. Do you want me too, kitten? Do you want even more cum inside you?"

The question makes me lose all sensibility. "Yes. All of you."

Cassius has both hands resting on the hood of the car, breathing hard as he watches me get railed. "Those fuckers down at Strife thought they could take you from us, but you're ours, *bambina*. Do you feel how much you're ours?"

There's a distant grinding sound, and a moment later, Lorenzo's 4WD races down into the garage and stops in a squeal of tire rubber. He leaps out of the front seat and slams the door behind him.

"I hear we're making babies," he says with a wicked grin, pulling off his T-shirt and shoving down his jeans. He palms his length in his fist as he waits for his turn.

Vinicius smooths one hand up my back as he continues to thrust. "You see how eager he is for you, kitten? Lorenzo, her pussy is gushing. She's so wet and she's full of cum already."

Lorenzo's cock is right in my line of sight as he strokes himself up and down. "I can hear her. Hurry up, I want my turn."

"I'm not a...*ah*." I was going to say *a fairground ride*, but Vinicius ups his pace and he's hitting that perfect spot. I'm so turned on I can't think straight.

"Everyone will know you're ours with our baby inside you, kitten. We'll look at you with your swollen belly and remember this moment when we all had you, one after the other, and you were full of us."

Cassius and Lorenzo are staring down at me splayed over the hood of the car. Where's Salvatore? He needs to be here, too.

Vinicius slides a hand beneath my belly and grips me hard. "I can feel my cock going in and out of you," he says, voice ragged. "That's so fucking hot. I'm going to..." He groans and leans his weight on me as he comes.

He pulls out slowly and carefully. I feel how wet my pussy is and Vinicius pushes his cum back into me with his fingers. "Can't waste a drop."

"I'll make sure we don't waste any. Move aside." Lorenzo plugs my pussy with the tip of his cock but stays right there. "If I thrust deep, their cum will leak out around me. What a waste. I wish we could all nut in you at the same time, princess. I want you fucking full of us."

Cassius cups my chin, his dark eyes glittering. "She's full. Go on and fuck our pretty girl until she's bursting."

Lorenzo moans as he sinks into me. "You feel incredible. You know I love it when you're already soaking wet and worn out. This is something else."

"You like my messy pussy, Lorenzo?"

"I love your messy pussy and your slutty heels," he says harshly, pounding me with firm, deep strokes. "We should have been fucking you like this from the start. I should have screwed you in the church in your white wedding dress in front of all those wedding guests. My woman. *Ours.*"

As he finishes, there's the roar of a car engine and Salvatore arrives in his Maserati.

Lorenzo tips his head back with a lazy laugh and slowly drags his cock out of me. "Just in time. Stay there, princess, you've got one man to go."

Salvatore glances at the others, and then at me, a savage expression on his face. I push myself up. The hood of a car is probably the least comfortable place to have sex with one man, let alone four.

Salvatore puts a hand on my back and pushes me back down. "Where do you think you're going?"

"There are half a dozen beds in this place," I tell him over my shoulder.

"Baby, you're ass-up in red heels over the hood of a Ferrari. You think I'm missing this opportunity? Now hold still while I knock you up."

A delicious pang shoots through me as I feel him draw

his zipper down and the head of his cock slides through my folds.

"Fuck, you're dripping all down your thighs and it's still not enough for you, is it?"

"Are we laying bets on whose it is?" Vinicius asks.

"Blue eyes and blond hair will make it mine," Lorenzo says with relish.

"Blue eyes and blond hair just means it takes after its mother," Salvatore points out, and thrusts into me so hard and fast that I cry out.

"We'll know right away if it's mine," Cassius says, his tone smug. "The Ferragamo coloring is unmistakable."

"You're all talking like I'm already pregnant," I point out.

Salvatore drags his fingers down my back and then slaps his hand over my ass with a *crack*. "We'll fuck you like this until you are."

Lorenzo leans on the hood of the car and puts his face close to mine. "You like that, don't you, princess? All of us screwing you, impatient to take our turn with our woman. If you thought we were competitive before, you're about to find out just how fiercely we compete."

Salvatore's breathing is growing labored and his fingers are digging into my hips. His thrusts become harder and deeper, barely pulling out before he's slamming into me again. I squeeze my eyes shut as my world turns golden, and I spasm on his cock as I come.

Salvatore slams his hand onto the hood of the car, pumping his hips into me as he finishes a moment later.

"Jesus fucking Christ, Salvatore," Vinicius says. "Watch my car."

"You watch your fucking car. I'm watching Chiara with her pussy full of all our cum." He pulls out and spreads me open with his fingers and then groans. "Oh, fuck yes, baby. That's what I need. Are you guys seeing this?"

My face flames red as they all crowd around him to look at me dripping with them, legs parted and ass in the air.

"Perfect, *bambina*," Cassius purrs.

"Kitten, you've never looked hotter."

Salvatore helps me up, and then sits me down on the Ferrari between his thighs, a wicked smile lighting his eyes as he cups my chin.

"How about a kiss for Daddy?" Salvatore slants his mouth over mine and kisses me deeply. He tweaks my nipples, tucks his shirt back into his pants, and winks at me. "Back to work. Rest up. Eat a good dinner."

I watch him and Lorenzo get ready to go, worry curling through me. I'm used to watching them leave, but the thought of being pregnant and losing one of them is the worst thing I can imagine.

"Be safe. Be careful, please."

"We will. Don't worry, baby, we're just looking for De Luca," Salvatore assures me, smoothing my hair back from my face.

"And then we'll rip his fucking fingernails out," Lorenzo growls as he slams the door closed on his 4WD and roars out of the garage.

"Please don't torture Mr. De Luca," I say to Salvatore. "He and Nicole have been used by my father. Dad's the real culprit here."

"We won't hurt him. Lorenzo's just frustrated." He kisses me again and heads for his car. "Take care of yourself. Lorenzo and I won't be back for hours, so don't wait up."

I glance down at myself, naked except for high heels and red pressure marks on my breasts and knees. My thighs are slick and shiny. My hair is tangled.

Vinicius cups the nape of my neck, his eyes glowing as he gazes down at me. "Just look at you."

"I'm a mess."

"Yes. A wonderful mess." He scoops me up in his arms and carries me upstairs, unable to wipe the smile from his face.

"Someone's happy," I say, wrapping my arms around his neck.

He puts me on my feet in my shower, undresses, and joins me under the hot water. His smile has turned dreamy. "You know what? I am happy. It's exciting, trying for a baby. It's new and it's something we can all do together. Are you excited, kitten?"

I wash my hair slowly, imagining being pregnant. Imagining the moment that I can hold my own baby. My men holding our baby. Could that sweetness really be ours? "My head still hasn't caught up with the idea, but I am excited."

"I never thought we would get to this place."

"So soon, you mean?"

He shakes his head. "Ever. Salvatore wants children but Cassius never said one way or the other. He's either totally for something or totally against it and I can never guess which it will be. Lorenzo's not that different."

"And you?"

"I never made up my mind, one way or another. Then we met you, and it just feels right. The others feel the same way. It feels right because it's you."

A delighted smile spreads over my face. "Really? That's the loveliest thing anyone's ever said to me."

"You're who we want for the mother of our children. Someone who's sweet and loving and who will protect them at all costs. I know you'll give them all the love they could want and more, and you'll fight like a tigress to keep them from harm."

I wrap my hands around his waist and gaze up at him. "All that's true, but there's another reason, too."

"What is it?"

I look up at him. "It's because I love you."

His eyes glow and he cups my face in his hands. "You do?"

"You're my beautiful, clever man who never fails to make me feel wonderful."

"Well, that's the loveliest thing anyone's ever said to me." His smile fades, but his eyes are as bright as ever. "I love you, too, kitten. Not just for who you are, but for what you've done for all of us. We were waiting for you for nine long years. Thank you for not making us wait a day more."

He kisses me beneath the rushing water, his arms wrapped around me. They found me, and I'm never leaving their sides.

We get out of the shower together and dry off. As he's rubbing his hair with a towel in my bedroom, he glances at his phone. "Are you fucking kidding me?"

I see that my own phone is lighting up with messages and pick it up to unlock it. Salvatore has texted the group chat, *Sorry, Vinicius. I think I dented your car when I punched it earlier.*

Vinicius starts toward the door and replies, *What??*

Salvatore sends a picture of a red Ferrari with a cartoon anvil crushing the hood. Lorenzo and Cassius reply with laughter and emojis, and I stifle a giggle.

Vinicius sends back, *Oh, haha*, and tosses his phone onto the bed. "What are you grinning about, kitten?"

I'm still getting used to the idea of getting pregnant and I will worry about them even more if they have a baby to protect, but right at this moment, I feel nothing but in love with four beautiful men.

I shake my head, smiling. "Just that the fathers of my future children are a bunch of big kids."

9

Lorenzo

I stare at the message Chiara sent to the group chat a few hours ago. *I love you all.*

She loves us.

All of us.

I don't know who she told first and who was last, but I'm surprised to find I don't care and I have no interest in finding out. Chiara's words are a warm weight in my chest. She loves me.

She loves *us*.

It's been a week since Ginevra had the baby and we all fucked Chiara over Vinicius' car. Every chance I get I've been sliding my hand over Chiara's stomach, feeling her belly. The others are doing it, too. There's nothing to feel, but there will be soon. She's probably not pregnant yet, but we're in there.

In fact, I hope she's not pregnant yet because getting her that way is so fucking hot I almost don't want it to end.

Everyone's suddenly obsessed with sex. Even more so than usual, that is. The others keep turning up at the compound at random hours of the night. I hear the gate grinding open, footsteps coming along the corridor, and the sound of Chiara's bedroom door opening and closing.

I give them a few minutes to settle in, then quietly open Chiara's door and enjoy the show. Salvatore likes her on her back so he can kiss her. Cassius loves her on top, his hands cupping her breasts while he thrusts up into her. Vinicius prefers her from behind so he can watch himself screwing her in the mirror. No one's finishing on her tits, in their hand, or pulling out. These men are on a mission.

Two weeks into Chiara's sleep being broken every other night, she sits at my kitchen counter yawning over her morning coffee. There are shadows beneath her eyes and she looks exhausted.

"If you want to sleep through the night, just tell me and I'll lock the front gate."

She rubs her eyes and yawns again. "You know that they're all coming here?"

"Princess, I fucking watch."

"You do? Lorenzo, you big perve. How come you're not creeping into my room like the others?" Chiara stops rubbing and frowns at me. "Come to think of it, we haven't had sex for more than a week. Why?"

I have my reasons. "Do you need more dicks in your life right now? Are you not swamped with dick?"

Chiara laughs. "God. So much dick. But what happened to the competitive man I know and love?"

I give her a wicked smile. "I have your cycle written down. You're not fertile for another three days."

She suddenly chokes on her coffee. "Oh, my God, you're monitoring my cycle? I don't even know that."

I go over to her and wipe milk foam from her lip and lean in close. Does she think I'm going to leave this kind of thing to chance? "Of course I am. I've been circling the days on my calendar. So guess what? When you're fertile, the gate is going to be locked that day. And the next day. And the day after that. It's going to be locked at night as well. No one's getting in or out, and that includes you."

Her eyebrows creep up her forehead. "What?"

I smile and rub my thumb over her lower lip. My princess, all mine for three days while I fuck her senseless until I'm sure I'm the one who's knocked her up. I can't wait.

"What happens when the other three turn up and can't get in?"

"They can fucking cry about it. You'll be in my bed, phone off, coming on my dick. I don't live in the most secure house in Coldlake for nothing."

She gives me an amused smile. "I thought that was to keep the gangs out, not so you could knock up the mayor's daughter in peace."

"You know me. I'm always thinking ahead." I press my

mouth to hers and part her lips with my tongue. I murmur in between kisses, "Are you going to tell on me princess, and ruin my plans?"

"What plan? I didn't hear a thing."

I laugh softly and kiss her again. She slides her arms around my waist and presses her tits against my chest, and I turn to tempered steel in my jeans. She can't still be horny. If we fuck now, I won't be in the best condition to get her pregnant.

"Stop giving me those sex eyes. I thought you weren't going to ruin my plans."

"I just miss you, Lorenzo," she murmurs, stroking the nape of my neck.

I never thought I would turn down sex from my woman. I don't want to turn down sex from my woman. I want to wrap her thighs around my hips and fuck her against the refrigerator.

"Ah, Christ. Uh...I have a patient to deal with down-stairs. One of the fighters at Lasher's gym got into a bar brawl and I'm hiding him from the cops until he heals." The Strife men don't like me treating Lasher or anyone associated with him, but the Strife men can shove it up their asses.

"But, Lorenzo," she whispers so sweetly, "it doesn't feel right that I've had sex with the others this week but not you."

Her eyes are hazy with desire. There's no way she needs more sex but as I try to pull away from her, her arms keep wrapping around me like tentacles. "If you're by some miracle still horny, go upstairs and play with your toy."

I quickly disentangle myself and head for the basement. I have no problem playing the long game. I push the heel of my hand against my erection and groan. Almost no problem.

Two days later, my dick is perpetually hard and all I can think about is ramming it into Chiara and bursting with one thrust. I'm going to lose my fucking mind if this goes on for much longer. I meant to abstain from coming for a week so I'd have plenty of my swimmers stored up, but the other night Salvatore wrapped his hand around Chiara's throat and growled that she was his sweet little cum slut while she was coming on his dick.

I stood in that doorway and rubbed one out in my fist then and there. Salvatore noticed me, but Chiara didn't. Thirty minutes later, I got a text from Salvatore.

SALVATORE: *Why are you lurking like a creeper in Chiara's doorway? You could have just joined in.*

Lorenzo: *I would have been in the way. That looked like a perfect fuck.*

Salvatore: *It was. JFC.*

I LEAN both hands against one of the metal tables in the med room. I'm on the verge of losing it again just thinking about that. The fighter is convalescing at Lasher's place and I'm done cleaning up and restocking.

It's just past seven in the morning. Time to check Chiara's temperature.

I've been doing this in secret since we started trying for a baby, monitoring her morning temperature so I know when she's ovulating. With a laser thermometer in my hand, I slip stealthily into her bedroom.

This morning I've caught her as she's just waking up, and her eyes flutter open as I sit down on the mattress. She spots the thermometer in my hand.

"Lorenzo, what are you doing?"

"Taking your temperature."

"But I feel fine."

I lower the thermometer and smile at the readout. "Princess, you're more than fine. You're about to ovulate."

"I am?"

I give her a kiss and head downstairs to find my head of security. He's in the basement and I give him my orders. "Lock the gate and don't open it until I say so, under any circumstances. If the other three show up, I'm home and so is Chiara, everything's fine, but we're not taking visitors for the next seventy-two hours. If anyone else arrives, I'm not here and you don't know where I am or when I'll be back."

When I turn around, I see that Chiara has followed me downstairs with bare feet and dressed in one of my T-shirts. I stare at her hungrily. All mine for three days.

I push her into the med room and slam the door behind me, then claim her mouth in a kiss. Fucking finally.

"You're really going to do this?" she asks as I lift her onto one of the metal tables. "The others are going to be so mad at you."

She shakes her head like she doesn't approve, but her knees are hugging my hips and she's hooking her fingers into the waistband of my jeans.

"Then they should have thought of it themselves." My mouth descends on hers again and I kiss her hard. I'm so fucking horny that I just want to bend her over my desk and release all this pent-up desire in one glorious, intense fuck.

But we've got the whole compound to ourselves and plenty of time. Let's be romantic.

"You know what we never do?" I say, heading over to the door, grabbing the white coat that's hanging on the back and putting it on.

"What?" she asks.

"Play doctor."

She tips her head back and laughs at my joke. Then her smile fades as she realizes I'm serious. I grab a stethoscope and wrap it around my neck, holding on to the ends with both hands as I saunter back over to her. Her gaze runs up and down my body and I can tell she likes it, but she didn't expect this.

"Isn't playing doctor too corny for you?"

Not the way I play. "I don't know. Try me."

She thinks for a moment, her legs swinging back and

forth. "Doctor, I've been so stressed. Is there something you could do about that?"

I watch her with narrowed eyes, saying nothing.

"You see, there's this gorgeous man who hasn't touched me for more than a week and it's driving me crazy. My muscles feel tense. I can't sleep at night."

"Tense where?" I ask, fitting the stethoscope in my ears and pressing the bell over her chest. Her heartbeat suddenly fills my ears, steady and strong.

"Um, you know. Places."

I fight to keep a straight face. "Miss Romano, please. You can tell me. I'm a doctor."

Her face suddenly flames pink. I've done all kinds of deviant things to her and a little roleplay has her flustered.

"This temperature you've been having. Is this another one of your problems?" I press the backs of my fingers against her hot cheeks.

"Sometimes. When he's teasing me."

"Have you ever felt like things are out of your control? Restlessness? Mood swings?"

She nods, gazing up at me with big eyes.

"Mm-hmm. I see. Is everything all right at home?"

"Well, yes and no. I have four beautiful boyfriends, but I still haven't had...enough."

My eyebrows raise in surprise. "Four? That must be exhausting. Unless they're all weak and impotent. Is that it?"

"No, they're all very strong, virile men, it's just..." She

flicks her gaze up at me. "One of them hasn't touched me in so long, and everything feels wrong."

I gaze down at her with total seriousness. "I see. It's an emergency."

Chiara bursts out laughing again. "I'm so sorry. I'm not laughing at you. I've never done roleplay before but isn't this a bit cutesy for you?"

I give her a faint smile. I'm not offended in the slightest, and she won't be laughing in a minute.

"Miss Romano, have I said something funny?" I pull on a pair of black latex gloves, then reach into a drawer for a bottle of KY Jelly.

She watches me with rapt attention, her eyes growing wider. "Maybe I'm getting hysterical because of my, you know, problems."

"This is more serious than I thought. Take off your clothes from the waist down and turn around."

Chiara grips the edge of the table, hesitating, her lower lip caught between her teeth. Then she hops down from the table and does as she's told, unbuttoning her skirt and slowly shimmying out of it along with her panties.

As soon as her back is turned, a wicked smile spreads over my face. She's self-conscious and uncertain. Perfect.

"Move your legs apart, please, and bend forward."

Chiara does as she's told. The air in the basement is cold and her cute ass pebbles with goosebumps. I admire the view for a moment. Her pink slit getting wetter and darker by the moment. With my gloved fingers, I spread her open like I'm inspecting her.

"Is this where your problem is?"

Chiara replies with a breathy, "Yes."

I spread KY Jelly over my fingers. "Breathe out for me, Miss Romano."

As she does, I push my middle finger deep inside her, and she gasps. "Here?"

"Yes, there."

I feel around inside her, feeling the texture of her inner walls. When I reach a spongy place behind her clit, she yelps as I rub slowly back and forth.

"Oh, yes, I can feel it," I murmur, adding my forefinger. "I often find that if there's a problem here, there's also a problem...here." My thumb is slick with lube and I swipe it over her ass, pressing into it a little.

"I'm not sure—*ah*."

The tight ring of muscle gives way and I push into her ass up to my first knuckle. Chiara breathes hard, one of her legs shaking.

"Aren't you being a good girl for your doctor?" She's leaning far over the metal table and I cup her throat and draw her up, her pussy and ass stretched tight around my fingers. I hold her tight by the neck and keep thrusting my fingers into her. "Spread your legs. Arch your back."

Chiara braces her arms against the table and does as she's told, and I'm able to drive myself further into her. I drag my nails down inside of her forearm. "You know what I've been fantasizing about? Shooting Acid. Not to kill him, just to fuck him up enough that he bleeds a whole lot. Any excuse to stick a needle in your arm and watch your pretty blood drain out of you."

She licks her lips. "You like taking my blood?"

"The times that I've cut you or stuck you have been my favorite fucking things, but I never get to do it just for me. I cut you to get to that tracker. I gave your blood to Acid. When is it my turn?"

"I'm locked in with you. It's no one's turn but yours."

I groan and bury my face in her neck. "Fuck, baby, you know I get excited by the sight of your blood. You think I wanted your virginity just so I could say I was first? I wanted to make you bleed for me."

Chiara gazes at me over her shoulder with hazy eyes. "Then why don't you cut me?"

I fist her hair and pull her head back. "Cut your pretty flesh? What if I like it too much, princess? What if I can't stop?"

"I guess we'll find out."

I test her neck with my teeth, just hard enough to make red marks. "Oh, you really want to play doctor."

Letting go of her throat, I reach for a scalpel and hold it up before her eyes. The instrument glints as I twist it in the light.

"Where should I cut you, princess? A little nick in the side of your neck so your blood runs over your tits? How about your lips so I can taste your blood every time I kiss you? Or down here on the backs of your thighs so I can watch it drip down your legs as I fuck you?"

Before she has a chance to answer me, I ease my fingers

out of her and rip off my gloves. Chiara's bare, beautiful thighs are just begging for the kiss of my scalpel. I place my hand on her thigh, just below the fleshy part of her ass, and hover over the place with the scalpel.

"Here?" I ask.

Chiara grips the table and nods.

"Are you ready? Count slowly to three."

When she reaches two, I slash her skin. A quick, shallow cut that makes her cry out. Her flesh is pink for a moment, and then blood wells up. I groan and put the scalpel on the table, watching her, mesmerized, as I pull off my T-shirt and jeans. As the first rivulet of blood runs down her leg, I grasp the base of my cock and sink into her wet pussy.

I hold her throat and turn her head so I can kiss her as we fuck. "Aren't you good for me, princess? I get to make you bleed and knock you up at the same time. How does a devil like me get into heaven?"

I reach down to her cut and drag my fingers up her thigh, and then hold my bloody fingers up in front of her face.

"Or are you my pretty angel I've dragged down to hell?"

With red, sticky fingers, I find her clit and rub her in fast circles while I fuck her slowly. She keeps her back arched and her head tipped back so I can kiss her.

"If I'm your angel, then hell feels pretty good."

I smile against her lips. My balls are aching and I want to fuck her fast, but now that I've got her like this with no one to interrupt us, I don't want to stop.

"Rub your clit for me. I need both hands for this." I pull out of her and touch the point of the scalpel against her thigh again, right next to the first cut. "Hold still, princess. You don't want me to mess this up."

With the blade at the ready, I listen to her panting and soft moans as she brings herself to orgasm, and just as it starts to pass, I slash her with the scalpel. She breathes in sharply, her eyes wide.

"Can you feel your blood dripping down your legs?"

Chiara nods, still panting.

"One more, princess, a little longer this time. Be a good girl and hold still."

Just one more cut. Don't get greedy.

Savoring the moment, I position the scalpel carefully, and cut her slowly, blood beading up around the sharp metal. Chiara's head bows and she whimpers.

I groan and toss the scalpel onto the table. When I thrust into her, I feel her wet blood on my own thigh. I can't hold back now and I thrust into her deep and fast, one hand braced against the metal table and another fisting in her hair, keeping her in place.

"How's that, princess? You like being a good girl for your doctor?"

Chiara's breathing hard, her eyes closed in ecstasy, and she nods. I pull out for a moment, drag my cock through the blood on her leg and then shove myself back into her.

"Your ripe little pussy is going to be full of my cum, and I'm going to fuck it deeper to make sure I'm the one who breeds you."

I'm brimming with the need to come. Pleasure surges through me and races from my balls to the head of my cock. I grab one of her thighs and hook it up so her knee is on the table and she's spread wide. I keep thrusting even once I'm finished, getting my cum as deep as I can.

I pull out and admire the sight of the blood dripping down her legs and my cum leaking out of her swollen pussy. With the flat of my hand, I smack her ass once, and smile as an exultant feeling spreads through my chest. That should do it, but I've got three days to fuck her to make sure.

I gather Chiara to me and press my lips to the side of her throat. "Who had sex with you last?"

Chiara pushes her hair off her face and takes a deep breath. "Ummm...Vinicius. Last night."

Last night she might have been fertile. It would be just like Vinicius to sneak in ahead of me. "We'll know eventually. If the baby has hazel eyes, it's his, and if it has blue eyes, it's mine."

She shoots me an amused look. "If I am pregnant, and that's a big if, it could be any of yours. Counting days and taking temperatures is all well and good, but my body isn't programmable like a computer. It could just as easily be one of the other's babies."

Yeah, we'll see.

"Come with me and I'll patch you up, princess." The cuts I made in her flesh are already clotting. I grab what I need and take her upstairs, laying her on her side on the sofa. Carefully, I clean the cuts and apply antiseptic. She hisses in pain as the cold, stinging alcohol cleanses her wounds. I work slowly but thoroughly, murmuring to her as I go.

"You're still playing doctor, aren't you?" she asks, head pillowed on a sofa cushion as I cover the cuts with gauze.

A smile spreads over my face. "I am. This is how I play doctor. I cut you and bleed you, and then I'm so fucking nice to you when I clean you up after."

"Will I have scars?"

"Not if you do as you're told and keep these covered." I want to watch these cuts heal day by day until her skin is perfect once more thanks to my attention. Then, I want to pick up my scalpel and cut her all over again.

When I'm finished, Chiara turns to me and takes my face in her hands. "Look at you. You're happy, aren't you?"

I brush my lips over hers. "Who, me?"

"Competition. Machiavellian schemes. Sex. Blood. These are the things that make my Lorenzo happy."

I smile and cup the bandage on her thigh. "And what makes my princess happy?"

She traces my lips with her fingers. "You do."

I gather her closer and lift her up in my arms. Upstairs in my room, I check my phone as I take off my clothes. "Missed calls from Cassius. About a dozen text messages, too."

Chiara gets beneath the blankets and rests her head on my pillow, her expression sweet and trusting despite all the shit I do to her. "Asking why he can't get in?"

"Maybe." I throw my phone aside with a grin and turn back to her.

"Are you going to let him in?"

"Hell, no. I'm not done with you, princess. Now come here."

10

Chiara

After three days of having sex with Lorenzo at all hours of the day and night, I've had more orgasms than I can count and I'm absolutely famished. I don't know where he's found the strength to keep going because he's been existing on nothing but black coffee and sex. I sit up carefully in bed and glance over. Lorenzo's head is on the pillow and his eyes are closed in blissful sleep. He should be pale and fatigued the way he's been carrying on, but he's glowing. I guess a sex diet agrees with him.

My stomach gurgles. Not me. Sex is great but I need food.

As I ease myself out of bed, a strong hand wraps

around my wrist and pulls me back down. "Where do you think you're going?"

"Lorenzo, I'm hungry." I find myself laughing as he nuzzles my neck even as my stomach growls.

"I've got something for you," he mumbles, pushing down the sheets and wrapping his hand around his stiff cock.

"Unless you want me to bite it off, let me go and make a sandwich."

"If you bite my dick, I'll spank your pussy until you come all over my fingers," he threatens with a growl, getting an arm around my hips and pushing my legs open. "Now hold still, I want to make sure you're good and pregnant."

"What if I am pregnant? Shouldn't I eat?"

His eyes open and he frowns. "You're right. Go eat something, and then we'll go again."

I kiss him and slip from the bed, pulling on my underwear and one of his T-shirts to wear as a dress.

Downstairs in the kitchen, the contents of the fridge are dismal. There's been no fresh food restocked since Lorenzo put the place on lockdown. I hunt through the freezer and find a frozen pizza with a cartoon of an Italian chef on the box.

"Oh, Cassius would *hate* you," I tell the pizza with a smile as I open the box and pre-heat the oven.

Twenty minutes later, I'm standing in the kitchen munching happily on pepperoni pizza when Cassius himself strides into the room. He glares at my bed hair, my outfit, and then at the pizza.

"What the hell is going on?" he seethes.

"I was hungry, and Lorenzo didn't have anything else. Honestly, Cassius, it's not that bad. You should try—"

"Not the pizza. He's been fucking you for three days straight, hasn't he?"

Oh yes, that. I hurriedly take another bite as an excuse not to answer.

"Scava!" he roars at the top of his voice. "Get down here, you *cazzo di merda*. I want a word with you."

A few minutes later, Lorenzo appears in the doorway, dressed in jeans, a cocky smirk, and nothing else. "Cassius, how have you been? We've missed you."

Cassius lets forth a stream of angry Italian.

Lorenzo's eyes widen in amusement. "Now, come on, you know I never learned Italian. What's he saying, princess?"

I will cut your balls off and stuff them down your throat, you asshole. How dare you lock Chiara away from the rest of us? Don't you fucking smirk at me.

"Uh, he says hi." I take another bite of pizza.

Cassius goes on ranting until Lorenzo finally loses his patience. "For fuck's sake! If there's some rule I've broken, then tell me what it is. Did we set any fucking rules? Did I bitch about the three of you showing up at my house at all hours of the night to screw our girlfriend? No, I let you all get on with it."

"We never locked Chiara up so you couldn't reach her,"

Cassius snarls. "*Bambina*, pack a bag. We're going to my penthouse."

Lorenzo doesn't break eye contact with Cassius. "Princess, don't fucking move."

I'm not going anywhere. I'm having my lunch.

"Cassius, Chiara is safer here. The gates are open to you and you can see her as much as you want now. Knock yourself out." Lorenzo says this as if he really would like to knock the bigger man unconscious.

Cassius' eyes narrow. "Why did you lock Chiara up for these three days? What's special about these three days?"

Lorenzo grins and rubs his hand over his jaw. "I was tracking Chiara's cycle and taking her temperature, which any of you could have done if you'd thought of it."

"You didn't think to share this information with the rest of us?"

"Fuck, no. I want her carrying my baby."

I wince and take another bite of pizza, wondering if I should call Vinicius. He's so good at diffusing arguments. I'm surprised that Salvatore hasn't shown up yet, shouting his head off. Please, God, don't let Salvatore turn up right now or hands will be thrown.

Cassius is ranting in Italian again, and I put my lunch down and swallow. "Cassius, we'll set some ground rules and Lorenzo won't do this again. I doubt it even worked. I'll probably take a year to get pregnant."

That seems to soothe Cassius' temper. He takes a deep breath and comes over to me and kisses my forehead.

"Damn right he won't do it again." Then he mutters at the pizza, "*Disgustoso.*"

I grin and take another bite.

Lorenzo pats Cassius' shoulder as he moves toward the coffee machine. "Now we've dealt with that, how would you like a cup of coffee, you bad-tempered fuck?"

"*Grazie,*" Cassius murmurs. His hands slide down to my ass and he squeezes me. Then he frowns as he feels the edge of the bandage. "Are you hurt? How did you get hurt?"

I dart a look at Lorenzo and look away again quickly. Somehow, I don't think Cassius will take Lorenzo cutting me with a scalpel in his stride right now. "It's nothing. Never mind."

"Why are you blushing?"

"I'm not."

"Honestly, princess, could you look more guilty?" Lorenzo says as he adds coffee grounds to the machine.

"Do you know what's going on here, Scava?" Cassius asks him.

"Of course."

"How did Chiara get hurt?" Cassius asks, teeth clenched.

A heated smirk slides over Lorenzo's face. "We were playing doctor."

"*What*? You cut her?"

Lorenzo slams a mug onto the counter and rounds on the other man. "I'm about done with you losing your temper and raising your voice to me in my house. Yeah, I cut Chiara. So what? I don't get up your ass when you spank her. I can do what the fuck I want with our princess if she's willing."

And the fight starts all over again, only with Lorenzo fighting back as fiercely as Cassius this time, his expletive-ridden English competing with Cassius' Italian.

I call out, "Stop shouting, it's not good for the baby."

Both of them shut up mid-sentence and turn to stare at me.

"It's me. I'm the baby."

The corner of Lorenzo's mouth twitches but Cassius glowers at my attempt at humor.

"But soon there might *be* a baby," I remind them. "Are you two going to carry on like this when you're fathers?"

They exchange glances, still furious with each other.

I turn to Cassius. "You're frustrated and concerned, but shouting at Lorenzo isn't helping." I turn to Lorenzo. "You knew that locking me away was going to piss the others off. I know you love to win, but having a baby isn't about you. It's about all of us."

The two men glare at each other in hostile silence while I wait. I don't need to spell it out for them. They're not third-graders.

"I'm sorry for shouting, Scava."

Lorenzo rolls his eyes. "Fine. I'm sorry for locking you out."

"Apology accepted."

Lorenzo goes back to making coffee, and I smile at them both. Our first disagreement and we managed to resolve it without any blood being spilled. A few minutes later, the three of us are sitting at the kitchen counter with our mugs.

I take a sip of my latte and look at Cassius. "Why do you call him Scava and not Lorenzo like the rest of us?"

Lorenzo answers for him. "Because he's a pompous, classist asshole with a stick jammed so far up his ass that he can taste wood."

"I thought we were done fighting," I tell him with a meaningful look.

"It's a habit from the old days," Cassius explains with a shrug. "I was a *capo*, a captain, under Francesco Fiore. Scava led a street gang. His family and mine have never been equals."

I wince. "So when you call him Scava it's like you're speaking to an underling? Isn't that inappropriate seeing as you're friends and equals?"

Maybe this is the source of the problems between them, the perceived status differences. It seems to me that these two might not try and one-up each other so often if they spoke to each other with more respect.

I put my hand on Cassius' arm. "Will you try calling him Lorenzo, please? For me?"

Cassius scowls deeply and says nothing.

"Vinicius isn't from an important family, but you don't call him Angeli," I point out.

"Look at Scava's ripped jeans. Look at his hair."

With his arms and chest covered in tattoos and his messy blond locks, he doesn't look anything like Cassius in his designer clothes with his perfectly groomed beard and hair. His manicured nails. Cassius even smells expensive, while Lorenzo smells like blood and sweat.

I love the way both of them look. I love the way both of them smell. Different, but perfect in their own way.

"I am looking, and I love the way Lorenzo looks. I love the way you look, too. I love your voice. I love the way you talk. I love you both for different reasons, but the important thing is, I love you *both*. It would make me so happy to hear you call Lorenzo by his name. And Lorenzo, I would like it if you didn't deliberately annoy Cassius."

"But, princess, that's half my fun."

"I want us all to be as close as five people can be. We should respect each other and not try to compete with each other."

Cassius glances at Lorenzo. "Do you care what I call you?"

Lorenzo rumples his hand through his messy hair, amused. "Whatever makes our princess happy. Why don't you try calling me Lorenzo?"

"Fine. If it will make you happy, Chiara, I will call him Lorenzo," Cassius mutters, his accented voice stiff and awkward.

"Thank you. Maybe it's silly, but it does matter to me." I press a kiss to his cheek, and his face softens.

Lorenzo watches us in silence for a moment, and then he folds his arms, the need to gloat filling his eyes. "You fucking pushover. So much for being Cassius 'women should know their place' Ferragamo. She just twisted you right around her little finger."

Oh, my God.

Cassius' spine straightens in outrage and he roars, "Scava, I will wring your fucking neck!"

"*Lorenzo,* I will wring your fucking neck," Lorenzo corrects. "Thanks for the show, princess. I'll watch you bring this obstinate old bull to his knees any day of the week."

I sigh and rub my forehead. "Lorenzo, what did I just say? He won't call you Scava if you don't wind him up. This has to work both ways."

Lorenzo comes around the counter toward us, a very different expression on his face. "If you really want to bring me and Cassius together, I've got a much better idea."

Cassius seems like he wants to grab Lorenzo and sink his fist into his face as he growls in Italian.

"What idea?" I ask.

Lorenzo's wicked smile widens. "Cassius' thick, veiny dick and mine, fucking you at the same time."

Cassius breaks off and his eyes suddenly kindle with interest. I remember what Lorenzo said to me in bed a few weeks ago.

One day soon I'm getting my dick in here along with someone else's and we're both going to fuck your pussy at the same time. Who shall I choose? How about Cassius. Cassius' big, fat dick and mine railing you together. Will that be enough for you? You greedy bitch. You little cock slut.

Lorenzo slips a hand around my throat and turns my head toward Cassius. "Show him how much you missed him, princess."

"But I—" I break off as Cassius kisses me. All trace of anger is gone and his lips are demanding. My body is caught between the two of them as they slip their hands beneath the T-shirt I'm wearing.

"Tell him how much you missed him," Lorenzo whispers.

Cassius waits, one brow raised. I stroke my fingers through his beard. "I missed you so much."

"Say, please, Cassius, won't you fuck me with your thick cock? I want even more than you in my tight little cunt."

I start to repeat his words, but I'm being led up a horny garden path and I'm not sure how this is going to work.

"*Bambina*, you're not saying anything."

"I think she fucking could, Cassius. Don't you?"

"Absolutely she could."

I look from one man to the other. "*Now* you're agreeing and getting along?"

Cassius kisses my throat and murmurs in my ear, "Who, us? Lorenzo and I are the best of friends. Let us show you."

He lifts me up onto the counter, pulls my panties down my legs and spreads me open, his eyes gleaming as he lowers his head to lick me. Unable to resist, I lean back on my hands. I could tell Cassius' tongue from any of the others' by feel alone. Strong, insistent swipes that taste me as much as they give me pleasure.

"I'm aching to fuck you, *bambina*. You're all I could think about while I was locked out. It was torture."

"Let me help you, best friend." Lorenzo picks me up from behind with his arms hooked underneath my knees and holds me open. With his back against the counter, he waits while Cassius undresses.

I hold on to Cassius' shoulders as he steps toward me, his thickened cock in his hand. With a kiss, he thrusts himself home, and I'm pushed back into Lorenzo.

Lorenzo groans, the sound vibrating through my chest. "I could watch you getting fucked all day, princess."

We both watch Cassius' generous girth disappearing inside me.

"You still think you could both fuck me at the same time?" I gasp between thrusts.

I'm supported by Cassius' arms and so Lorenzo is able to let go of one of my thighs and his fingers find my clit. His devilish voice is in my ear. "You're getting wetter at just the suggestion. You want this so bad."

Just as I'm getting close to coming, Lorenzo stops touching me. He does this over and over until I'm panting in frustration. "Just let me come, please."

"Not like this. Let's go upstairs."

Cassius helps me to my feet and we walk naked through the house and upstairs to Lorenzo's room.

"Get her on top like you love to do," Lorenzo says.

But Cassius is already on it, laying back on Lorenzo's

bed and pulling me on top of him. This feels even more deviant than taking both Salvatore and Vinicius in my ass and pussy, because I could get pregnant this way.

I feel Lorenzo behind me and he has a bottle of lube in his hand that he's applying to his cock. Cassius slows his thrusts and I feel the head of Lorenzo's cock pushing at my entrance. He's squeezes hard and it feels impossible, but then an inch or so of him slips inside me.

My head tips back and I groan. "I can't believe you're actually doing this."

"Just you wait. Relax now, princess, and let us fuck you."

With every slow stroke of Cassius' cock, Lorenzo works himself deeper.

"That's so fucking tight, both of us jammed into you like this," he whispers in my ear.

So *full*.

Too much but just perfect.

Cassius and Lorenzo move together in unison, slow thrusts that have me nearly blacking out from pleasure. I turn my head and watch us in the mirror, my body supported by strong arms, my men breathing hard, their cocks wet and shiny as they slowly push into me and out again.

"Does it feel weird that your dicks are rubbing together?"

"Inside you, it's perfect," Lorenzo says.

Cassius' head falls back and he groans. "We're going to

nut in you at the same time, *bambina*. I hope you like it messy."

"You know she does."

I moan and reach down between my legs to rub my clit. I'm so close after all of Lorenzo's edging and I'm so over-stimulated that I barely need to stroke myself before I feel my orgasm rising up like a tidal wave.

Lorenzo says through clenched teeth, "Cassius, I'm going to blow. Do I need to stop or—"

Beneath me, Cassius' body is hotter than a furnace and every muscle is straining. "Fuck, no, holy fucking hell, Chiara."

In unison, they thrust deeper, hands clenching my arms and waist as they climax, driving my own peak higher. We collapse against each other in a panting, sweating heap.

Cassius supports my body in his hands as they draw out of me. Lorenzo groans and flops down on the bed. I lower myself on rubbery arms and wriggle between them.

"I can't believe you both made that work. If my baby has a fiery temper, blue eyes, black hair, and a taste for good Italian food, I'll know why."

I glance between Cassius and Lorenzo, and both of them are smiling with their eyes closed.

"I'm glad you two are friends again."

Lorenzo grins. "When were we not? We're best of fucking friends."

"*Completamente giusto*," Cassius murmurs sleepily. *Exactly right.*

Snuggled between them, it's hard to believe they were shouting at each other a short time ago. I reach up and touch both their jaws. "I have one small request. I want you to say one nice thing about each other."

"I said, like, ten nice things about his dick earlier," Lorenzo replies, and Cassius laughs softly. "Doesn't that count?"

"You did, but there's more to you both than your dicks."

He glances at Cassius, and I hold my breath, wondering if he's about to wind the Italian man up again. "Sure, princess. If it's what you want. Cassius isn't happy unless the people he loves are happy and safe. The syndicate. You. The dancers in his clubs and everyone in between. No one's beneath his notice."

I smile and thread my fingers through his hair. "That's beautiful and so true."

Cassius still has his eyes closed. "I've never met a man more loyal than Lorenzo. He would never let us or anyone on his team down, and he would never think of looking at a woman who isn't you." He opens one eye. "But don't lock my woman away from me ever again, or I'll punch your fucking teeth out."

"Got it." Lorenzo raises a brow at me. "Are you happy now?"

I snuggle down between my two handsome men, a huge smile on my face. "Happier than you could know."

"You'd better look after those cuts on her thigh, Lorenzo."

He strokes my hair back from my face. Taking care of

these cuts seems like half the satisfaction for him. "I'll take good care of her, don't you worry." He rubs his thumb over my lips. "Say thank you to Cassius for worrying about you."

"Thank you, Cassius."

"Three cuts...and she held so still. Her pretty blood dripped down her leg as I fucked her. No complaints as I cleaned her up. So brave, our princess."

Cassius' face relaxes into a smile. "Of course she was."

11

Vinicius

"Do you really think this is going to work?" Thane asks.

I sigh as I make a left-hand turn. On the other end of the line, Thane is silent, waiting for me to reply. "I don't know, but it's the only plan I've got."

"It sounds like a suicide mission," he mutters. "Do you want me there with you?"

Even if we took off all his jewelry and put him into normal clothes, Thane would still be Thane. Tall and as ominous as a raven. "Thanks for the offer, but you don't blend in and you can't act normal."

"Fair. Bye." He hangs up.

That's one part of the plan put in place. Now for the hard part.

Ten minutes later, I pull into Lorenzo's basement garage and hear sounds coming from down the concrete hall. I follow the noises, a folder of printouts tucked under my arm.

When I walk into the med bay, Chiara's got both hands braced on a metal table, her panties around her knees, and her legs spread. Lorenzo has his fingers against her clit and he's working it quickly while he whispers into her ear. I stop dead and watch them, a smile spreading over my face.

As she comes, her body bucks against his and he wraps a hand around her throat. Lorenzo doesn't stop fingering her even as her orgasm passes.

"Again."

"No, please, I can't, it's too much—" she sobs.

"Do as you're fucking told," he growls, pinning her in place with his arm and mercilessly rubbing her clit. She writhes in his grip, desperately trying to get away from him. A moment later the agony on her face morphs into pleasure and she comes again.

Finally, he releases her and she collapses over the table on both forearms, breathing hard.

"Perfect, princess." Lorenzo puts on black gloves and reaches for a white tube, and with a careful finger, he smooths salve across the cuts on her thigh. So gentle now. So careful of his girl. He covers the cuts with a sticky bandage, then draws her underwear up over her ass and settles them into place.

"Knock, knock," I call, sauntering into the room. "Lorenzo, I hurt myself too. Is it my turn?"

He tosses me the white tube with a lazy grin. "Knock yourself out."

I throw the salve back to him. "The others are upstairs. I want to talk to you all about something."

Chiara comes over to me with flushed cheeks and a happy smile, and plants a soft kiss on my jaw. I love seeing her like this, but I wish she didn't look so happy right now. In a few minutes, I'm going to destroy that blissful expression.

When we're all gathered in the lounge on the sofas, I put the folder on the coffee table. "Thane and I have been working on a theory. This is going to be a tough conversation. If anyone needs a break at any point, just say so."

Cassius frowns and so does Salvatore, but no one says anything. I open up the folder and lay out a series of print-outs on the coffee table. Newspaper articles with gruesome headlines.

BODY DISPLAYED AT TWISTED MURDER SCENE.

TORTURE VICTIM SURVIVED FOR DAYS BEFORE DEATH.

MISSING WOMAN FOUND MUTILATED AND BEHEADED.

Finally, I lay a map on the table with cities marked with red dots. A dozen or so cities clustered around Coldlake.

Salvatore leans forward and reads the map upside

down. "Washington. Pittsburgh. Philadelphia. Chicago. Coldlake. What do the dots mean?"

Chiara has picked up the newspaper articles and is skimming them. "Are the dots murders?"

I nod. "Unsolved murders, all within the last twenty years. All the victims were women who were abducted and then found dead, and all had been tortured or their dead bodies were displayed in some grotesque manner."

Chiara glances up at me. "Do you think these deaths are connected to your sisters?"

"I think it's a possibility." I look around at the others. "Think about it. Whoever killed our sisters, they knew what they were doing. You don't just wake up one morning a law-abiding citizen and—I'm sorry for bringing up Ophelia, Salvatore—make someone scream herself to death. Ophelia was the first to die, but that wasn't a first-time kill."

"Yeah, you're right," Salvatore says, his voice hoarse.

Cassius is reading an article about a woman found hanging from children's play equipment in a park. "Your theory makes sense to me. Evelina's killer knew what he was doing and kept her alive as long as he could. He enjoyed every fucking second of what he did to her."

"The police haven't connected any of these murders, just so we're clear," I tell them, gesturing at the printouts. "This is research I've been working on with Thane. It might be nothing."

Lorenzo narrows his eyes. "Or it might be something. Thane's been helping you?"

"Thane's been great. I think he feels bad that he didn't notice that the pictures of Nicole were fake." Or his professional pride is hurt and he's trying to make up for his mistake. That's more likely. Either way, I'm glad for his help.

Chiara keeps reading. "I don't see anything about the killer leaving black flowers behind when he abducted the victims in these articles. Or putting black flowers in the women's mouths."

I nod. "Yes, you're right. That's something special about the Coldlake murders. Our sisters were killed to send a message to us. Someone wanted us to suffer. I've been wondering if these other murders were done purely for pleasure."

"You think a serial killer came to Coldlake and murdered our sisters?" Lorenzo asks.

"I'm saying it's a possibility. That, or the killer is from Coldlake and they made it a rule never to kill in their own backyard, but they hate us so much that they made an exception."

Chiara looks sadly at the newspaper articles. "All these unsolved murders. Do you think the police didn't care about these women, either?"

"Maybe. Or maybe they tried and didn't get anywhere. Murders go unsolved when there's nothing to connect the victims to the killer. Usually, the husband did it or it was a jealous lover. A co-worker. Someone in the victim's circle. When it's a total stranger, the cops don't know where to turn."

"Or they just don't give a fuck about the victims and don't even try to investigate," Cassius mutters.

"You're right, there was no investigation for our sisters. But that doesn't mean there's no evidence."

Lorenzo perks up. "Oh?"

I look around at each of them. "The day our sisters' bodies were found, photos would have been taken of the crime scenes. Evidence put into little plastic bags. DNA swabs taken. A pathologist must have done an autopsy on each of our sisters, even if it was only cursory. Some reports would have been filed. It's standard procedure. What should have happened next was the detectives looking at the evidence and starting to investigate."

"But they didn't," Salvatore mutters.

"No, they didn't. My guess is all that evidence has been languishing in a box for nine years, gathering dust."

Chiara stares at me over a printout. "If that's true, then the killer's identity might be in that box. Their DNA. Their fingerprints. CCTV recordings. If we got our hands on it, we could investigate their deaths ourselves."

"We'd have to see what evidence there is first, assuming it hasn't been accidentally on purpose destroyed." I smile at her. "But yes, you're right. That's exactly what I want to do. Acid and Zagreus are connected to private investigators. Lorenzo knows medical people. Between us and Strife, we could launch a pretty good investigation on our own. If Strife can be persuaded to help us."

"Strife owes me a favor," Chiara points out. "A big one."

"They sure do, kitten." I pick up one of the printouts.

"This murder in Shady Point caught my interest. It's a town off the Interstate between Philadelphia and Coldlake."

Salvatore takes the page from me and starts reading aloud. "Unsolved murder of a nineteen-year-old woman from thirteen years ago...name's Kira Campbell...body mutilated and posed...missing four days before she was found dead." He grimaces. "Sounds familiar. What caught your interest about this one?"

"Thane and I can't find any connections between the Coldlake cops and the Shady Point cops. Shady Point is a small town. No corruption. Not much crime. They hold a vigil for Kira Campbell every year. A place like that wants its cold cases solved." I look at each of them in turn. "That makes it perfect for us."

"Perfect how?" Chiara asks.

"Imagine that the Shady Point detectives have been doing this research," I say, indicating the articles and the map laying on the coffee table. "They see that there were four unsolved murders in Coldlake around the time Kira Campbell was killed. They also discover that there wasn't much of an investigation and they're hungry for leads that might help them solve their own cold case. They approach the Coldlake cops and ask if they can come and talk to them about the Black Orchid Killer, and the Coldlake cops say sure, knock yourself out."

"How are you going to persuade the Shady Point cops to do that?" Cassius asks.

"I'm not. I am the Shady Point detectives." I turn to

Salvatore with a smile. "Me, and maybe you. We could pass for detectives. Are you up for it?"

Salvatore stares at the printouts on the coffee table. All this time, we've been assuming that the murders were a Coldlake phenomenon. I don't think the possibility crossed anyone's mind that other women could be suffering like our sisters.

He nods sharply. "Yeah, I'm up for it."

"Hold up. What about your faces?" Lorenzo asks. "You two are known criminals."

"Suspected criminals," Salvatore counters.

"Whatever. The point is, the Coldlake cops know you, and there are bounties on your heads. You're going to walk into police HQ and have a friendly chat? You'll be fucking arrested."

"Yes, we are just going to walk in, and no, we won't be arrested. Don't you remember the Main Street bank robbery three years ago?"

"I remember that," Chiara chimes in. "A man walked into the biggest bank in Coldlake and talked his way into the vault in the middle of the day. He stole millions in jewels and bonds."

"Two and a half million, to be exact," I say with a smile. "I would have managed more but my bags and pockets were full."

Her eyes grow round. "That was you? But the robber didn't look anything like you! I saw the CCTV images."

"It's a wonder what makeup, prosthetics, and a bit of acting will do. The Coldlake cops know Salvatore and me as the handsome, well-dressed, confident men you see before you. I'll turn us into two over-caffeinated, over-worked cops in cheap suits in less than an hour. Fake badges and IDs are no problem. And I haven't told you the best part of our plan yet."

"Well?" Cassius asks.

I hold out my hand to Chiara. "Our beautiful junior detective who'll have the Coldlake detectives falling over themselves to help us. Kitten, do you mind working a room full of jaded men with your charm?"

Since the night of the poker game, I've known that she'd do anything to help us. For this mission, I need her.

"For you and for your sisters, I'll do anything. I think that's a wonderful idea and I'd love to be part of your plan."

Salvatore smiles at her. "Wonderful, baby."

"I don't like this," Cassius mutters, but he knows as well as I do that it's Chiara's decision, not his. He glances at Lorenzo. "What do you think, Lorenzo?"

Lately, Cassius has been saying Lorenzo instead of Scava. I don't know why he's switched, but I like it.

Lorenzo peers at me and then at Chiara. "I think you'd better make fucking great disguises, or our next plan will be me and Cassius breaking the three of you out of jail."

"Vinicius can do it," Chiara says, turning to me with shining eyes. "What happens next?"

"Thane and I have already made email contact with the Coldlake detectives. It looks official and they don't suspect a thing. Next, we try and make an appointment to meet with them at the station. When we do, I'll take Salvatore and Chiara to the factory and we'll see what we can turn ourselves into."

"What's the factory?" Chiara asks.

"That's my place, kitten. You've never been to my loft or the place where I work before. I can't wait to show it to you."

Cassius takes Chiara's face in his hands and kisses her. "See that you're careful. You're walking into the lion's den and those cops could take you straight to your father if they realize who you are."

Lorenzo gets to his feet. "I'm not turning cartwheels at the thought, but Chiara's always said she wanted to help. You'll be careful, won't you, princess?"

"I will," she tells him with a smile.

He points a forefinger at her. "See that you are. I'm not kidding." Then he walks off, muttering, "What a fucking plan. I prefer my plans."

"That's because when you make plans, Chiara ends up naked in your bed," I call after him.

"Exactly," he calls over his shoulder.

After that, things come together faster than Thane or I anticipated. Within a week I'm looking at an email from the detectives at Coldlake Central Police Station confirming our appointment.

"Well, fuck. We did it." I put my phone into my pocket and head to my car, smiling. It's not my usual Ferrari, but a dark blue mid-range sedan with tinted windows.

Chiara is at Salvatore's house having coffee with

Ginevra and playing with the baby. When I walk into the lounge twenty minutes later, Chaira has Camillo in her arms and she's feeding him from a bottle. I smile at the sight, because she just looks so sweet with a baby in her arms. Cassius and Salvatore were annoyed that Lorenzo locked her up for her fertile days, but if it worked, I don't care. I won't put up with Lorenzo doing that again, but the sooner Chiara is pregnant, the sooner the four of us will be fathers. I'm nearly thirty. Cassius will be forty in a few years' time. We're in our primes and we don't have children, but goddamn it, we should have lots of children. Chiara's only eighteen and that means she has plenty of childbearing years ahead of her.

She says she only wants four. Screw four.

I head over to her with a smile and drop a kiss on her lips. "Aren't you a pretty picture?"

Chiara only wants to gush about the baby. "He's so sweet, and Ginevra says he's such a good sleeper and he barely cries. My mom always says I was a good baby so maybe we'll have one just like him."

Maybe we will, but it depends on who the baby takes after. Among the four of us, there's bound to be an Olympic-level screamer. "If our baby takes after me, he'll be cute as a button. Or perhaps you'll have twins, like me and Amalia."

"Twins, I hadn't thought of that." She looks both nervous and excited at the thought.

Ginevra says, "Chiara's been telling me that my little

Camillo has been making my brother and his friends as broody as hens."

I let Camillo grasp my forefinger and I wiggle it gently up and down. "How could he not? Look at this adorable bundle."

"Did you come here to coo over the baby or did you have business with Salvatore?" Chiara asks.

"Business with you, actually, kitten. Things are moving forward on that plan we talked about."

Chiara's eyes open wide. "That's wonderful. Give me a few minutes and then I'm all yours."

I stroke her cheek and smile. "No rush. Get your fill of baby cuddles."

"What's that boring car doing in my driveway, Vinicius?"

I turn around and see Salvatore standing in the doorway. "Oh, hello. That car? We have plans for that car. You, me, and Chiara."

Realization flashes over his face, and I head over to him. In a soft voice that won't carry to Ginevra, I murmur, "Detective Johansson, Detective Bartlett, and Junior Detective Bianca Azzuro have appointments this Thursday with the Coldlake cold case team."

"You're a magician. I can't believe you've managed it."

"Believe it. I'm a master. When Chiara's finished with the baby, I'm taking you both to the factory and we're trying on disguises."

I watch Chiara talking to Camillo, her forefinger

brushing the tip of his nose. "Doesn't that sight just melt your heart and harden your dick."

Salvatore gazes at her, a lopsided smile on his face. "Absolutely."

Half an hour later, when we're on the freeway going northeast, I make a call. "I'm headed to the factory. Meet me there in twenty minutes."

"On my way," a flat voice replies.

"That was Thane, wasn't it?" Chiara asks from the back seat. She's sitting in the middle seat and she's cuddled against Salvatore. "Is it difficult working with him after what they did?"

I give a humorless laugh. "Yes. Part of me still wishes Salvatore and Lorenzo had shot him for what he and the Strife men did. That's what my heart wants. That's what my guts want. But you made the right choice, and you're the only one who could have granted them mercy. Salvatore and Lorenzo wouldn't have listened to anyone else."

"I still fantasize about murdering them," Salvatore mutters, stroking his fingers down Chiara's thigh.

When I exit the freeway, Chiara leans forward to talk to me. "I'm excited to see where you live. Yours is the only home I haven't seen."

"It's not palatial like Salvatore's house or as secure as Lorenzo's, and it's not sleek and modern like Cassius' apartment, but I'm proud of it."

The north of Coldlake doesn't have the riches that the south and east do, but it's not as rough as Lorenzo's quadrant, either. Residential streets and rows of cafés, hardware

stores and fried chicken shops give way to old brick facto-
ries. Some have been converted into apartments or offices.
Others stand empty and boarded up.

My home stands on a wide, leafy street, an old light-
bulb factory across the road from a motorcycle and car
repair shop with two dozen vehicles slowly rusting on
their lot. It's not a pretty location, from the outside anyway,
but it's home.

I pull into the lot in front of my building and cut the
engine. "Welcome to the factory, kitten."

We get out, and Chiara gazes up at the four floors.

"Level one, a legitimate printery." Half a dozen people
run the printing machines and take orders from
customers. The accounts are scrupulously kept and all
taxes are paid. "Level two, offices, computers, storage,
many locked rooms with interesting things behind doors.
Maybe two-thirds legal." I flash Chiara a smile. "Level
three. Counterfeit operations and my private offices. Only
a third of what goes on there is legitimate. And finally,
level four. My loft apartment. All mine and entirely illegal." I lower my mouth to Chiara's and kiss her as she
laughs.

An engine throbs behind us, and a tall, broad-shoul-
dered man on a black-and-silver motorcycle pulls into the
lot. He's dressed head to toe in black leather with a shiny
black helmet. He looks at me, then at Salvatore, and finally
gets off the bike and pulls his helmet off.

"Hey, Thane," I call, and he nods.

Salvatore says nothing as his eyes narrow. Thane gazes

back at him, unzips his leather jacket, tucks his helmet under his arm, and strides into the factory without a word.

"Isn't he chatty," Chiara murmurs, and takes Salvatore's hand and gives it a squeeze.

I give Chiara a brief tour of the first and second floors as we head up the broad, concrete steps. "The building was built in the 1920s. I've renovated the whole place but kept the charm of the exposed brick and brass fittings."

"It's very stylish, just like its owner," Chiara says, gazing up at the high ceilings and huge windows that let in the light.

"Thank you, kitten. I like it very much."

When we reach my offices, Thane's sitting at the huge oval meeting table and he's opened his laptop. He doesn't look up as we approach and goes on typing.

"What a stunning view," Chiara says, moving to look out the window that takes up the entire wall that faces south. All of Coldlake is spread out before us.

Thane turns his laptop around to face us and stares at me, baleful impatience written on his cold features.

He can wait. My woman is admiring the view from my building.

Finally, Chiara turns to Thane with a smile. "Hello. Have you got something to show us?"

Thane launches into an explanation of the schematics on his screen. "Here are the floor plans of the police station. You're meeting the detectives here." He points at a place on the screen and moves his finger. "The evidence lockers are here, and also here in the basement. Cold case archive boxes are probably in the basement. The case number is on this piece of paper. There'll be CCTV cameras everywhere so try not to look sus as you snoop around the building."

I shake my head. "We're not going to snoop. The nice detectives are going to give us the evidence."

"Human beings don't always do what they're told." Thane's lip ever so slightly curls. He prefers the mathematical predictability of machines and systems.

"They'll do it for me. It's called charm." I glance at Chiara. "And if my charm isn't enough, we have Chiara."

Thane flicks his gaze up and down Chiara and turns back to his computer. "I gave all the Shady Point detectives' data to Vinicius and he's made your badges and IDs. Unless you have questions or need tech support on the day, I'll be going."

"That's everything we need," I tell him.

He closes his laptop and stands up, addressing me. "All the files are in our shared folder. Later."

Thane moves toward the door and then turns back to us.

"I have a message from Acid." Thane glances at Chiara, black hair falling into his eyes and the merest suggestion of a smirk on his lips. He places the toe of one boot behind the other and ducks his head, almost a bow, but not quite. "Good luck, your highness."

Chiara smiles at him, genuinely amused. "Acid's so thoughtful. Tell him thank you. And thank you too, Thane. I appreciate all your work."

Thane scours her expression, searching for sarcasm.

Salvatore folds his arms and glares at him. "Chiara means what she says, unlike you."

Thane shrugs and heads for the door, raising one hand in farewell before he's gone.

I turn away with a shake of my head. "I have our disguises upstairs. Come with me."

I lead the two of them upstairs and unlock the door to my apartment. It takes up the entire top floor of the building. The ceiling is high and there's plenty of natural light. I've decorated it in an eclectic style. Interesting pieces of furniture and décor that don't match but somehow work together to give the place an air of elegance and comfort.

Chiara gazes around. "Vinicius, your place is amazing. How come I've never been here before?"

"It's not as secure as Lorenzo's and Cassius' places, and it's not as sprawling as Salvatore's, but it's home. I like it."

"I *love* it," Chiara says, walking across the open space. I suddenly see her here with a baby. A little boy. They're sitting together on the rug beneath the huge windows playing with colored blocks.

For a second, I can't breathe.

I want that.

I want that so much.

It doesn't have to be my son. It could be any of our sons, and I will love him so fiercely until the day I die. If I can't have this, then everything else in my life will feel meaningless and I don't know what I'll do.

I realize Chiara is staring at me with her head on one

side and she's asked me a question. "Are you all right, Vinicius?"

Salvatore clasps my shoulder as he passes me and shoots me a knowing look. "He just loves you, baby."

I come back into myself and smile at her. "Have I told you lately how beautiful you are?"

"You probably have, but I'll happily hear it again," she says, returning my smile.

"You're beautiful, kitten. Now come with me and we'll go play dress-up."

I have our planned disguises laid out on my dressing table next to my bottles of cologne, and I pass Chiara a wig.

"Try this on. If it suits you, we can tie it back in a low ponytail. These detectives will have seen you with your glorious blonde hair and wearing designer dresses. In a plain skirt suit and with a wig and darkened eyebrows and lashes, they won't recognize you."

She scoops up her blonde hair and pulls the wig on. Long, dark brown hair cascades over her shoulders, and with the bangs in her eyes, she looks different already.

"I like it. What are you and Salvatore wearing?"

"Cheap suits. An auburn hair rinse for Salvatore and a mustache for me."

"Auburn," Salvatore says with a grimace. "I'll look washed out."

"That's the idea. We want to look like ordinary country cops, not the devilishly handsome city mafiosos that we are."

I pass Salvatore a box of hair dye and apply a fake mustache to my upper lip. It's hideous. My hair is too long and I need a haircut, which is on purpose. I want to look like an unkempt country detective. I pull a shoulder holster on over my shirt and muss up my hair.

"What do you think, do I look the part?"

Chiara runs her fingers up and down the straps of my gun holster. "I don't know about the mustache, but this is pretty sexy."

"Oh, yes?" I say, enjoying the expression on her face. My cock stirs in my pants. Her wig is interesting, too. The dark hair gives her a bad-girl appearance. She seems to think so, too, as she runs her forefinger down the buttons of my shirt.

"Detective Bartlett, is there anything I can help you with?"

Salvatore looks up from scowling at the box of hair dye and throws it aside. He strides toward Chiara, scoops her up in his arms, and carries her over to the bed. "Yes, there is. I'm tired of thinking about this mission. Let's get back to the fun mission."

"Which is?" Chiara asks.

Salvatore grins as he loosens his tie. "Getting you pregnant."

12

Chiara

Salvatore looms over me as he takes off his clothes, his gaze sharp and hungry as I wriggle out of my own.

"Are you getting in on this?" he asks Vinicius over his shoulder.

Vinicius lays along the bed with his head propped against his palm, a smile on his lips. "Don't mind me. I'll just watch for the moment."

Salvatore cups my jaw and purrs, "Oh, I enjoy an audience. Shall we show off for him, baby?"

"I love to show off," I say, reaching between my legs to drag the wetness from my pussy up over my clit, enjoying both men watching me do it.

Salvatore grasps my legs, pushes them wider, and spits on my pussy. I moan as it trickles down.

He looks up sharply and his lips curve into a vicious smile. "You like that? Open your mouth."

I do as he asks and he leans over me and spits in my mouth. My eyes open wide, and then he slams two fingers into me as I swallow him down.

"You dirty bitch." Before I can answer, he grabs my throat and squeezes. Hard. He's the Salvatore I encountered on my seventeenth birthday, hard expression and eyes glittering with wickedness.

I can't tear my eyes away from him.

I'll happily be his dirty bitch.

Still squeezing my throat, he walks his knees up the bed and grasps his cock, sinking into me.

"Salvatore," I manage to gasp around the tight grip he has on my throat.

"Yes, baby?" he asks, his voice dripping with fake sweetness.

"Hit me."

He shoots me a look of molten desire and lets go of my throat, slapping me across the face.

Hard.

Leaving me gasping.

My head snaps to the side and my eyes water. Heat burns right through me and condenses in my clit.

"Salvatore, for fuck's sake," Vinicius exclaims.

"What? She likes it. Don't you, baby?" His voice is full

of sweetness again and he draws my face back to his and kisses me.

I'll show him how much I love it. I grasp his wrist and run my nails down his muscled forearm as he pushes his thumb into my mouth. I suck on it, closing my eyes and enjoying the burn in my cheek.

"Good girl," he purrs.

I could come just from the way he's talking to me.

"She's sucking so good. Get over here and choke her with your cock."

Vinicius sits up on the bed and takes off his clothes. A moment later I feel the mattress next to my head sink as he kneels there, and I turn my head to take him in my mouth.

Vinicius' fingers trail over my reddened cheek.

"Pretty, isn't she?" Salvatore asks.

"She's always pretty."

"She sure is. Especially getting railed at either end."

I open my eyes and lock gazes with Salvatore as I work Vinicius with my mouth. Salvatore's breathing hitches and his gaze grows unfocused. I look between the two of them as their breathing grows ragged. Now I'm the one in control as I suck slowly up and down and keep my hand firmly on Salvatore's hip.

Vinicius half laughs, half groans. "Not so hard, kitten. I don't want to nut in your mouth."

I run my tongue up the underside of his cock. That sounds like a Vinicius problem, not a me problem, and I keep going.

"How I love your mouth when you do that, baby,"

Salvatore says, his hair falling into his eyes as he works his thick cock in and out of me.

He lets go of my throat and tweaks my nipples, and I moan around Vinicius.

"Fuck, I'm going to nut." Salvatore groans as he comes deep inside me. He breathes hard and smiles, gazing at me before pulling out. He starts to lean down so he can lick my clit, but Vinicius pulls him away from me.

"I want to do that. You come up here and hold her, you fucking animal," Vinicius scolds him, but he's smiling as he says it.

Salvatore slips behind me on the bed and pulls my back against his chest. His lips are against my ear and he cradles my head as he murmurs, "Am I a beast to you, baby?"

I can't reply for a few seconds because Vinicius has swiped his tongue over my clit, and then starts working it. "Yes," I gasp, my back arching.

"We're all a little beastly. Lorenzo putting a gun to your head. Cassius putting you over his knee. Vinicius sneaking into your room and pinning you down with his dick before you even knew what was happening."

"You got soaking wet the first time we met you," Vinicius murmurs against my clit between laps of his tongue. "Did you ever work out which one of us it was?"

He darts a look up at me, his green-gold eyes flashing.

"All of us, kitten. Wasn't it?"

As my breathing grows harder, I feel Salvatore's hand creeping around my throat. He whispers savagely in my ear that I love being their dirty little slut as Vinicius keeps working me with his tongue. "Full of cum already and just aching for more, aren't you?"

I climax with a strangled cry. Vinicius sits up and grasps my hips, and I feel his cock sink into me. He fucks me fast before my orgasm can finish, making it go on and on while Salvatore squeezes my throat. All the blood rushes to my head.

"You don't need to breathe, do you? You just need to come," Salvatore whispers in my ear.

I couldn't breathe even if he wasn't choking me. I'm sky-high on what they're doing and I don't come down until Vinicius thrusts deep with his own climax and slowly pulls out.

I slump back on the bed, breathing hard and feeling boneless.

Salvatore smiles down at me, and then glances at Vinicius. "Good work, team. I think we're ready for our mission."

"Dream team," Vinicius agrees, pushing his hair off his sweaty forehead, his eyes glowing.

THE MORNING OF OUR MEETING, we drive to the police station in Vinicius' blue sedan. My stomach is a riot of nerves and I can't stop fidgeting in the back seat.

Salvatore reaches back from the front passenger seat and takes my hand, squeezing tight before letting go. His hair has an auburn tint, his suit isn't nearly as well-tailored as usual, and his tie is ugly, but he's still my handsome Salvatore. "Nervous, baby?"

"I feel like I'm sneaking around behind my father's back and he's about to jump out and catch me."

Vinicius grins at me in the rearview mirror. "We're always sneaking around behind the mayor's back, if you think about it."

True. I take a deep breath and remind myself what I need to do. Smile at the male detectives and ask questions that two hard-boiled detectives wouldn't stoop to ask. My skirt is knee-length but tight and I'm wearing high heels. My long dark wig is pinned half-up, with the rest cascading down my back.

Salvatore and Vinicius have their badges clipped to their belts and I have mine around my neck. When we park outside the station and head through to the front desk, the officer on duty gives our badges the merest of glances before buzzing us through.

Vinicius told us this would happen. If you're relaxed and look like you should be there, badges and ID almost don't matter.

Two Coldlake detectives greet us and shake our hands, introducing themselves as Detective Hardy and Detective Simmons. We decided that Vinicius should do most of the talking as he's the most practiced at coercion and subterfuge, and he seems in no hurry to get to the point, chatting about the precinct, the city, that one time he came to Coldlake on a family holiday.

Eventually, once we're sitting at the detectives' desks with mugs of coffee, Vinicius brings up the murders and asks the men who they think killed the four sisters.

Simmons waves a careless hand. "The brothers did it themselves. They're like Roman emperors, cleansing all the competition. You take power, and you kill your family so no one can take it away from you."

Detective Hardy nods, his expression grim. "I'm sorry, but you wasted your time coming up to Coldlake. These deaths are cold cases, but it's an open secret in this city who murdered those girls. A shame we'll never be able to pin it on the brothers."

Next to me, I feel Salvatore tense up like he wants to argue with them, and I quickly say, "These organized criminals are such animals. By the way, I heard a curious thing about your upcoming election. One of the candidates for mayor is..." I trail off with a smile. "A bit strange?"

Both detectives burst out laughing.

"Oh, you mean Christian 'corpse-fucker' Galloway. Yeah, we have weirdos all over this city," Detective Hardy tells me.

I exchange banter with him, pretending to be shocked yet fascinated by the gossip and giving him as many smiles as I can. We're not *that* interested in the murders, I'm trying to convey. We're not going to cause you more work or imply that you're lazy or stupid.

When the detectives are relaxed again, Salvatore asks, "Out of curiosity, was there much evidence collected for this cold case?"

"Oh, yeah. There'll be some downstairs in the basement."

"What sort of evidence?" I ask, eyes wide.

Detective Simmons passes a hand over his jaw. "Items collected at the crime scenes like ligatures, weapons, clothing. Reports. Any DNA swabs will be in cool storage off-site, though."

"Could we trouble you to take a quick look at what you have here? Then we'll be on our way," Vinicius tells them. "I should go back to Kira's family with something concrete to report. Kira's our local girl who was murdered."

The Coldlake detectives exchange glances. They clearly think this is a waste of their time and effort.

"I think about that poor girl all the time," I say sadly. "My mom knows her mom and she's set her heart on me finding out who murdered Kira."

Detective Hardy shrugs and stands up. "Sure. No one's poked around in that box for years, though. There's no guarantee there's anything interesting in there."

"No problem at all," Vinicius says, getting smoothly to his feet. He catches my eye as we follow the detectives downstairs, and he gives me a quick smile and a wink.

Nice work, kitten.

The evidence room is packed with shelves all filled with archive boxes. Detective Hardy walks along the rows muttering the case numbers under his breath until he finds what he's looking for.

"Here we go." He weighs it in his hands and frowns

before setting it on the table in front of Salvatore. "Have at it."

My heart is beating in my throat. Salvatore pulls back the lid and Vinicius and I crowd forward to stare inside. My mouth falls open.

Whatever I expected, this wasn't it.

13

Chiara

Vinicius rips his fake mustache off and throws it onto the dashboard of the blue sedan. "Motherfucker."

We're silent on the drive back to the compound, each of us sunk in disappointment. All our hopes, Vinicius and Thane's hard work, all gone to waste.

When we pull into the underground garage at the compound, Cassius comes downstairs, his expression alight with anticipation. Lorenzo emerges from the med room and even his eyes are brighter than usual. Both their faces dim as we get out of the car.

"It didn't work," Lorenzo guesses.

"Worse," Salvatore says. "It worked, but there was nothing to find. The evidence boxes were empty."

Cassius swears in Italian and slams his fist against the concrete wall. "Is it not enough that they never bothered to investigate our sisters' murders? They had to destroy the evidence as well?"

"Let's go upstairs," Vinicius says with a sigh. "I need a drink."

In the lounge, Lorenzo passes around glasses and a bottle of Grey Goose vodka, straight from the freezer. When he offers me one, I shake my head. Neat vodka makes me gag. I grab a bottle of water from the fridge instead.

Cassius swallows a large mouthful of vodka and sits down, his glass clenched in this hand. "Tell us what happened."

Vinicius explains how everything unfolded beautifully and the Coldlake detectives never doubted we were who we said we were. They led us right to the evidence boxes.

"Is there a record of who signed the evidence out?" Cassius asks. "Can't the detectives go to them and ask where it is?"

"Oh, there's a record," Vinicius says in a bitter tone. "The chief of police was the one to empty the boxes. We asked to talk to him, but the detectives shut that idea down right away. Said that the chief must have had his reasons and that was that."

"He's a friend of Dad's," I tell them. I've got a horrible,

twisting feeling in my stomach. Was Dad the one to ask the chief to move the evidence? Maybe even destroy it? I gaze out the window at the skyscrapers in the distance, and tendrils of dread curl up my spine. He's out there somewhere, the Black Orchid Killer. If the Mayor of Coldlake is covering up for him, he's even more terrifying than I thought.

The men finish off the bottle of vodka and open another one, and they all stay for dinner. A last-minute dinner at Lorenzo's means raiding the freezer for pizza rolls, mozzarella sticks, French fries, and apple pie.

We heat everything up in the oven and spread it out on the coffee table. I don't even want a plate. I just want to sit on the floor and eat with my fingers, and I do.

"This is just what I needed," I say, dunking three French fries in spicy aioli. The food reminds me of being a kid and eating in the kitchen with Mom when the staff had gone home and Dad was out.

Lorenzo bites into a mozzarella stick. "Serious gourmet shit."

"How's that pizza roll treating you, Cassius?" Salvatore asks.

"There is no pizza. This is a roll with sauce and cheese. And it's fine as long as I don't think about it too much," he concedes, biting into it.

While we're eating hot apple pie with ice cream, I notice that Vinicius is doing his best to be cheerful but he's barely speaking. "I'm sorry about your plan. It was a wonderful idea."

He gives me a sad smile. "Thanks, kitten. I should have realized that the evidence could be long gone."

"It's not much of a comfort, but at least we know more than we did this morning," I tell him. "I haven't given up hope that we'll find out who the killer is."

Vinicius nods, but his eyes are bleak. "Yeah. We'll think of something."

Even though I'm drained, it takes me a long time to fall asleep that night. When I eventually do, I fall into blood-soaked dreams and I toss and turn in my bed. I wake up in the darkness covered in sweat and the nightmares fade. Then I fall headlong into another as soon as I drift off.

The Black Orchid Killer is stalking me through the home I grew up in. There's blood all over the floors and the walls and I just know it's Mom's. I follow the wet, red trail through the hallways until the killer lunges at me out of the darkness. I scream and grab hold of his mask as he plunges his knife into my throat. Then I'm falling in slow motion down the staircase, and as I fall I tear the killer's mask away, revealing my father's face. He watches me fall, laughing maniacally.

The dream changes and I'm in the churchyard dressed in black, sheltering beneath a black umbrella as it pours with rain. There are four somber caskets before me waiting to be lowered into freshly dug graves. Tombstones stand at the heads of the graves, each one carved with a name.

The first one is inscribed with *Salvatore Fiore*. My heart filled with despair, I walk past each of the caskets, reading the tombstones. *Vinicius Angeli. Cassius Ferragamo. Lorenzo Scava.*

I sit up with a cry, clutching my chest.

"It was just a dream," I pant, throwing the bedclothes off. I need some water.

In the bathroom I drink straight from the tap and splash cold water over my face. Thank God it's finally morning and I can get up instead of going back to sleep. Wiping my mouth with the back of my hand, I mutter, "Too many mozzarella sticks at bedtime."

My gaze falls on a stack of pregnancy tests on the vanity. They appeared in my bathroom the morning after we had sex on the hood of Vinicius' car. I'm guessing Lorenzo put them there, being the helpful doctor-type that he is. I turn away to go and make my bed. I suppose I'll use one if my period is ever...

Late.

I stare straight ahead, counting back the days to my last period. But when was it? I've lost all sense of the days of the week since coming to live at the compound.

Am I late? Lorenzo would know, or he'll have it written down on his calendar. I wonder if I can get a look at it without him knowing because I don't fancy peeing on a stick while he breathes down my neck. Also, I don't want to get his hopes up only to disappoint him if it turns out I'm not pregnant. We've had enough disappointment this week.

At the top of the stairs, I listen for the sounds of anyone moving about. At this time of day, if Lorenzo has nothing else to do, he works out in the basement. I head down to his med room and approach his desk, a guilty feeling spreading through me. The last time I was caught reading something of his, it caused a huge fight. The desk drawers are closed, but I know they're full of notebooks that contain his violent, intrusive thoughts. His nightmares and his fantasies, all written in a messy scrawl. Their sisters are in those books. I'm in those books. I was horrified at first by what Lorenzo had written. Now, the sight of him bent over a notebook lost in his writing makes my heart hurt, but it also makes me proud. He's faced demons more terrifying than most people could bear, but they didn't break him. My Lorenzo is strong.

Thankfully, I don't have to go through his drawers for his calendar as it's sitting on the desk. There's a red ring around one of the dates last month, and I count forward twenty-eight days. My period was due six days ago.

Six is nothing. My period could come at come any moment.

And yet my heart is suddenly beating faster.

I head for the stairs just as Lorenzo appears at the far end of the corridor. He's dressed in sweats and a T-shirt with a towel over one shoulder, and his face is glowing with perspiration.

I pretend I don't see him and hurry up the stairs.

"Princess? What are you up to?"

Damn him. How does he know I'm up to something?

"Nothing!" I call over my shoulder.

I walk straight through to my bathroom and pick up a

pregnancy test. I'm definitely not pregnant but I won't be able to relax today until I take one of these things. The instructions from the box are simple enough. Pee on this end, wait a few minutes, and a plus sign means you're pregnant.

On a whim, I take out a bunch of tests and rinse out an empty box of cotton swabs and pee in that. One test might not be accurate. I should probably do more, and why not four? Four is my lucky number. I smile to myself as I imagine doing this ritual every month. Four pregnancy tests, one for each of my men.

A few minutes later, I have four tests lined up on the counter and I'm sitting on the closed toilet, heels bouncing up and down. I'm certain the results will be negative, but do I want them to be positive? The sensible thing would be to hope that I'm not pregnant yet as none of us are prepared for a baby. But sense went out the window when Cassius decided he wasn't going to pull out anymore.

As I stare at the four tests, déjà vu surges through me. These sticks remind me of something but I can't put my finger on what.

Then I realize. They look like the neat line of tombstones from my nightmare.

There's a footfall outside my bedroom door and Lorenzo calls my name. I pull open a drawer, scoop all the tests into it, and push it closed. When Lorenzo comes in I'm applying toothpaste to my toothbrush.

"I asked you what you're up to," he says, his eyes narrowed.

I smile brightly. "I'm brushing my teeth. Good workout?"

"Fine, thanks." He frowns and glances around the room, but nothing seems amiss. "I'm going for a shower and then I'll make us coffee, okay?"

"Sure!"

I must sound too chirpy because he hesitates in the doorway, those intense blue eyes of his scouring my face. "Is there anything you want to tell me?"

I shake my head, still smiling. It's not a lie, technically, because I don't *want* to tell him anything right now. After he leaves, I stare at the drawer. The results will probably have developed by now.

I put down my toothbrush and walk away.

I'm distracted for the rest of the day, gnawing on my nails and staring out the window. Lorenzo keeps giving me funny looks until he finally slaps my hand away from my mouth.

"Would you quit doing that? What's wrong?"

"Nothing, I'm just thinking about things."

"Is it yesterday? Are you thinking about your father?"

I give a noncommittal nod and say uncertainly, "Yeah."

"You don't sound very sure. If you don't tell me, I can't fucking help you," he growls and stalks off.

He's right. I know he is. I'm afraid that if I look at those tests I'll see the row of tombstones again, and I'd rather dream of being stabbed in the throat by my father than think about my men dying.

Around seven in the evening, I hear the gates out front

opening and cars driving into the underground garage. A moment later, Salvatore, Cassius, and Vinicius walk through the door.

"What's going on?" I ask them.

Cassius presses a kiss to my mouth. "We're having dinner together. I hope you're hungry because Lorenzo suggested ordering Chinese."

I give him a tight smile, realizing I've lost my appetite. Lorenzo is watching me silently from the other side of the room. It's not unusual for us all to eat together, but I have the feeling that he invited the others over so that one of them could discover what's eating me.

No one seems in a hurry to order food just yet. Lorenzo throws a bag of peanuts on the table and the men chat about their day. I sit silently in an armchair, the same thoughts revolving through my mind.

If I am pregnant...

It was a nightmare, not a vision...

Just get it over with...

I mutter something about using the bathroom and go upstairs. I close my eyes, open the drawer, and stuff all the tests in my jeans without looking at them. I also grab the instructions out of the trash and slip them into my back pocket.

Downstairs, the four of them stop talking as I stand in the middle of the room.

"You okay, baby?" Salvatore asks, his blue-green eyes filled with concern.

I take a deep breath. "Over the past few weeks, I told

you all something individually. Now I have something to tell you all together."

Vinicius smiles at me. "We love you too, kitten. It's all right. Don't look so terrified."

"It's not that." I look from one of them to the next. "I'm late."

Lorenzo's face splits into a grin. "I fucking knew it. You were creeping around doing secret shit this morning. Why didn't you tell me you were taking a pregnancy test? I could have helped you."

"You think you're pregnant?" Salvatore asks, shooting to his feet. "Let's do a test now!"

"I already did. I took four tests this morning, one for each of you. But I haven't looked at the results yet."

I indicate my jeans pocket, and Vinicius' eyes widen. "Can we see?"

Haltingly, I dig the tests out and place them on the coffee table. They stare at them, and then at me.

"What do they mean?"

"Is that positive or...?"

"Chiara, are you pregnant?"

"Oh, shit. The instructions." I tug them out and place them next to the tests.

Salvatore snatches up the paper and peers at it. The others cluster around him, trying to see. He suddenly shouts, "*Baby, you're pregnant.*"

I watch their faces closely as they process what I've just told them. Salvatore stares like he's been hit over the head by a mallet. Vinicius raises his eyes to mine and breaks into a smile. Cassius nods slowly and straightens his cuffs, chest puffed out. Lorenzo picks up each of the tests and examines them closely.

"Oh, my God," Salvatore says in wonder, a smile spreading over his face. "We're going to be fathers."

I was hoping that knowing the results would dispel my sense of dread, but it suddenly doubles.

"It's really early," I remind them. "I don't even have morning sickness yet. Something might happen—"

Cassius pulls me into his arms and holds me against his chest. "Ah, *bambina*. It's normal to be scared. Are you feeling scared?"

I squeeze my eyes shut and nod, my cheek pressed tightly against him. I'm scared for them. Scared for the baby. We went from trying to get pregnant to actually being pregnant in what feels like five minutes. Something might happen to the baby. I don't know how to protect it and there are so many people who wish us harm.

He kisses the top of my head and his deep voice rumbles in my ear. "I forget how young you are sometimes. Things are exciting when you're eighteen and then suddenly the world turns upside down and seems terrifying. Is that how you feel?"

"I had such terrible dreams last night. They feel like an omen."

He cups the back of my head and holds me tighter. Cassius' warmth. His big body is the comfort I need. "There are so many good things in this world, *bambina*. Everything that's good is a little bit terrifying, and children are the very best. You're one of those things for me. The biggest thing." He releases me and cups my face, his eyes sparkling. "And now our little one is, too."

Cassius is unequivocally happy. I look around at the others and they're all gazing at me with a mixture of love and excitement.

Lorenzo jerks his head toward the door and says softly, "Come on, I'll check you over."

He takes my hand and we go downstairs. He's not looking me in the eye as he grasps me around my waist and lifts me on one of the tables. He takes my blood pressure and temperature without a word.

My heart races. Is he worried, too? I don't know what I'll do if Lorenzo is afraid. "Say something, would you?"

He swallows, hard, pulling the blood pressure cuff off my arm. "I'll take care of it like it's mine, even if it's not. Do you understand that?"

I put my hands on his shoulders. "I know you will. I never thought you wouldn't."

He nods sharply. "Good. Just so we're clear. And you'll have to put up with me poking and prodding you a lot from now on. I need to know everything about how you're feeling and what your body is doing. How are you feeling, by the way? You said you didn't have any morning sickness yet."

I rub my belly and grimace. "I don't know, maybe this is morning sickness. I feel awful."

Lorenzo pauses, one brow raised. "Anxiety?"

"Can I tell you the truth?"

"You better tell me nothing but the fucking truth every day of your life, princess."

"I don't feel happy," I confess in a whisper. "That makes me a horrible person, doesn't it? The moment I laid eyes on the tests all lined up in a row as I waited for the results, I started to panic."

"Do you want the baby?"

"Yes, I do. But..."

Lorenzo braces his hands on either side of me against the table and gives me a severe glare. "Hey. You know all my gruesome thoughts. You're not going to shock me. Say what you're really thinking."

The four little tests lined up like tombstones. My men don't just have Coldlake, each other, and me to look out for now. Soon we'll have a tiny, vulnerable baby.

"I'm scared this baby is going to get one of you killed," I confess in a whisper. "That *I'm* going to get one of you killed. I'm scared that there might come a day when one of you will sacrifice your life for us, because this baby will be something you love more than yourselves."

He gives me a lopsided smile and puts his palm flat against my belly. "Ah, princess. Always looking out for us. You don't doubt that we would do that? Sacrifice ourselves for this baby, even if it's not biologically ours?"

I shake my head. "Not for a second."

"Good. Because that's what we would do," Salvatore says from the doorway.

I look up at him, then at Vinicius and Cassius as they

step into the room. They've heard everything that Lorenzo and I have said to each other.

Cassius kisses the top of my head and murmurs, "But just because we would, doesn't mean we'll have to."

I take a deep breath and nod. They're all being so brave about this, and I have to be just as strong for them.

Vinicius squeezes my shoulder. "Listen to Cassius. We are four of the biggest, meanest assholes in Coldlake. We are going to keep you and this baby safe, and we are going to love every second that we have the privilege to do so."

"No one's going anywhere," Salvatore whispers, dropping a kiss onto my lips.

"You hear that, princess?" Lorenzo says, packing away his equipment. "Now take a deep breath and relax because your blood pressure is through the fucking roof. I'll take it again tomorrow and I want to see that you've calmed down."

I smile at him. "Yes, doctor."

Cassius and Vinicius are on either side of me, and I put my arms around their waists and pull them close. They hug me together, with fierce embraces and many kisses.

"I'm going to order Chinese food for delivery," Salvatore says, heading for the door.

"You can't order food to this house," Lorenzo calls after him.

Nothing and no one comes in or out of Lorenzo's compound without his permission, and he has a blanket rule about deliveries. Not even noodles and dumplings are allowed past his security team.

"Fuck! I'm going out for Chinese food. Back soon."

Forty minutes later we're sitting on the sofas unpacking boxes of Chinese food and passing out chopsticks.

"Obviously, the baby is all of ours," Vinicius says, eyes glinting with mischief as he scoops stir-fry onto his plate. "But whose do we think it is? Any bets?"

"Vinicius, you are not going to lay bets on who the father is," I tell him.

"Dammit. I never get to have any fun."

"It's going to be obvious if Cassius is the father," Salvatore points out.

Cassius sits up straighter and pushes his fingers through his hair, dark eyes glinting. "The Ferragamo genes are good, strong genes."

"But if the baby has blue eyes, it could be either mine or Lorenzo's," Salvatore adds.

"Or mine," Vinicius says. "My mother has blue eyes. Light brown or hazel means it's definitely mine, though."

Lorenzo is eating Singapore noodles directly from the box, a smug smile on his face. "I counted the days. I took Chiara's temperature. I was there for her most fertile days. I don't know why this is even a discussion. It's my baby."

Cassius scowls at him. "You arranged things in your favor, you cheating *bastardo*, but that doesn't rule the rest of us out."

"Chiara, whose baby do you think it is?" Lorenzo asks, picking through his Singapore noodles with his chopsticks, but his hawklike gaze is on me.

"Yes, mother's instinct," Cassius says. "My grandmother

knew right away she was pregnant without taking any tests. All nine times."

"Nine?" I say, horrified. "*Nine* babies? Just so you know, I'm drawing the line at four."

"One for each of us," Salvatore says.

"Let's make it five," Lorenzo says. "One for Chiara, too. And one more go at knocking her up."

"Four," I insist. "And as for who the father is..." All four men sit up with interest. "I have no idea. I'm not an Italian grandmother."

"Will we take a paternity test?" Salvatore asks.

The four of them exchange glances, but none of them have an answer.

Vinicius chews a dumpling thoughtfully. "If you want to have four, kitten, then do we try for one from each of us or just let nature take its course?"

Lorenzo reaches for the stir-fried greens. "Let's just mess with her birth control until we have ten kids, and then at least two of them should belong to each of us."

I nearly drop my plate. "Lorenzo!"

Salvatore points his chopsticks at Lorenzo. "No way, Doctor Evil. We agree to that, then the next thing we know, there are ten baby Lorenzos running around. Can you imagine? What a nightmare."

"I'm kidding," Lorenzo says, but there's a glint in his eyes that tells me he's more than a little serious.

Cassius swallows his mouthful of noodles. "We all want at least one child, yes? So how do we make sure that happens?"

Lorenzo already has an answer. "Next time we're trying, only one of us is allowed to cream pie her at a time. Everyone else has to pull out."

Vinicius is drinking wine, chokes, and nearly spits it out. He wipes the back of his hand over his mouth and asks, "Kitten, do I have to explain what a cream pie is?"

"I can guess from context. Lorenzo, you're so romantic."

"I'm so fucking romantic," he agrees.

"If you all want charts, paternity tests, and cream pie schedules, that's your business. I prefer to leave things up to nature." I rub my belly. "She's done pretty well for us so far."

Cassius smiles at me. "Look at you. So motherly already."

Right now I'm rubbing a food baby, but there's a real baby in there somewhere. My fears have vanished as we've talked. "Oh, I forgot to say something."

All four men freeze and stare at me, Salvatore and Lorenzo with their chopsticks halfway to their mouths.

"I love you all."

Salvatore's expression relaxes into a smile. "We love you too, baby."

Cassius is sitting next to me and pats his knee.

I move closer and he scoops me into his lap and I wrap my arms around his neck. "*Ti amo, bambina.* I'm so proud of you."

I wriggle my way into the comfiest position on his lap and rest against his strong chest. "Will you still cuddle me like this if I'm as big as a house?"

"You are going to be so beautiful when you start to show, and you had better cuddle me. With your cute belly, I'll still be bigger."

I close my eyes, a blissful smile on my face.

I'm happy, I realize.

We're going to have a baby.

Our baby. All five of us.

The next morning I'm in the kitchen with Lorenzo when Salvatore comes downstairs. He stayed the night in my bed and he looks fresh-faced and happy when he kisses me good morning.

"Baby, I've booked you the same obstetrician as Ginevra, is that all right? She says he's been wonderful."

"Thank you, I think that's a great idea."

"Wonderful. Your appointment is at the end of the week."

"Put it in the group chat," Lorenzo tells him. "Make sure everyone knows what's going on."

"Good idea," Salvatore agrees, taking out his phone.

Hearing them talk like this makes me smile. Nine years, I remind myself. They've been closer than most friends are for the last nine years. Sharing Coldlake came easy to them, and then sharing me. They couldn't wait for us to all be together, and that's not just because of the sex. They love seeing each other happy and getting what they crave.

My hand drifts down to my belly. *And now they're sharing you, little one. You have the most handsome and good-*

hearted fathers. They already love you so much. I can see it in their faces.

"Was there ever a time when the four of you didn't get along?" I ask.

"Apart from Cassius and I nearly coming to blows when I locked him out of the compound?"

Apart from that. Thankfully they're getting along now.

Lorenzo scratches the side of his face. "Well, there was a Halloween incident that involved a mask and a chainsaw..."

Salvatore grins. "But we don't talk about that."

On Thursday afternoon, I drive with Cassius to my appointment, and he holds my hand most of the way and hums in a deep baritone. Lorenzo follows in his car, and Salvatore and Vinicius meet us in the parking lot.

The obstetrician's office is in a leafy, wealthy neighborhood in Salvatore's territory. I surreptitiously glance at the other pregnant women in the waiting room, wondering how many weeks along they are. They gape openly at my four men, three of them in suits and one of them in tight jeans and an even tighter T-shirt that leaves none of his muscles to the imagination.

I can't help a small smile of pride. My men are smoking hot.

I haven't been in public for so long that I forgot how strange we must look to other people. When I accept a paper cup of water from Cassius and kiss him, then take Vinicius' hand, people's eyes grow even wider. Lorenzo gets up and stands in front of me, shoving his hands into his pockets and glaring around the room. Everyone looks quickly back down at their magazines.

"Chiara?" calls a man who just appeared in the doorway at the far end of the room. He's tall and skinny with haphazardly curly hair and is wearing a doctor's coat.

I get to my feet and so do all my men. As we walk en masse toward the obstetrician, he pushes his glasses up the bridge of his nose and frowns in confusion.

"Ah, who's the father?"

The four men glance at each other, amusement and pride glimmering around their lips. Cassius smooths his tie. "All of us."

"Can we all come in with Chiara?" Vinicius asks.

The obstetrician's eyebrows creep up his forehead. He glances at Salvatore, realizes who these men are who are accompanying the formidable son of Francesco Fiore, and quickly covers his astonishment.

"Of course. Just wait here a moment. Let me get Chiara settled into an appropriate room and then I'll come back for you all."

I smile up at the doctor as he leads me down the corridor. "Sorry, I thought Salvatore had explained. Thank you so much for accommodating us all."

"Of course. Just in here." He opens the door of a consulting room, and in a brusque and efficient voice, says, "This one should be roomy enough. I'll have a nurse take some blood to confirm the pregnancy and then I'll do an examination. Take off your clothes on your lower half, and then hop up onto this table. I'll be back in a few minutes with the, ah, fathers." He gives me an awkward smile and pulls the curtain closed around the bed. A moment later I hear the door close behind him.

I laugh to myself as I take off my jeans and underwear, imagining the obstetrician trying to get one father's name, any name, for his forms, while they insist that he put all four of them. The vinyl-padded table is cold and covered in scratchy paper, but there's a blanket, and once I'm undressed I drape it over myself to keep warm.

The door opens and closes and I presume it's the nurse coming to take my blood. Someone just visible beyond the curtain reaches up to open it.

"I wasn't sure which arm is better. I know I have a good vein in the left..." My mouth goes dry as the curtain is pulled back and I realize the man dressed in a white coat isn't my obstetrician. He isn't a nurse, either.

His narrowed, hate-filled eyes sweep over me. He seems to like the fact that I'm half naked and alone with just a blanket to protect me.

Cornered.

Without so much as a hairpin to use as a weapon.

His mouth draws into a nasty smirk. "Hello, Chiara. What a happy day this is. Congratulations to you and the fathers."

14

Lorenzo

"Where's that fucking doctor?"

"Trying to find a room big enough for us all," Salvatore says, refilling his paper cup of water from the cooler.

"It's not hard," I mutter. "We'll make ourselves fit."

Vinicius grins. "Did you see his face when he realized we're all the father? You think he would have come across something like this before."

Salvatore laughs. "Here? This is the most uptight part of Coldlake. Not being married when you're pregnant is enough to raise eyebrows."

Cassius glares up the corridor. "That doctor better not

be asking Chiara about our relationship. She needs peace and quiet while she's carrying our baby."

The back of my neck is prickling. Leaving Chiara alone with a strange man for even a second doesn't sit right with me. I go over and stand by Cassius and peer up the hallway with him. Where *is* that doctor?

"You know what? Fuck this."

I stalk down the corridor after Chiara and the obstetrician. A nurse passes me and stares at my bare arms and tattoos. I guess I'm not the usual sort of father she sees in this fancy place. I round on her with a snarl. "Where's Chiara?"

"I don't..." she begins, backing off with wide, scared eyes.

"I'll find her myself."

"No, you can't—"

I push past her. Don't fucking tell me can't. I'll find my woman if I damn well want to. The first door I rip open, the room beyond is empty. As I close it, someone emerges from another door at the other end of the corridor. He's dressed like a doctor but something about the way he's keeping his face averted doesn't sit right.

"Hey."

I take long strides toward him, and he speeds up.

"*Hey.*" I break into a run, and so does he. I'm torn between giving chase and finding my woman, but only for a second.

I need Chiara. Now.

I slam open the door the stranger emerged through

and glance around. It's not a very big exam room and the far wall is concealed by a privacy curtain.

"Chiara?"

My heart pounds in my chest as I hear dead fucking silence from behind that curtain.

I lunge forward, bracing for the sight of blood. For shattered dreams and horror. I can see it in my mind's eye, a lurid composite of everything the Black Orchid Killer did to our sisters, only this time he's done it to Chiara.

When I rip the curtain back, Chiara's laying on her side and curled into a ball with her arms wrapped around her belly.

And she's shaking.

Not dead. Relief pours through me, but only for a second.

The baby.

I put my hands on her. "Princess, what's happened? Did he hurt you? Did he touch you?"

Please, God, no.

Slowly she unclenches and turns toward me. Her face is chalk white. I can't see any blood. I touch her belly, her thighs, feeling for wetness, for injuries.

"Lorenzo," she whispers, her teeth chattering.

"What did he do to you?" I call over my shoulder as the other three come into the room, "There was a dark-haired man dressed as a doctor. I didn't see his face. Find him."

Salvatore is closest to the door. "I'll go after him."

Cassius casts Chiara a troubled look and follows Salvatore, and I hear their footsteps pounding down the corridor.

"Help me with her," I say to Vinicius, and we coax Chiara into a sitting position. I peel back one of her eyelids and her pupils look normal.

Chiara takes a deep breath and grasps my shoulder. "I'm okay. He didn't touch me. He just gave me a shock."

Thank fucking Christ.

Vinicius groans in relief and pulls her into his arms.

"Who was it?" I ask. "Did you see his face?"

She nods. "It was Dad."

I clench the blanket in my fist. The mayor. The fucking *mayor* was here. That piece of shit came down here to terrorize his pregnant daughter.

Vinicius disappears for a moment, then comes back with a can of lemonade from the vending machine. "For the shock."

"Good idea." I pull the tab and hand it to her. "Here, just a sip."

As she drinks, I push her hair back from her face and then rest my hands on her shoulders. Reassuring myself that she's fine. That the baby's fine.

I exchange glances with Vinicius. He looked as horrified as I feel. That was too fucking close. "I can't believe we let her out of our sight. What were we thinking?"

I picture shoving Sienna toward the stairs at Strife before heading back onto the street, assuming she would be fine. Believing, when I had no good fucking reason to believe, that she would be okay because she was only meters away from me. Distance doesn't matter. The only way to know someone's safe is to keep your own fucking eyeballs on them at all times, or better yet, under lock and key.

All around me is this asshole obstetrician's expensive equipment. All the tools of his trade that make him seem safe to the women who come to him at their most vulnerable.

He did this. He let that fucking monster in here with Chiara.

"Where's that doctor?" I growl, stalking out of the room.

I find him hiding in one of the empty exam rooms. I grab him by the collar of his white jacket and march him back to Chiara and Vinicius. On my way, I pass Cassius and Salvatore returning from hunting for the mayor.

"It was Romano. Did you see him?"

Salvatore shakes his head. "We didn't find anyone. What are you going to do with him?"

My jaw is too tight for me to reply. I haven't decided yet, but it's going to fucking hurt.

I shove the shaking obstetrician back into the exam room. Cassius and Salvatore follow me in and close the door behind them.

"You stay there, princess," I tell Chiara, and pull the curtain around the bed so that she can't see what I'm about to do.

When I turn around, the doctor has his hands up and he's backing away, half begging, half fending me off.

"Please don't kill me. The mayor said he just wanted to talk to his daughter. I had no choice, he's the mayor. What about my business?"

"No choice? No fucking *choice*? There's always a choice, and you made the wrong one." I grab the obstetrician's right hand and yank it down on a counter, the world turning red.

"Wait, not my—"

I take hold of the ultrasound monitor and slam it onto his hand, over and over again. He breaks off and screams in pain. I keep slamming, listening to the crunch of bones and the smashing of glass.

I let him go and he crumples to the ground, gripping his wrist with his left hand, staring in horror at the mangled mess.

"Be grateful you're not dead," I seethe. "Lock your doors and don't walk alone at night. I might return and finish the job."

I pull back the curtain and check on Chiara. She's sitting on the edge of the bed wearing her jeans, and her complexion is better, as if hearing me beating on the asshole who put her in danger has put some color back in her cheeks.

That's my girl.

I hold out my hand to her. "Come on, princess. Let's get out of here."

Chiara puts her hand in mine and glances at the blood spattered across my T-shirt. "I'm going to need another obstetrician."

I give the man a kick as we pass by and he yelps and scurries away from me. "All of his patients are going to need another obstetrician for a while."

Back at the compound, Salvatore paces up and down the living room floor. "This is all my fault. I shouldn't have booked Ginevra's obstetrician. The mayor must have realized you'd be pregnant soon and found out that the Fiores use that doctor."

"None of us realized," Cassius tells him. "We're all to blame, not you."

I lean against the wall, arms folded tight, my mind too full of blood and violence to think about anything but finding out where that doctor lives, smashing the front door in with a sledgehammer, and breaking his fucking legs.

Vinicius kneels down before Chiara, putting gentle hands on her thighs. "Did the mayor say anything to you, kitten?"

She swallows and looks sick again. "He said, *Remember, this is my city. I can get to you and this child anytime I want.*"

The muscles in my jaw get even tighter and my head starts to pound. Once I'm done with the doctor, I imagine taking that sledgehammer to Mayor Romano's front door and crushing his fucking skull.

Cassius spits curse words. "His city? It's not *his* city. It's ours."

"Is that all he wanted? To threaten you?" Vinicius asks.

She nods. "I managed to ask him a question, though.

Why he made the chief of police remove the evidence from the Black Orchid Murders case from the archives."

Vinicius' mouth falls open. "He admitted it?"

Chiara shakes her head but her eyes are suddenly burning. "He didn't need to. He looked shocked, and he started to say, *How did you know about that?* Then he must have realized I could be bluffing and shut his mouth. But it was too late. I could see the truth written all over his face."

Salvatore passes a hand over his jaw. "Holy shit. Is he mixed up in the Black Orchid Murders somehow, or is he just hell-bent on the four of us never getting justice?"

"Dad never wanted the police to investigate the murders and the evidence was languishing in the archives. The fact that he went out of his way to have the evidence moved or destroyed makes me wonder if he knows who the killer is."

We exchange ominous glances.

"Did he say anything else?" Cassius asks.

"I asked him what his voters would think if they knew the Mayor of Coldlake was covering up for a serial killer. He looked even more shocked. Then he called me some horrible words and stormed out."

Fury burns in my chest. All this time, the Mayor of Coldlake has been covering up for a serial killer. "But who would he cover up for?"

Chiara stares blankly across the room as she considers this, and shakes her head. "I don't know."

Could it be someone in the mayor's family? Does he have a brother, an uncle, a cousin? Someone he feels he has to protect? Maybe the killer is blackmailing the mayor somehow to hide the evidence.

"What did he call you as he walked out?"

"*Traitorous bitch*. But it doesn't matter. He thought he could appear suddenly and scare me, but after I started talking about that evidence I think he was more frightened of me."

Salvatore smiles and brushes the backs of his fingers against her cheek. "That's our girl."

Yeah, that's our fucking girl, and we're going to protect her properly from now on. I point a finger at her. "You're not leaving the compound from now on."

"Lorenzo, please don't lock me up. We agreed I'd be safe as long as I'm with one of you. Dad won't kill me, not before the election, anyway. I'm too useful as his poor, kidnapped daughter." She gives me a small, unhappy smile.

More useful alive than dead, for the moment. She's probably right. Through my gritted teeth, I growl, "Remind me again why we haven't taken him out yet?"

"Because it's not enough for me that he dies. I want Mom to get justice for what he did to her."

I jab a thumb at my chest and shout, "I can give you justice. I've been saying that from the start."

"Lorenzo," Salvatore says sharply.

I growl and push my fingers through my hair. My heart hasn't stopped pounding since we left the obstetrician's office.

I feel someone touch my forearms and I look into Chiara's beautiful face.

"If Dad knows something about your sisters' murderer, that's all the more reason not to kill him. I'm not saying never, but I'm not ready for that."

"I can still help you." Listen to me, I'm practically begging for permission to beat that man to a pulp. "If he knows something about the Black Orchid Killer, I'll torture it out of him. I could break him within an hour."

It wouldn't be hard, either, but I'd take my time over someone like the mayor. Really make a meal out of it.

"I know you could." She glances at the others and then back at me. "Maybe it's unfair to stop you if you really want to do this. Your sisters are as important as my mother."

I rub my thumb over her lower lip and slowly shake my head. "No, you're right."

"He's your father," Cassius murmurs. "It's your decision what happens to him."

"If it's what you want, we won't touch him," Vinicius assures her.

"What I want most is for everyone in Coldlake to know exactly who Dad is and what he's done, and I'm not ready to give up on that hope yet. I'm sorry." Her eyes are suddenly filled with tears. She hates that she still has hope.

I draw her into my arms. "Don't cry, princess. Never fucking apologize for loving your mom."

She holds me tight for a second and then pulls back. "If the Black Orchid Killer was in this room right now, would you seek justice, or would you just want him dead?"

"Dead," I say. I don't even need to think about it. A monster like that needs to be put down.

The others nod.

Morbid silence stretches through the room. I stare at Chiara's belly. My woman's pregnant, and she's thinking about revenge killings and her piece-of-shit murderer of a father. She should be happy and without stress. I need to do better.

Chiara swipes her fingers under her eyes, a determined expression on her face. "All right. I know what I want to do next."

"*Bambina*, you shouldn't be doing anything. You need to relax after what you've been through today."

She shakes her head. "Women all around the world and throughout history have managed to do amazing things while they're pregnant, and I will too." She turns to me. "Lorenzo, will you please take me to Strife?"

My eyes nearly bug out of my head. The dodgy dive bar right on the edge of gang territory, also known as the last place on this fucking earth that I want Chiara to be right now. "Why the hell would I take you to Strife?"

"Because I want to talk to Acid. I'm calling in the favor he owes me."

~

"WELL, well, well. I'm honored, your highness."

Acid saunters out from behind the bar, his green eyes gleaming. It's the middle of the afternoon and there are only a handful of hardened drinkers in the front bar. Through the door into the main bar, two women in G-strings dance onstage to "Partition" by Beyoncé.

"Hello, Acid. It's nice to see you, too."

"Ah, for a moment I thought you really meant that." He glances at me, and there's a flicker of anger in his expression. He still hasn't forgiven me for pointing a gun in his face and telling him he's a dead man.

"I do mean it. Can you spare me half an hour of your time?"

Acid's gaze moves from Chiara to me and back again, as curious as a cat. "Sure. Anything for you, your highness."

"I'd like to speak to Thane, too. If he's around."

Acid takes his phone from his pocket and makes a call. "Thane, her highness is here. Come downstairs like a good boy and pay your respects."

I could smash his fucking face in for calling Chiara that, and Acid knows it. Chiara, on the other hand, doesn't seem to mind, and she has her head held high like she really is a queen.

A moment later, we hear heavy footsteps coming downstairs. Thane's wearing a black tank top and pants with too many pockets and straps. Is it fashion? Are those pockets actually useful? Who fucking knows.

His eyelinered gaze flickers over us and lands on Chiara, and his head tips ever so slightly to one side. His attitude is somewhere between curious and impatient as he folds his arms and waits.

"Good afternoon, Thane." Chiara turns to Acid. "Is there somewhere we can talk?"

"Sure. Let's go into the bounty bar."

The bouncers with tattooed faces open the doors for us. Zagreus is in a booth at the back of the bar on his laptop and he looks up automatically as we walk in. He seems surprised to see Chiara, but his expression flattens into dislike as he sees me. I'm even less welcome around here than I used to be.

Tough fucking titties.

There are a handful of hunters scattered throughout the darkened bar, in pairs or alone. They follow Chiara's progress across the room with sharp interest. It's not every day that a beautiful blonde dressed in jeans and a baby doll T-shirt walks through here. They're wondering what she's doing in the bounty bar at Strife, accompanied by Acid, Thane, and Lorenzo Scava, no less.

Acid shows Chiara to a table and they sit down with Thane. I stand by Chiara's chair with my arms folded and glare around the room until everyone goes back to minding their own fucking business.

"You can sit if you want," Acid tells me.

No shit I can sit if I want. "I'll stand."

"What can I get you to drink?" Acid asks Chiara.

"Lemonade, please." He signals to the bartender, and she asks, "How's business lately?"

Thane's eyes narrow and he and Acid exchange glances.

"You don't even know what we do, do you?" Acid asks.

She gives a careless shrug. "I know some things. Would you like to tell me more?"

Acid cracks his knuckles, watching her. "Your men go to work in fancy suits, pretending like what they do is legitimate, meanwhile, we're out here on the streets risking our lives to make their money for them."

"Out of the goodness of your hearts," I say through my teeth.

Acid smiles slowly. "Out of the goodness of our hearts, and for a fuckload of cash. The difference is, we get our hands dirty."

Chiara's doubtful gaze travels over him. She's seen all of us get our hands dirty at one time or another.

He points to me but leans toward Chiara. "Your man here used to be one of us. Down here on the streets. Then he got expensive tastes." Acid's eyes run pointedly up and down Chiara's body.

She blinks slowly at him, her expression bored, and there's a flicker of disappointment in Acid's eyes that she hasn't risen to the bait.

"Lorenzo's tastes are my business, not yours."

The bartender brings a lemonade for Chiara, puts a beer down in front of Acid, and hands Thane a glass of water.

"Oh, I bet Lorenzo's got really interesting tastes."

Chiara doesn't bother to reply.

Seeing that he's not going to get under her skin, Acid's attention swings to me. "When are you going to tell me to go fuck myself?"

I pretend I'm not this close to stabbing him in the throat. "She can tell you herself if she wants to."

Chiara takes a sip of her drink, her eyes never leaving Acid. "Your attitude is cute. I can see you're enjoying yourself but remember, I saved your life. Twice. If I asked for it, I could have those two pints of blood back, with interest, and then have this place razed to the ground."

I reach out and stroke the nape of Chiara's neck.

You sure could, princess.

Acid sits back, shaking his head. "You really are the Princess of Coldlake."

She smiles at him. "I am. Can we talk business now?"

"Sure, your highness. When you're in trouble you need the best of the best, and that's us. What kind of problems can we help you with?"

Thane raises one dark, sardonic brow. "Daddy issues?"

Acid tries to keep a straight face, but his lips twitch as he takes a mouthful of beer. "We, ah, might not be the men to help you with those. Try Ferragamo."

"I wish I could join in your fun. I've had a hard time joking about my father since he murdered my mother right in front of me."

Both Acid's and Thane's expressions turn blank with shock.

"We thought that was gang shit," Acid says.

She smiles sweetly at him. "No. Just my daddy issues."

All humor and teasing drops from Acid's demeanor, and he puts his beer aside. "That fucking sucks, your highness. All right, what's your business here?"

"I want to set a bounty. Two, actually. One for a hunter to handle. One for Thane."

"If you wanted to set a bounty, you should have said. I'll get Zag."

He starts to get up, but Chiara holds out her hand. "No, I want to talk to you two first."

Acid sits back down again, his brows drawn together. "Strife bounties don't come cheap, and neither does Thane. Can you pay?"

Chiara hesitates and then takes her diamond ring off her finger.

"No!" I reach for the ring but she holds it out of my reach and gives me a meaningful look. That ring belongs on her finger. I love seeing it there, fuck-off big and sparkling. I helped put it on her finger and I'm proud of that. I look at it sometimes while I'm balls deep in her and it reminds me that she's mine.

That she's *ours*.

Chiara explains what she wants done while sirens are blaring in my ears. She's not offering up that ring. I'll pay for her goddamn bounties myself.

"That's part one. What do you think?" Chiara asks.

Acid is shaking his head. "I think you're fucking crazy."

"Will you do it?"

"Hell, yes. I'll handle it personally."

"Thank you." She turns to Thane. "What I want to ask of you might be more difficult, but Vinicius has told me about the things that you can do. I don't know if this is possible, but can you please look into my father's emails and text messages and see if there's anything that might connect him to the Black Orchid Killer?"

Chiara explains about the mayor ambushing her and the reason she suspects he might know the killer and is protecting him.

Thane rubs a hand over his jaw. "The mayor got to you? Where were you?"

"At a doc—at an appointment." Chiara's poker face has been firmly in place since she stepped into Strife, but suddenly it slips, and she blushes.

Thane's gaze flickers to her belly, and my hackles stand to attention. One word, one fucking innuendo and I will leap over this table and punch his teeth out.

He gives a lazy shrug. "That's not hard. If something's there, I'll find it."

"Thank you." Chiara puts her ring in the middle of the table.

Acid contemplates it and shakes his head. "Keep your fancy rock. Just consider us even after this."

"All right. I'll consider us even if you get my bounty for me, and if Thane scours every corner of every device that my father owns." Chiara picks up her ring and puts it back on her finger.

"Pleasure doing business with you, your highness."

She stands up to go, and I cup her lower back and murmur in her ear, "Could you give me one moment, princess?"

She nods and heads for the door, and I signal one of the bouncers and he moves to stand beside her.

I turn back to Thane, grab a fistful of his tank top, and yank him toward me. "You say one word to anyone and I'll cut your fucking balls off."

I don't need everyone and his dog at Strife knowing Chiara's pregnant before she even starts to show.

Thane smirks up at me. "I wouldn't dream of it. Congratulations, daddies."

I release him with a shove, shoot a poisonous glance at Acid, and head out of the bar, holding Chiara's hand.

When we reach my car, I push her up against it and my mouth descends on hers. "That was so fucking hot. You handled them beautifully, princess."

She smiles and kisses me back. "Thank you."

"I don't know how you do it. They get so far under my skin I can't think straight."

"You do realize that Acid thrives on pissing you off? Pissing everyone off, come to think of it. If you let it roll off your back he'll stop trying."

"I was letting it roll off my back! For the last few years, I've barely threatened to punch any of them or even thought about it. Then you came along and they're *looking* at you and *smirking* at you and undressing you with their eyes. And they fucking *kidnapped*—"

She kisses me again.

I huff angrily. "You're ours. We don't share. I should just fucking tell them that." I turn toward the bar and she grabs me, laughing.

"Lorenzo, there's no need. They know I belong to the four of you and no one else. You don't have to go in there and lay down the law." She runs a finger down my cheek and smiles. "Though I have to say, you're pretty sexy when you're all possessive like this."

If that's what she wants then she can have it. From all of us.

"In. Get in the car. Just because you're pregnant doesn't mean we can't run a train on you."

"What's a train?" she asks.

What's a train? The innocence of this girl.

I give her a devilish grin. "Guess."

15

Chiara

"You could just tell me."

"I'd rather show you. Where are the others? Send them a text. *Lorenzo invites you on a train.*"

I get out my phone. "It's a sex thing, isn't it?"

"Why would you think that?"

It's definitely a sex thing. "You won't embarrass me, just so we're clear. Pregnant women can't be embarrassed by sex. We know too much."

"Sure, princess." He's still grinning as I type a text message into the group chat.

.   .   .

CHIARA: *I don't know what he means but Lorenzo invites you on a train. We'll be back at the compound in twenty minutes.*

Salvatore: *Lorenzo, you crude fuck.*

Salvatore: *On my way.*

Cassius: *Bambina, we will all be there. You're beautiful and I love you.*

Vinicius: *A FUCKING TRAIN. I can't with you, Lorenzo.*

Chiara: *Will someone please tell me what it means?*

Vinicius: *It's what we did on the hood of my car.*

"OH, SO ONE AFTER THE OTHER," I say, and feel my cheeks heat. Maybe you *can* embarrass a pregnant woman.

"You're so cute when you blush. I'm sorry, I'm an asshole. I have to take advantage of your innocence while you still have it."

I reach out and touch his cheek. He's still smiling, and my heart feels very full. "Look at you. You're happy for the first time all day."

He glances at me, his expression astonished. "What?"

I run my fingers down his muscled arm and hold his hand. "You've been so angry and upset and I wanted to make you smile. Mission accomplished."

"You little brat," he murmurs, still smiling.

When we arrive back at the compound, Lorenzo marches me upstairs to his bedroom and tells me to take off my clothes. I sit on the bed with my arms around my bare legs.

Lorenzo pulls off his T-shirt. "Look at you. So fucking cute."

When the others arrive, Lorenzo paces up and down in front of them like a general giving orders.

"Those Strife fucks have been staring at our woman. Their eyes have been all over her, so we need to get all over her."

"They might have gotten their eyes all over her, but we're inside her," Salvatore points out.

I wince as Lorenzo's temper ratchets up to twelve.

"They know about that, too! Bunch of nosy fucks who—"

I sit up on the bed and reach for the button on Lorenzo's jeans. He trails off as I open his fly and lick the thick root of his cock.

"Why do you never wear underwear? You own underwear."

He shrugs, giving me a lopsided grin. "Underwear is bullshit. You shouldn't wear it either."

Vinicius slides his hand down my ass and strokes my pussy from behind. "You are now freed from the tyranny of panties, kitten."

"And what about you? Will you free yourself as well?" I happen to know that Vinicius only wears expensive designer underwear and I doubt he wants to give it up.

"I will for now," he says, undressing quickly and getting onto the bed with me.

"I have to wear underwear or people stare." Cassius nudges the outline of his semi through his pants.

"Yeah, yeah, we know you could stop traffic with that monster," Salvatore says, shrugging out of his shirt. "Now quit talking about your cock and make yourself useful with it."

I laugh as I watch them all bantering and undressing. There's no need for Lorenzo to feel jealous. No other men could replace these four.

I end up in the middle of a cuddle pile with all of them touching and kissing me. Someone is licking me and someone else is pushing one thick finger in and out of me. I take one of their cocks in my mouth and find two more to rub up and down. There are so many hands on my body. All of them are hungry for attention and I feel myself gently but firmly pulled from one man to the next. Salvatore sinks into my pussy while I'm teasing the tip of Cassius' cock with my tongue.

Then Vinicius pushes me onto my knees and thrusts into me from behind. Lorenzo's hands are in my hair as he guides his cock into my mouth.

"I always love to see our girl covered in cum," Lorenzo says. "Let's finish that way."

Salvatore's eyes gleam. "Good idea."

Someone has found my vibrator and I hear the buzz a moment before someone pushes me onto my back again and applies it to my clit. Heavenly sensations pour through me.

Suddenly there are four men kneeling over me while they work their hands furiously up and down their jutting cocks. I grasp Salvatore's thigh and the underside of one of my own and hold on for dear life as the strong vibrations course through me.

I'm in the middle of an orgasm when I feel the first man come, striping my waist with his seed. I hear a groan that sounds like Vinicius' and feel him spurt over my thighs.

"Fuck yes, make a mess of her," Lorenzo says in a tight voice before coming with a gasp over my pussy.

When I open my eyes I see there's just Cassius left, and he grabs one of my breasts, swearing in Italian before he shoots his cum all over my chest.

I glance down at myself, striped with shiny, wet ribbons. Cassius lays down on the bed beside me and clasps me against him, pressing kisses to my throat. The others collapse around us.

Lorenzo's smile is feral as he looks at me in the midst of all their bodies, my face flushed from coming.

"Who do you belong to?" he demands.

I arch my back and stretch luxuriously, smiling as I touch their chests, their cheeks. "I'm all yours, my loves."

16

Cassius

Life settles down for a while, as much as it can settle with the mayor on the news every night. Every time we see his face we remember that the Black Orchid Killer is roaming free with that man's protection. Strangely, Christian 'corpse-fucker' Galloway is still in the running, with his popularity neither growing nor shrinking.

Chiara has a new obstetrician, a woman, and we all go to every appointment with her and breathe down the doctor's neck the entire time. She's patient with Chiara and even more patient with us as we question everything she says and demand to know what this heart rate means and what that is on the ultrasound.

Every time I lay eyes on Chiara, I'm stunned by how beautiful she looks. Like a walking miracle with her glow and her baby bump. It's a small bump, but it's growing bigger every day.

One evening when she's into her fourteenth week, I fit my hands over her belly from behind and nuzzle her neck. "Such a sweet little bump. Barely more than a handful."

She smiles up at me. "We love being your handful."

"Will you hide it for the fight tonight, or will you show it off?"

I'm taking Chiara out for the evening. My best cage fighter, Lasher, has a championship fight tonight and I want to introduce her to my other passion.

She covers my hands with hers and admires how we look. "I kind of want to show it off. What do you think?"

Very few people know that Chiara's pregnant yet. She'll be well protected tonight, by me and others. I plant a kiss on her mouth. "I want to show both of you off."

"I'll go and get ready, then," she tells me with a smile.

Forty minutes later, Chiara comes downstairs with smoky eyes and red lips, wearing a tight black jersey dress with long sleeves and heavy gold earrings.

I smile slowly at her, my gaze raking her body. "Wow."

"Cassius, you said *wow*. Since when do you say wow?"

"Seeing you has driven all words from my mind, both Italian and English. You're stunning, *bambina*. Let's go and show you off."

I take Chiara by the hand and we head down to my car. As we emerge into the basement, Lorenzo comes out of the med room. His gaze instantly sharpens when he sees Chiara.

"Look at you. Hot as fuck and with your bump out. Come here."

I watch Lorenzo as he pulls her into his arms and kisses her. One hand is in her curls and the other is squeezing her ass. She melts into his arms for a moment, and then breaks the kiss and turns back to me with a smile.

"Have fun tonight, princess."

I neaten her lipstick with a swipe of my thumb and smooth her hair down. There. Perfect again.

"I will, thank you."

"Don't wait up, Lorenzo," I say, still gazing at Chiara. "There's a lot happening tonight."

"I already checked on the itinerary. The pre-show. The fights. The after-party."

Lorenzo will have mapped out every minute that she's out of his sight. "Did you make those extra arrangements I asked about?"

He's staring at Chiara like he wants to devour her. "Of course. You two have fun."

Oh, we will. It's a beautiful clear night as we drive through the streets of Coldlake. We need to head through the city and into the east. The fight is being held in my territory.

"I'm surprised Lorenzo didn't insist that he comes, too."

"He won't want to piss Zagreus off by attending one of Lasher's fights. Lasher used to run Strife with the others."

"I heard. It's sad that they all had a falling out, and it makes me even happier that you and Lorenzo are getting along."

"Our little spat is nothing like what went down between those men. You don't have to worry about me and Lorenzo, *bambina*."

She gazes out the window at a passing billboard. It's for a boxing match, not a cage fight. "How come I never heard of Lasher before I met you? You made it sound like he's famous. All the boxing stars get billboards before their big fights so why doesn't he?"

"Cage fighting is illegal in Coldlake. Mayor Romano claims it's too dangerous."

"Is it?"

I consider this. "Many sports are just as high contact. Boxing. Football. Cage fighting has a reputation for being violent and lawless, but there are rules." I shoot a look at her. "Besides, it's entertaining and unlike any other sport. You'll see."

Chiara's never been squeamish and she's been growing more ballsy. I think she might get a kick out of tonight's fight.

The venue is an indoor basketball stadium with an octagonal cage on the court and more seating added ringside. Chiara and I have front-row seats to the fight, and as we sit down, lights flash overhead and the music pounds. Everyone in the crowd is hyped up.

I nuzzle the side of Chiara's face, sliding the blade of my nose against her cheek before kissing her temple.

"Cassius, everyone's looking at us." Chiara smiles as her gaze darts around at the spectators. Hundreds of people are crammed into the gymnasium to watch the fight. Lasher, my prizefighter, versus the comeback champion Peril. It's a powerful drawcard, despite being illegal. No one tells us how to have fun in Coldlake.

"Everyone's looking at *you*," I correct her and palm her belly, fingers splayed. My son is inside Chiara—or my daughter. Tiny and vulnerable. As I glance up, I see that dozens of heads are turned in our direction, marveling at the sight of Cassius Ferragamo with his arms around a woman. Cassius Ferragamo, smiling. And is that the mayor's daughter?

I kiss Chiara again and keep my arm around her waist as I feel the gossip buzzing around us. Chiara Romano, beautiful and untouchable, so recently engaged to Salvatore Fiore and now in the arms of another member of the Coldlake Syndicate, and at an illegal fight.

Vindictive delight spreads through me as I kiss the mayor's daughter. I can't wait until the news of this gets back to him.

17

Chiara

Awoman drops into the seat on my other side and nods to Cassius. "Good evening, Mr. Ferragamo."

Cassius nods to her. "Good evening. Alecta, this is Chiara Romano."

The woman smiles at me. She's a few years older than me and has long, dark curly hair with purple streaks, and she's wearing tight jeans and a black tank top. Her nails are painted purple and there are black bands tattooed around her fingers. "Nice to meet you, Miss Romano."

I glance between the woman and Cassius, wondering if this is the extra arrangement that Lorenzo mentioned. "Alecta, are you my bodyguard?"

"I work down at Strife. Mr. Scava requested a woman tonight as Mr. Ferragamo can't accompany you everywhere, like the ladies' room." She smiles wider. "But you probably don't need me. I heard you can handle yourself."

"Are you a bounty hunter? I've always been curious about Strife's bounty hunters. It sounds like such a cool job."

She laughs. "Excuse me, I heard you pulled a gun out of a designer purse and shot dead the leader of the Geaks. What's cooler than that? Also, you've got Acid calling you *your highness* and bragging about how you personally saved his life. Twice."

I roll my eyes, but I'm smiling. "That sounds like Acid."

"Oh, yes. Acid loves to talk about himself."

Over in the eight-sided cage, the fighters are warming up and the ring girls are posing for the crowd. Cassius explains that there will be two fights before the championship, and he seems less interested in these fighters but claps and cheers along with the rest of the audience. The referee steps into the ring and takes hold of the microphone, enlivening the crowd as he introduces the fighters.

The fight begins and the men circle each other, before raining down a series of kicks and punches and trying to wrestle each other to the ground. Cassius and the rest of the crowd get into it, cheering, shouting, and groaning when their favorite takes a bad hit. Soon, blood is streaking down the chin of one of the men and he seems dazed. The match ends by points, and I'm not surprised to find that the one who isn't bleeding is the winner.

There's another round of fighting, and then another break.

"How do you like it so far, *bambina*?" Cassius asks me.

I grin at him. "I can see why you enjoy it. There's plenty of unpredictable action."

"The technique," he says in reverential tones. "It's all about technique and knowing your opponent. Lasher is one of the most flexible fighters I know, and his technique is..." He kisses the tips of his fingers.

"Did you ever want to be an MMA fighter?"

Cassius smiles at me. "When I first came to this country, I did. I was very good, but business kept me from making a go of it. Now I only sponsor fighters, though I still train in a fighting gym and it keeps me fit." He pats his flat, muscled stomach.

So that's his secret. Cassius is more than fit, he's a beast. I imagine him up there in the octagon cage, facing down another man with his fists raised. He would make a formidable opponent.

"Do women do cage fighting?"

"Of course."

I glance at the cage, thinking about the moves and what Cassius said about technique. Learning to punch and kick sounds therapeutic and I wouldn't mind feeling stronger. "When I've had the baby, will you take me to one of your gyms? I'd like to try it. Not to fight. Just to train."

His hand slides over my belly. "Once you've had the baby, of course we can. We'll bring Vinicius. He keeps telling me he wants to be stronger but he's worried about being hit in his pretty face."

I laugh. "Vinicius and I will train in the no-hit club."

"No one is laying a finger on you. But you can punch me as hard as you like, *bambina*. I'll enjoy it."

The lights and music suddenly change. The championship fight is about to begin.

If the earlier fighters seemed fit and tough, the two who emerge and strut about in the cage are awe-inspiring. Their eyes blaze with determination and a competitive spirit crackles between them.

"That's my fighter," Cassius tells me, nodding to a blond man in red shorts and an open red robe.

Lasher surveys the crowd, spots Cassius, and leaps smoothly over the ropes toward us. Cassius and Lasher bump fists and Cassius embraces him before turning to me.

"Chiara, meet my best fighter, Lasher. Lasher, this is Chiara Romano."

"Good luck tonight," I tell him and hold out my hand. "I hope you win."

He flashes me a smile that's one hundred watts of pure charisma and shakes my hand. He's wearing fingerless hand wraps. "If Miss Chiara Romano wants me to win, then how can I lose?"

His attention wanders over to Alecta and his smile widens as he takes in her tight clothes and beautiful face. "Did you come to cheer for me, too, Alecta?"

"Keep your fists up," she tells him, her tone acerbic. "Don't let that pretty face get ruined."

He swipes his thumb along his jaw and winks at her. "Don't worry, baby. I'll still be this handsome after the fight if you want to party."

Alecta flicks her eyes up and down his body, one sardonic brow lifted. "You wish."

"Stay focused," Cassius tells him, then launches into a stream of advice about his opponent's weaknesses and fighting style. Lasher listens and nods, clenching and unclenching his fists.

Finally, Cassius pats Lasher's cheek, tells him he's going to win, and we sit back down in our seats as the fighter goes back to the cage.

Despite her dismissive words, Alecta can't seem to take her eyes off the blond man. Most of the women nearby are staring at him. It's the way he moves. The way he holds himself. If he's as good a fighter as his confidence suggests, then the championship is his.

He's joined in the ring by a mean-looking, dark-haired fighter in black shorts with a tiger tattooed on his back. The crowd cheers for both of them, but when Lasher lifts his fists, the screams are louder and more enthusiastic.

Alecta folds her arms and glowers, but she doesn't look away from him.

"Do you know Lasher?" I ask.

She makes a dismissive noise. "He was part of Strife when I first started hanging out there. He was always a cocky shit."

Aren't they all down at Strife? "It seems like he remembers you."

"He flirts with anything that moves. I'm not cheering for him tonight. I don't think you'll find many people from Strife who will." She glances at Cassius and then back to me. "But I try and keep my personal feelings out of my work. I hope you enjoy the fight."

I'm about to ask what Lasher and the Strife men fell out over when a bell rings and everybody screams as the fighters begin circling one another. They fight in flurries of punches and kicks. I can hear them landing and they make me wince, but neither fighter seems to notice the pain.

Despite his muscles, Lasher is light on his feet and viciously fast, but in the third round, his opponent gets him down on the ground and starts twisting his foot. Agony flashes across Lasher's face.

"He's going to tap out," Alecta says, sitting forward and gripping her seat. Despite her resolution not to cheer for Lasher, she's watching him with apprehension.

"He won't," Cassius replies.

"What's tapping out?" I ask.

Cassius leans closer so I can hear him over the crowd. "If a fighter's had enough, they call out, or tap on the floor or their opponent's body and the ref ends the fight."

A moment later, Lasher throws Peril off and drives him viciously into the ground. Then Lasher is behind his opponent and has his elbow around the man's throat.

Cassius shouts in triumph. "If he can hold this, he's going to win."

Alecta has her hands over her mouth now. "Peril needs to tap out."

"He's too stubborn. Lasher didn't tap out so neither will he."

The seconds tick by agonizingly slow. Finally, the referee rushes in to break up the fight just before Peril passes out, and Lasher is declared the winner.

With sweat pouring down his body, Lasher leaps to his feet with a roar, both fists raised.

The crowd goes nuts. Cassius is shouting louder than anyone. Alecta is applauding and whooping at the top of her lungs. When I catch her eye, she covers it up with a cough and grins at me.

"Fucking superb," Cassius is shouting while he applauds.

"Need that bathroom break?" Alecta asks me.

"Actually, yes," I tell her, giving Cassius a quick kiss before walking with Alecta to find the ladies' bathroom.

We have to wait for a few minutes and then we use the stalls. As we're washing our hands side by side at the sinks, I say, "I don't know anything about cage fighting, but I thought Lasher fought pretty well."

She smiles and smooths down her hair. "He was pretty good. Don't tell Acid I said that, though," she adds.

"Never."

As we're grinning at each other, there's a clunk, and all the lights go out. The bathroom is plunged into inky blackness and women gasp in shock. Beyond the door to the bathroom, voices are suddenly raised in panic.

Alecta grabs me in the darkness and takes a firm grip on my hand. "Chiara, is that you?"

I'm surprised by how calm she sounds. My nerves have suddenly shot through the roof. "Yes, it's me. What's happening? Do you think it's the police?"

The police raided one of Cassius' clubs on opening night a few months ago, but they didn't cut the power first.

"Possibly," she says in the same calm tone.

I don't understand why she sounds so chilled out until I realize it must be her bounty hunter training. She's assessing what's happening around us. Thinking rather than acting blindly. I make myself take a deep breath and follow her lead.

Alecta produces a small but powerful flashlight and suddenly the bathroom appears around us. Women are fumbling their way along the sinks, trying to find the exit.

She shines the flashlight around, searching for something.

"Cassius—" I start to stay.

"Mr. Ferragamo isn't your bodyguard right now. I am," she says firmly. "We're getting you outside to my car and then we'll worry about him."

Lorenzo hired Alecta so I know I'm in good hands, and Cassius would want me to let her do her job. "All right. How are we getting out of here?"

Her flashlight illuminates a window above the row of sinks. She jumps up and pushes it open. "Up here. Wriggle through and drop to the ground. Try and roll so you don't hurt your ankles if you can."

She helps me up onto the basin, and I look through the window and my heart sinks. It's a twelve-foot drop, maybe more. "I can't do this."

"Yes, you can. Deep breath and go. I'll be right behind you."

"I can't do this because I'm pregnant."

Alecta's face falls. "Oh, Jesus, I forgot. Okay. We'll use the fire exit. There's one thirty feet down the stadium, and if that's blocked, there's another on the east side of the building." She jumps down from the sinks and holds out her hand to me to help me down. Once I'm by her side, she says, "I'm going to turn off this flashlight so we don't attract any attention. Don't let go of my hand, okay?"

My heart races faster. If there are enemies out there I suppose she's doing the right thing. They'll be looking for bodyguards with flashlights and other equipment. If we can blend in with the panicking crowd, we can make it outside.

I take a firmer grasp of her hand and nod. "Okay."

Out in the gymnasium, there are hundreds of stumbling, panicking figures trying to use their phone lights to find their way outside. I search for the green-and-white exit signs that should be lit up in the dark, but either they've been smashed or the fuse has been ripped out.

"This doesn't feel like an accidental power outage," I tell Alecta.

She squeezes my hand in response, either *I know*, or *It's okay*. It doesn't feel okay. I put my hand over my belly as if I'm comforting the baby. Really, it's comforting me.

I stare across to where our seats were. Cassius could be just feet away from me. "Do you think we should find Cassius?"

"Mr. Scava and Acid will skin me alive if we go looking for him. Just keep moving this way and—" Alecta breaks off with a moan of pain. Her hand in mine loosens, and I feel her fall to the floor.

"Alecta!"

Several people have materialized around me in the darkness. A piece of tape is slapped over my mouth and my hands are wrenched behind my back and tied. A bag is pulled over my head and torso, and two strong people on either side of me hustle along with hands under my arms.

I kick and scream as hard as I can, but I can barely hear myself over the pandemonium that reigns in the gym. No one can see me. No one knows where I am. I whimper in my captors' powerful grasps. If I resist them too much, they might punch me and hurt the baby. But if I don't resist them, they'll take me away and even worse things might happen.

My dilemma is decided for me when I'm shoved down onto what feels like the back seat of a car, and a door slams. Someone holds me down with a hand on the back of my neck and another on my back. I've been kidnapped twice before, once by Lorenzo, who was terrifyingly efficient at it, and once by Acid and Thane, which was messy but successful.

This kidnapping falls into the terrifyingly efficient category.

I remember Alecta at the gym when the lights went out, and I try to channel her composure. I wriggle onto my side so I'm not pressing on my belly, and the person holding me allows it and then pushes me down again.

There's total silence in the car. No muttering. Not even a cough to tell me if the people who have captured me are men or women. After a long drive, we take a few turns in rapid succession and then the car comes to a halt.

I'm hustled out and the sound changes from outdoor night noises to muffled indoor noises. The floor beneath my feet is tiled, and then concrete, and then I'm being forced down steps. My knees nearly buckle and I try to resist, but all I get is a threatening shake and I'm compelled forward again.

Down into the cold.

Down into dampness.

The walls echo with the sounds of our footsteps, and then quickly become muted. Swallowed up by earth and stone.

The edge of a chair hits the back of my knees and I'm forced to sit. Thick ropes coil around my arms and torso. A hand reaches beneath my hood to rip off the tape covering my mouth, and then as footsteps recede, a door slams.

I'm left in silence, except for my own terrified breathing.

"Dad?" I call, hoping I'll hear his hard, unfriendly voice replying. Please, God, let it be Dad who's had me kidnapped. Dad might still have enough humanity left in his heart not to murder me and his unborn grandchild.

If it's not Dad, if it's the Geaks who have taken me, or if it's the Black Orchid Killer...

Bile rises in my throat as I remember the imaginative ways the murderer tortured and killed the syndicate's sisters. Horror-movie images of what a sadistic, psychopathic killer might do to me and the baby flicker through my mind.

"Let me go, whoever you are!"

I picture a man in the dark. Watching me. Laughing at me. The hood still covers my head and I can't see a thing, but I know that I could scream louder than I've ever screamed before and no one would hear me. My kidnapper didn't strip the tape from my mouth so that I could call for help. He took it away so he could hear me scream.

He loves it when they scream.

Purple spots dance before my eyes. I'm breathing too fast. I count slowly as I inhale and exhale, forcing myself not to lose control. It's all I have as the minutes tick by, counting my breaths and trying not to think. Listening for anything that might tell me where I am and who has taken me.

Cold starts to seep into my hands and feet. My mouth is dry and my muscles ache. I'm wondering whether I've been down here for one hour or two when I hear a door clang and the sounds of a scuffle. Someone else is being forced downstairs.

The door into this room is flung open and the scuffling grows louder. Two people seem to be forcing another across the room toward me. A deep, male shout of rage and pain fills the air, followed by harsh breathing. Someone's standing behind me and suddenly, the hood is ripped from my head. They're gone before I can see who it is. The only person I can see is tied to a chair beside me.

Oh, shit.

I had three guesses about who's taken me. I can rule one out. Shaking his dark hair out of his eyes and blinking in the dim overhead light, his suit rumpled and his wrists tied behind his back is—

"Dad?"

He stares back at me. "Chiara? I saw on the news that you were taken. I didn't believe..." He trails off and closes his mouth. There's blood dripping down the side of his face from a cut on his eyebrow.

The news. Cassius and the rest of my men must be panicking if they've reported my kidnapping. "What's on the news about me? Who took us? What's going on?"

But Dad's too busy shouting and trying to wrestle his way out of his bonds. All he's doing is exhausting himself, and he finally gives up with a growl of frustration. "Pieces of fucking shit! I'll have you all arrested. I'll kill you all with my bare fucking hands! Don't you know who I am?"

"Dad, I'm pretty sure they know who we are," I mutter.

He whips around and stares at me. His eyes flicker from side to side as he thinks, and a dreadful realization seems to crash over him.

I sit up. "Wait, do you know who's taken us? Who is it?"

Dad turns away and stares straight ahead.

"Dad, who is it? It's not...*him* is it? The Black Orchid Killer?"

Say no.

Oh, my God. Please say no.

Dad goes on staring straight ahead.

"Dad, what have you done? Why has he grabbed both of us? Did you do something to make him angry, or does he—"

"Shut up," he says, quietly, his voice as hard as steel.

This murderer killed the syndicate's sisters in order to punish them. If Dad threatened the killer and told him he wouldn't keep his secret any longer, what if the killer is going to torture me and make Dad watch?

"He'll kill you once he's done with me. You're not getting out of this alive, either," I snarl at him. Dad doesn't reply.

An hour goes by, maybe more. Time seems fluid in this windowless void. I can't bear the silence and so I sing under my breath, the song Mom used to put on the old record player when we would dance on the carpet. The tune that I danced to with my men as I cried happy tears remembering her.

"Stop that," Dad says.

I turn to look at him. "Why? Because it reminds you of Mom?"

His lip curls, and I know I'm right. He knows she loved this song. Maybe they danced to it together before they had me, back when Dad was still the dancing type.

"I want to sing to my baby. It might be the last chance I

get." I hum a few more bars under my breath. "She would have been so happy to know I was having a baby. Did you ever notice the way her eyes would light up whenever she saw a stroller? Mom loved babies."

"She behaved like a good politician's wife should, that's all."

"Don't be so cynical. You know that's not true." Sure, it was good publicity, the mayoress fawning over the babies of Coldlake, but Mom really did cherish every single child she came across. Mom will never get to hold my baby. Smile at my baby. Teach me how to bathe them and rock them to sleep or tell me all the little stories about the ways she raised me. I blink hard as tears crowd my eyes.

"I have to do this without her because of you," I say, my voice husky with emotion. "If I make it out of here alive. I don't know the first thing about babies. Sure, I'll learn. I'll get by. But it won't be the same as having my mother with me."

Crushing silence from Dad.

"What saddens me most is that she died for nothing because we thwarted all your plans. And you're supposed to be the clever one, Dad."

Dad's jaw flexes like he's grinding his teeth.

"The syndicate and I are against you, and you're not going to win the next election."

Dad gives a mirthless laugh. "When my opponent is Christian 'corpse-fucker' Galloway? I'll be just fine."

We'll see about that. There are plenty of ways Dad could lose the mayorship. I swear that if by some miracle I get out of here alive, I'll make sure everyone knows the truth about him.

"How did it feel, killing my mother?"

Stony silence.

"At first, I thought Lorenzo killed Mom. It was his knife in your hand. I never expected to look up into the murderer's face and see my own father."

I may as well be talking to a brick wall, but he's got no choice but to listen to me.

"Do you want to know what happened to that knife? While we were desperately trying to find Nicole—great plan pretending she was dead, by the way—Lorenzo threw it away. He understood how much it hurt me to see it in his hand."

"What a prince," Dad mutters.

"Compared to you, he's a king."

"I'm glad you're happy together, you and your pack of mangy wolves."

"I am happy. I think I deserve some happiness after what you did."

Dad turns to look at me finally, hatred suffusing his face. I'm happy. I've *dared* to be happy while defying him. "That woman was a liability. Little did I know her daughter was a liability, too. I'm disgusted with you, Chiara. I never raised you to be such a slut."

"You didn't raise me. She did."

"That explains a lot," he says and turns away.

Asshole.

"You're not going to feel anything as he kills me, are you?

If you're not going to try and save me, at least think of my unborn child. I'm carrying your grandson or your grand-daughter. They'll have your blood. They're your legacy."

"A bastard brat of the Coldlake Syndicate? That's not my legacy. It's better that they die today with their whore of a mother."

I close my eyes and turn my face away. "You're going to die speaking such ugly words, and you're going straight to hell."

"He's not going to kill me, you stupid girl," Dad sneers. "He thinks he's going to punish me by murdering you, but he's doing me a favor."

"Who?"

But Dad stares straight ahead, his expression filled with disgust.

"If you get out of this alive and I don't, I'm going to haunt your nightmares," I seethe. "Me, and this baby. I know Mom already haunts you. She's in every room of that house. I can't wait to help her make your life a misery."

"I sleep just fine, thank you."

I don't believe that for a second. "The police had evidence about the Black Orchid Killer but you had it moved. Why did you do that? I know it was you."

"You have been a busy little bee," he mutters, his voice dripping with sarcasm.

"I'm better at scheming than you are. I suppose you thought you'd impress the Coldlake Syndicate when you killed Mom. You should have realized that murdering a woman you're supposed to protect is the last thing that would endear you to them, but it backfired."

"It doesn't matter."

"Why not?"

Dad turns to look at me, his eyes as cold as the day I tried to shoot him by the swimming pool. "Because slitting that woman's throat is the best thing I ever did."

I shake my head, tears filling my eyes. "But on my seventeenth birthday."

"Your mother was getting in the way. I told her my marriage plans for you and she became totally unreasonable. Screaming. Crying. If she were here now, tied to that chair, she'd be in full-blown hysterics." He glances over me with grudging admiration. "You seem to take after me at least a little."

I take a shaky breath. "Full-blown hysterics is tempting, considering where we are. Is this the killer's basement? The Black Orchid Killer?"

Dad turns away again. I can make him talk about Mom, but I can't make him talk about the killer.

"If the two of you were friends, you're not anymore. You used him to punish the syndicate, and you used him to try and set a trap. Has he grown tired of being used?"

Nothing.

I try again.

"You and Mr. De Luca impersonated the killer when you faked Nicole's death. Did that make the killer angry? A man like him must be proud of his murders. His works of art. Has he killed Mr. De Luca? Is that why we can't find him?"

I suppose Mr. De Luca had his throat slit and he's buried in a shallow grave for daring to mimic the true killer. Dad doesn't seem to possess even an ounce of regret over what's happened to his friend.

"Is the killer someone you've known for a long time? Someone you went to university with? Maybe he's another politician and you've got each other's backs when it comes to covering up crimes. His murders. Your corruption. For a brief moment, I thought the killer was a couple of gangsters from the west of Coldlake. I've heard what gangs like to do to their victims. The women are horribly tortured before they're killed, but it's not art. It's not like what your friend does, and besides, you'd never cover up for a street gangster. Not the high and mighty tough-on-crime Mayor of Coldlake."

"Chiara, have you ever shut up in your entire life?" Dad growls through his teeth.

"I always used to shut up when I was around you. I don't do that anymore. I never will again."

I pull against the ropes binding my wrists, but they're as tight as ever. What is going *on*? I'm not in a hurry to be killed but I'd at least like to know who's keeping us in this basement.

I sit back with an angry cry, and despair sweeps over me. When I'm killed? When *we're* killed. Me and the baby. "Maybe you can persuade him to let me go if you beg for the baby's life."

Dad gives a hollow laugh. "I suppose you don't even know who the father is."

"Please, Dad," I beg him, tears spilling down my cheeks. "This baby is your flesh and blood, too."

Dad's jaw bunches, but misgiving flickers in his eyes. Like he's experiencing an emotion he detests. Like compassion.

"If there's any way out of this, tell me now. You must be able to think of some way of persuading this man. By blackmailing him, maybe. If you tell me who he is then maybe I can help you think of something."

Dad opens his mouth, and my heart swells—but then he closes it again.

"Dad, we have to put the past behind us. It's you and me against..." But I trail off as I hear something that makes all the hairs stand up on the back of my neck.

Someone's coming down the stairs.

One person, walking with slow, deliberate footsteps. A moment later, the door to the basement swings open. A man enters, dressed head to toe in black with his face and hair covered. I can't even see his eyes. He's lean and holds himself with chilly stillness. He slowly scans the room, left to right, like he's the Terminator, taking everything in. This is the man that Salvatore described the night Lorenzo was nearly taken.

"Dad?" I whisper, staring at the figure. "Is this him?"

The man takes a step toward me and regards me, his head tilted to one side. A predator assessing his prey.

Chills sweep over me and my chest lifts up and down

with short, frightened breaths. "This is the killer, isn't it? The Black Orchid Killer."

The man rolls his shoulders and pushes his chest out, as if pleased I've recognized him. He takes a step toward Dad, whose eyes are filled with wariness.

"I don't know what you think you're playing at," Dad growls. "We had an agreement that—"

The killer draws back his fist and sinks it into Dad's belly. He doubles over as much as the ropes allow him to and he groans.

"You moron," Dad says, panting through the pain. "Who'll protect you if I'm gone? Have you thought of that? *Answer me.*"

Apparently, the killer has decided he doesn't care anymore and he turns to me. Immediately, his gaze seems to zero in on my baby bump.

I shake my head from side to side, trying to push away from him with my feet. "No, please, leave me alone."

"I told you, Chiara has to stay alive until after the election," Dad shouts.

The horror of those words chill me to the bone. Chiara has to stay alive *until.*

"You never had any problem discussing this before. What the hell has gotten into you?" Dad frowns, and he examines our captor closely. Suddenly, his eyes flare with anger. "Wait, you're not—Who the fuck are you?"

The man in black stares at him.

I look from him to Dad and back again, frowning. "What's going on? I don't understand."

"Go on," Dad says to the killer. "Say something. Let me hear your voice."

Silence rings through the basement. Nobody breathes.

Dad says in a cold voice, "You're a fucking fake."

The figure in black scratches the back of his head. Then he shrugs, grabs his mask and pulls it off, revealing thick blond hair, bright golden eyes, and a clean-shaven jaw.

He smiles, revealing pointed canines. "Hey, kitten. How are you doing?"

I stop pretending to struggle against my bonds and sit back with a sigh. "Oh, I'm fine. We nearly had him."

Dad is spluttering with indignation. "Chiara? Vinicius Angeli? What the hell are you two playing at?"

"That was an Oscar-winning performance," Vinicius tells me. "From the cage fight to now, you never broke character."

It was the only way I could be sure that I'd convince Dad. He's known me all my life and always seemed to be able to catch me out in a lie. "Thank you. Telling the media I had been kidnapped was inspired. It really added authenticity."

"That was Salvatore's idea. The journalists had no idea what it meant, that a missing girl had been kidnapped, but they were hungry for stories about Miss Chiara Romano."

Dad's jaw is so tight his teeth might shatter. "Don't bother to congratulate yourselves. Your dirty trick didn't work."

Vinicius turns to him and spreads his arms. "What

gave me away? My body's too perfect, isn't it? Go on, I can take constructive criticism."

Dad glowers at him.

"I suppose you're not going to tell us who the Black Orchid Killer is? No?" Vinicius turns back to me. "I could just torture him until he tells us what we want to know. Most men will sing like canaries if you take a bolt cutter to their ball sack."

There's a voice from over by the doorway. "Did someone say torture?" Acid prowls into the room. "I'd be happy to oblige, your highness."

Thane stands next to him, staring at the mayor with a glacial chill in his dark eyes and examining Dad's body as if he's wondering where to get started.

"Can one of you untie me, please?" I ask.

Thane steps forward, his eyes glinting. Vinicius stops him with a hand on his chest. "Not you, pervert."

He hunkers down next to me and cuts through the ropes, and then rubs warmth back into my hands. His eyes are gentle as he gazes up at me. "I'm sorry it didn't work. It was a good plan. What do you want to happen now?"

He's my father, so he's leaving the decision to me. All my men plus Acid and Thane would be more than happy to go to town on Dad with knives, pliers, bolt cutters, and their fists, but it's not what Mom would have wanted. She believed in justice.

"Torture is probably what he deserves," I say, looking at Dad. "But I want the mayor found out, not secretly ripped apart in a basement and dying a martyr to everyone in Coldlake."

"It's been nine years since those women were murdered, your highness," Acid says, leaning against the dank walls of Strife's basement, his green eyes glinting. "You still think you can solve these murders yourself?"

I take a long, slow look around the room. This is the second time I've been in this basement, and while I know it's not *the* basement, the one where the Black Orchid Killer killed the syndicate's sisters, I feel like it's trying to tell me something. The feeling isn't déjà vu. It's more like there's something on the tip of my tongue that keeps slipping away.

A memory? An idea? Two dots that I need to connect?

Dad is gazing at me speculatively as if he, too, is wondering whether I can solve this puzzle. Thane's task these past few months has been to scour Dad's devices for any strange conversations about murders. When Acid and Thane snatched him tonight, Thane was going to check for any other phones or tablets he might have missed.

I raise a questioning brow at Thane. He gives an almost imperceptible shake of his head, and disappointment washes over me. I traded the favor owed to me by the Strife men for a kidnapping bounty and Thane's precious time and skills, and I've got nothing to show for it.

"Don't be squeamish, your highness. You don't have to watch if you don't want to."

"Thank you, Acid," I tell him. "But I'm saying no to torture. For now."

If there's a way to find the killer without everyone tearing strips off Dad, I'd prefer to do it that way. There's something just out of my reach, and I want to know what it is before I give up completely and resort to torture.

Vinicius is gazing at me with one eyebrow raised.

"I'm sorry. Do you all mind if we let him go for now?"

He takes my hand and helps me to my feet. "No need to apologize. Your family, your rules. The four of us already decided. Who wants to escort the mayor uptown?"

Acid's eyes flare with interest. "Oh, please. Allow us."

"Did you split his eyebrow?" I ask as Thane closes in on Dad to cut through his ropes.

"Yeah, we were a bit rough when we kidnapped him. I guess we need more practice." Acid grabs Dad by the scruff of his jacket and shoves him toward the door. "Move, you piece of shit."

"Thanks for letting me borrow the basement," I call after him.

"Anytime, your highness."

Vinicius pulls me into his arms. "Watching you work information out of the mayor was amazing. You have nerves of steel, kitten."

"I just wish it worked. I didn't find out what we wanted to know. I'm sorry."

He cups my cheek, his golden-hazel eyes soft. "No, but you got him talking. You came closer to the truth than any of us have before. If you still have hope, then I have hope."

I give him a sad smile. "Maybe I'll feel better about it after a good night's sleep."

"It's this basement that's getting you down. Come on, I'll take you home."

My mouth quirks in a smile. The compound. Home. The others will be waiting for us. Lorenzo will put a milky coffee into my hands and scour me for injuries with a fierce look. Cassius will kiss me and coddle me, and Salvatore will be impressed with how I faced my father and remind me how much I've changed since my seventeenth birthday. At times like these, I wonder what I've done to deserve these men. My heart aches to be with them all as soon as possible.

I take one final look around the basement, wishing I knew what it was trying to tell me, and then follow Vinicius upstairs.

18

Chiara

Lorenzo rips the Velcro open on the blood pressure cuff. "Perfect blood pressure. Welcome to week thirty, day one. This little one is the size of a cabbage. Their eyes can focus. They weigh about three pounds. Mama looks fucking gorgeous."

I cup my considerable belly in my hands. So far we don't know if it's a boy or a girl and I want it to be a surprise. From how big I feel, I'm starting to wonder if it's a baby elephant.

Lorenzo has kept up with his research and he knows more about the baby's progress than I do. I think it's his way of feeling in control of an uncontrollable situation.

"It might not be day one of week thirty. You don't know that it's yours."

"I'm counting from the day I locked the compound gates and there's nothing you can do to stop me." Lorenzo pulls his stethoscope from around his neck and puts it in his ears, then moves the bell around on my stomach. He smiles, and then pulls one earpiece out of his ears and offers it to me. "Here. Listen."

We listen to the baby's heartbeat together, a fast, strong whoosh in our ears.

"That's our baby," I whisper, my throat tight with emotion.

"Yeah, princess. That's our baby."

Lorenzo records a voice note of the sound on his phone and sends it to the group chat. The others reply almost immediately.

SALVATORE: *I'm out here being tough on the mean streets and you're going to make me cry.*

Vinicius: *I could listen to that sound all day.*

Cassius: *That's my bambino. Good and strong.*

"CASSIUS WANTS A BOY," Lorenzo says, shoving his phone in his pocket.

"I know. A little man to have running around the place, he told me. But if we have a girl, I know he'll be just as delighted and spoil her rotten."

"God, will he ever. Salvatore would be proud to have a boy at some point. I don't think Vinicius minds either way."

"And what do you want?" I ask.

"I want the baby to have the loudest cry, and the strongest kick, and the brightest eyes it can have. And for you to get through this and be smiling on the other side. That's all that matters to me."

"Not too strong a kick," I say, rubbing my hand over my belly. "I won't have any internal organs left in one piece by the end of this."

He makes a sympathetic face and kisses me. "How's mama? Dizzy? Headaches?"

"No, but my legs are aching all the time and I don't sleep through the night anymore."

"Stick your legs in my lap later and I'll rub your calves. I'll make sure the others do too, okay?"

I smile as I watch him pack up his equipment, wondering if I should tell him about the dreams I've been having. They're not nightmares, but they're unsettling. I'm standing in a basement and there are things around me in the dark. I don't know if they're objects or people, but I can't see them, and I can't make myself move. All the answers I crave are just out of my reach.

All the time, I'm thinking about basements and it's starting to drive me crazy.

"Lorenzo, can I ask you something?"

He must hear something in my voice as suddenly his

whole demeanor changes. He shoots a look at me, eyes narrowed with suspicion. "I don't know. Can you?"

"You might get mad, but I promise it's important."

He turns away from me with the blood pressure cuff and the stethoscope in his hands. "Then no."

I stay where I am, stranded on the metal table with my feet dangling a foot from the ground. "Something's been bugging me since I was tied up in the basement at Strife. The first time, but the second time, too."

"Why? What did those assholes do to you?"

"Nothing. It's a feeling I had. That the basement was trying to tell me something."

"Tell you what?"

I shrug. "That's just it. I don't know."

"Try and think about something else. I can't help you," he mutters, walking over to a cupboard and storing his medical equipment.

"You can. I wouldn't ask unless it's really important. I'm sorry if I'm going to upset you, but I've been over and over it and you're the only one who has the answer." I take a deep breath. "I want to ask you about the videos."

He slams the cupboard closed and rounds on me. I don't need any medical equipment to tell me that his blood pressure is suddenly through the roof. "We are not talking about those videos."

"I know it hurts. I wouldn't ask you if there were any other way. Maybe if you showed me—" Before I've even finished the sentence I can tell it was absolutely the wrong thing to say.

"You're not watching those fucking videos!" he shouts. Lorenzo pushes both his hands through his hair and growls. "I'm sorry. I didn't mean to shout. But I mean it, princess. I'll die before I ever let you watch those videos."

I didn't mean watch the murders, but he made it sound like the recordings began with just their sisters alone in a room and I want desperately to see that room. But I don't speak. There's barely controlled rage simmering beneath the surface that Lorenzo fights to get under control.

He walks over to me and grips the metal table on either side of my hips. His hair is wild and his cold blue eyes are troubled. "All right. I believe you when you say it's important. If there's something you really want to know, ask me, and I'll try to answer you. But I'm not showing you anything."

I nod, resolving to do this as quickly as possible, though not painlessly. I can already tell it's causing him horrible pain. "What did that basement look like?"

"It was just a basement. There wasn't anything special about it. Dark. Damp. The walls were crumbling in places. There was a vent high on the wall that let in a little light. It could be any basement in Coldlake or beyond."

Disappointment washes over me. I feared that's what he'd say. "Did you ever draw any conclusion about the killer from..." *The way he killed your sisters.* "How he did it?"

Lorenzo's eyes bore into mine. "That he's a sadistic fucking asshole and a coward who hates women as much as he hates the Coldlake Syndicate."

Hates women. I agree with him there. There's so much

hate in what this person did to the four sisters. They were murders so elaborate that they were elevated to an art form. A sick, twisted art form. I'd lay money on the killer being proud of their handiwork.

"I feel like there was a sense of irony about the way the killer murdered each of your sisters. That he was trying to send a message to each of you."

His brows draw together. "What do you mean?"

"Ophelia, for instance. The Fiores have always been immaculate and untouchable, so the killer mutilated and defiled Salvatore's beautiful sister, giving her the most grotesque death possible."

I remember what Lorenzo said that he told Sienna when she was tied up on his bedroom floor. *She hemorrhaged from her face. You wouldn't think it would be possible, would you? Those cuts in her cheeks severed the external maxillary arteries. My guess is he slashed her face first and then got on with torturing her and she screamed herself to death.*

"Cassius is from a proud, old Italian family," I continue, "so the killer wanted to mock him and his sister's history. Cassius said it himself. Impaling her on a spike was medieval."

The spike missed all the vital organs, traveled up through the body and out her shoulder. She could have been like that for hours, maybe days, before the bastardo *finally killed her.*

"Amalia was addicted to drugs and working in a brothel, so the killer cut her into pieces and threw her away. And Sienna..."

Pain flashes over Lorenzo's face. When she was found,

Sienna looked perfect, like a waxwork doll, but on the inside, she was filled with feces and dead insects.

"I think the killer was trying to say that she was pretty on the outside, but on the inside she was..."

"Trash," Lorenzo mutters, his tone bitter. "She was trash, her whole family is trash. I'm trash, and I have no business controlling any part of this city."

He pushes away from me and scrubs two hands over his face. I watch him in sad silence, hoping I'm not putting him through this pain for nothing.

"I never thought about their deaths that way before, princess. I think you're right. It's not just twisted. That monster was laughing at us."

"And he knew what he was doing. I think the killer must have some sort of medical training. He's intelligent and he thinks he's artistic, too. Exceptional. Someone important in Coldlake, or someone that has friends in high places."

"Yeah. Like your father. So who does your father know who fits that description? Medical background. Artistic. A flair for the sadistic."

I take a deep breath and scour my mind for possibilities. Maybe a doctor who loves to read the classics or an art gallery director who enjoys sculpture and tried his hand at sculpting with dead flesh. I wish I'd paid more attention to Dad's friends. Mom would know. I wish I could ask her. "Dad's connected with just about everyone important in Coldlake. Mom's funeral was a who's who of prominent people."

"I wish I'd been there," Lorenzo growls, his eyes narrowing. Then he glances at me. "I'm sorry. You know what I mean."

I do know what he means. It would have been an opportunity to take a good look at anyone who fits this description. "It's a creepy thought, that the killer might have been in the house that day, eating finger sandwiches and hiding in plain sight."

Lorenzo helps me down from the table. "I wish I could make you stop thinking about this stuff. You're having a baby. You're supposed to be radiant with sunshine and rainbows and shit."

Instead, I'm thinking about death and murky basements. I reach up and touch his cheek. "Thank you for talking to me about this. I needed to tell someone my theory and now I can move forward with the next part of my plan, if you'll let me use one of your computers. I want to go through newspaper articles about Dad since he became mayor and compile a list of everyone he's been connected with who is either artistic or medical."

He kisses my forehead. "No problem, princess. As long as you're where I can see you, I'll bear with it. But if I see your blood pressure going up, I'm changing my passwords and you can sit and knit."

I smile up at him. "Thank you for taking good care of me and the little bean."

He can't resist it when I'm grateful for his overprotectiveness, and the corner of his mouth twitches. "Damn you, woman. You've got us all wrapped around your little finger."

I blink my lashes at him, "Who, me?"

Lorenzo's phone rings and he answers it. "What?" He frowns and puts the caller on speakerphone. "Talk. She can hear you."

I stare at Lorenzo's phone, wondering who it is, and a female voice speaks. "Chiara? It's Alecta. How are you doing?"

I haven't seen Alecta since she fake-crumpled to the ground at the cage fighting match. She was a better actor than I was. "Alecta! I'm great, thank you. It's lovely to hear from you."

Her tone is serious. "I already reported this to Zagreus, but he thought you might like to hear this from me personally. I've been keeping an eye on the De Luca home under Mr. Scava's orders, waiting to see if De Luca appeared or if anything suspicious went down."

I exchange looks with Lorenzo. "And has he? Are Nicole and her mom all right?"

"They're absolutely fine," she assures me and then hesitates. "De Luca is back."

So he is alive. "When did he arrive?"

"Ten minutes ago. He pulled into the driveway, walked up to the front door and let himself in like it was a normal goddamn day and he hasn't been missing for eight months."

"Where is he now?" Lorenzo asks.

"Still inside the house, but I can't tell what's going on

because the curtains are closed. We've got another hunter watching the backyard in case he sneaks out that way."

"Thank you Alecta, I appreciate the call," I tell her.

"No problem. How's the baby?"

"It's absolutely fine. I think this one is already competing in cage fights the way it's kicking me."

Alecta laughs. "I bet Mr. Ferragamo is thrilled. Talk later."

Lorenzo hangs up and he takes my hand, his eyes hard and glittering. "I think it's time we paid a visit to your old school friend and her father, don't you?"

I call the others to tell them what's happened and they agree to meet us at the De Luca family home right away.

Thirty minutes later, I'm standing on the front doorstep at Nicole's house, and I ring the bell.

Nicole answers the door and her eyes widen as she sees the four men standing behind me, stony expressions on their faces. They widen even more as I shift on my feet and she catches sight of my bump.

"Oh, Chiara, you're—" Her smile is delighted for a split second, and then reality crashes down on her. "I guess you're all here to see Dad. You won't hurt him, will you?"

"No, we just want to talk to him," I assure her. "No one here is going to hurt him in his own home, I promise you."

Nicole gazes at each of my men. None of them laid a finger on her while she was at the compound. They kept her safe and then let her go when she asked. She steps back. "You'd better come in."

We file into the house, one by one, and Lorenzo calls

out, "Tell De Luca that there are armed hunters surrounding this house. There's nowhere to run."

"What's a hunter?" Nicole mutters as she leads us through to the lounge and disappears deeper into the house.

The five of us stand in the neat, carpeted room, waiting for Mr. De Luca to appear. In all the years I've known Nicole, this room has barely changed. There's a huge book-case covering one wall with leather-bound volumes of twentieth-century history, Roman history, *The Odyssey* and *The Iliad*. On the rare occasions Mr. De Luca was home when I visited Nicole, he'd usually have his nose in a book. One wall of the lounge is covered in framed photographs. Nicole as a baby. Family holidays. Mr. and Mrs. De Luca's wedding photos. Mr. De Luca's high school graduation picture. I spot him in the second row, and just behind him and to the left is Dad. My belly swoops at the sight of him. There's someone else familiar in the photo, seated in the front row. I didn't realize Christian Galloway went to school with them both.

I lean down to take a closer look at Galloway just as someone says my name.

"What do you want, Chiara?"

I turn around, and Mr. De Luca is looking at me with a mixture of irritation and fear. He's a thin, unassuming man with hunched shoulders. Nicole has his slender frame, but she has her mother's bright eyes rather than her father's shadowed ones.

"We just want to talk. Can we sit down?" I wait for him

to offer me a seat, and when he doesn't reply I ease myself down on the sofa. My legs are aching worse than ever.

Vinicius is gazing at him with intense suspicion and dislike. "You put on a wonderful show for me, De Luca. It's not often I'm fooled. *I didn't know where else to turn. He told me I couldn't go to the police.*"

Mr. De Luca's gaze darts around the room and he seems reluctant to leave the safety of the doorway.

"What happened the night you told the syndicate you were meeting the Black Orchid Killer?" I ask him.

Mr. De Luca starts to turn away. Lorenzo strides forward, grabs him by the shirt, and shoves him into a chair. "Answer her questions or I'll start asking some of my own."

He puts his arm up to protect his face as if expecting a beating. When he speaks, his voice is shaking. "Please don't hurt me. I'll tell you."

I wait patiently for him to get a grip, but I want to scream at him. He put his daughter in danger for my horrible father, and there's no excuse for that.

"That night, nothing happened," De Luca says, staring at the carpet. "I went to the meeting place, but I realized there was no point in me staying there. Mayor Romano didn't need me anymore."

"You didn't realize Nicole was in your car? She could have been killed because of you," I say.

He shakes his head, his expression mortified. "I swear I didn't know. I didn't find out until later."

I gaze at him with a mixture of pity and anger. I recognize the signs of someone who's been used by my father. Bewildered. Frightened. Alone. Where's Dad now that Mr. De Luca is being confronted by the men he was persuaded to entrap?

"The killer was there that night. Did you see or hear anything that might tell you who he is?"

Mr. De Luca shakes his head. "I was only there for a few minutes and then I left. I left *fast*. I made a horrible mistake when I went along with your father. I regret it every day."

So he ran away and hid, leaving his wife and daughter to fend for themselves. He didn't know that my men aren't the sort of people to get their pound of flesh from their enemies' families.

"You're weak, Mr. De Luca," I tell him. "But I didn't realize you were such a coward."

Vinicius takes a step toward him, and Mr. De Luca flings his arms up again, begging, almost screaming, "Don't hurt me, please!"

"I want one thing before we go." Vinicius holds out his hand. "Give me your phone. The one you were using while you and the mayor were planning your fun little ambush."

Mr. De Luca shakes his head. "I got rid of it months ago. It fell into the bath and it never worked after that."

Vinicius drops his hand with a sigh. The killer knew about their plan somehow. Thane could have scoured that phone for spyware that might have told us who the killer is. Another lead that's turned into a dead end.

I get to my feet. "You're a terrible husband and you're

not much better as a father. You put your work first. You put yourself first. Why don't you spend some time thinking about how you can make things up to your wife and daughter?"

De Luca puts his head in his hands and doesn't reply.

Out in the hall, Nicole embraces me. "You didn't find out anything you needed, did you? I'm sorry."

I give her a hug. "It's all right. It was worth a try. Are you going to be all right here with him? If you and your mom want him out, we can make sure he leaves."

Nicole gazes into the lounge where Mr. De Luca is still slumped on the sofa, his head in his hands.

Her expression fills with pity. "Dad's not very good at saying no to people like your father. He's let us down, but he's still my father." She turns to me with a smile. "Just look at you, a baby on the way. Are you having a baby shower? I'd love to—"

She's excited for a moment, and then her smile dims. She glances at the men around me, as if she doesn't believe they'd want her anywhere near any party I was throwing.

A baby shower. I've had so much on my mind that it never occurred to me. "A baby shower is a wonderful idea. I'll organize something and message you a date and time. Will your parents be okay with you coming to Salvatore's house?"

Nicole lifts her chin. "I don't care if they don't like it. My best friend is having a baby shower and I'm going."

I grin and give her another hug. "Wonderful. I'll see you soon."

As we walk out to the cars, Salvatore says to me, "You want a baby shower? We can arrange that. Ginevra would love to be there."

"And how about your pretty high school friends?" suggests Vinicius.

I haven't seen Rosaline, Sophia, and Candace in months. "Yes, that's a good idea. I'm sorry about today, though. We didn't learn anything new about the killer."

At Lorenzo's car, I turn back and gaze at Nicole's house. Her father is a broken man, but Nicole's going to be just fine, I can feel it.

"Let's go and eat at my house," Salvatore offers. "We can order some party supplies and plan the shower."

He's offering this in order to take my mind off things, and I'm grateful. "I'd love that, thank you."

We all drive over to Salvatore's beautiful house and he and I sit together on the sofa with his laptop and order pastel-colored banners and paper napkins, and a beautiful cake in the shape of a teddy bear asleep under a fondant blanket.

Cassius orders Thai food, and Vinicius pulls my legs into his lap to massage my calves while we eat and watch the evening news.

I'm starting to drift off, thanks to the massage, the food, and the sheer exhaustion of several broken nights' sleep, when I hear a familiar name on the news. Christian Galloway is being interviewed about his healthcare policies.

"...as a former medical professional, I can say with

authority that Coldlake's hospitals need a complete overhaul."

I sit up with a gasp. "Christian Galloway!"

The others turn to me in surprise. My heart is suddenly pounding hard in my chest.

"The other day Lorenzo and I were discussing who the killer might be. Someone prominent in Coldlake. Someone with a medical background, or maybe an artistic one. I've been racking my brain to remember people from Dad's circle who match this description, and it's just occurred to me. Christian Galloway."

It's not received by the others like the epiphany I was hoping it would be.

Salvatore frowns. "I thought we had established that your father was covering up for the murderer. He wouldn't cover up for his opponent."

I get to my feet and start walking up and down, rubbing my stiff lower back as I go. "But maybe he would! Listen, everyone's always said what a terrible opponent Galloway is because Dad always beats him and Galloway has never passed him in the polls. What if that's their intention? Dad has to have an opponent, so maybe he arranged for someone who would seem like he was putting up a good opposition but didn't have Dad's charisma or ability to inspire people? In return, Dad keeps Galloway's serial killer secrets."

It's not much to go on, and I don't have any evidence, but it's *something*. It's a possibility. The others are listening to me, and from their expressions, they seem to be at least considering the theory.

I keep walking up and down, thinking out loud. "I saw Galloway's photo in Nicole's living room. Her dad, my dad, and Galloway all went to high school together. They're the same age and they're from wealthy families. They might have some sort of secret friendship that goes back decades."

"Good point," Vinicius says. "I wonder if Galloway has any interesting data on his computers and devices. I'll get Thane to look into him."

Cassius' expression is hopeful as he watches me walk back and forth across the room. "It's the first time we've named a suspect. Do you all realize that?"

I give him a crooked smile, but the happiness I'm feeling that we might be getting somewhere is bittersweet. "It's somewhere to start, at le—" I break off with a wince and put my hand over my belly.

Lorenzo gets to his feet and crosses the room toward me. "What is it? What's wrong?"

"Nothing. The baby is demanding my attention."

"Kicking?" Vinicius asks as Lorenzo cups my stomach with his tattooed hands.

"Like it's in the Soccer World Cup," Lorenzo says as he helps me sit down in an armchair.

Cassius leans over and places a palm on my belly. A moment later, he grins. "My son could play for Italy."

Salvatore comes over and kneels down in front of me, placing his hands on the bump. "You, little monster,"

Salvatore says to the baby. "Don't kick your mother so hard. She's soft and beautiful and doesn't deserve it. Little kicks only, just to say hi to her and your daddies, okay?"

The kicking doesn't stop. "I don't think our little bean is listening to you, Salvatore."

My eyes are drawn back to the television where Galloway is still being interviewed. The others stare at him as well.

Lorenzo folds his arms, his expression cold and suspicious. "You know what? I've always thought Galloway was a fucking creep."

THE BABY SHOWER is held at Salvatore's house three days later. It's Sunday afternoon and the sun is shining through the big window onto the garden. Pastel-colored bunting is strung up across the room and the coffee table is covered in finger sandwiches, pink and blue cupcakes, and the sleeping teddy bear cake as the centerpiece.

I'm covered in scraps of cute wrapping paper. I lift a tiny pajama set printed with yellow ducks up for the others to see. "Oh, this is so sweet! Thank you, Rosaline."

She leans over and gives me a hug. "You're welcome. I can't wait to meet the little one."

"Ginevra, he's just *perfect*." Nicole is holding Camillo, gazing down adoringly into his face. Sophia and Candace are standing at her shoulders, making faces at the baby.

"He's a little tyrant," Ginevra says, amused, peeling the

paper wrapper from a cupcake. "But we love him. He's going to be a handsome devil like his daddy and his uncle Salvatore, I can just tell."

"He's an angel. Aren't you, Camillo?" Sophia coos.

Ginevra laughs. "Every woman who meets him turns to mush, but you should see him at bedtime when Antonio or I are trying to get him to sleep."

Lately, Camillo has found his lungs and I've heard the way he can scream when he's hungry or overtired. I wonder if he gets that from the Fiore side. I put my hand over my belly. God, I hope not.

"Time to cut the cake," I announce, brushing torn paper from my lap and reaching for the cake knife. The vanilla sponge is filled with cream and raspberry sauce, and my mouth waters as I hand out slices to the girls and then settle back with my own enormous piece.

Salvatore, Vinicius, Cassius, and Lorenzo are in the next room, and they've told me to enjoy myself and save them some cake. There's no problem with that as the cake is huge. And I am enjoying myself. I've given myself permission not to think about a certain father and killer for a whole afternoon.

Sophia sits down on the opposite sofa, hugs an enormous teddy bear and sighs. "When am I going to have children? I'm so broody sitting here with all this baby stuff."

"You need a man first," Candace points out, forking some cake into her mouth.

Rosaline cups her hands around her mouth and in a

loud whisper says, "You only need him for a few minutes. That's all it takes."

Sophia bursts out laughing. Turning to Nicole, she asks, "Do you want children?"

Nicole looks wistful as she gently bounces Camillo. "Oh, so much. I've wanted babies since I was a little girl. My family has a holiday house and I've always imagined taking my children there in the summer. Do you remember that house, Chiara? You came there a few times."

I finish my mouthful of cake and nod. "They were wonderful holidays."

There would be me and Mom, Nicole and Mrs. De Luca. Sometimes Dad would be there, and Mr. De Luca too, but work was always calling them away. Dad had mayoral work and Mr. De Luca is a medical researcher and always had to speak at conferences. Mom and Mrs. De Luca would cook, play cards, and drink wine, and Nicole and I would run around playing games all day.

"After the baby is born, you'll have to come out to our holiday house in the summer," Nicole tells me.

I give her a delighted smile. "I would love that, thank you. We always had the best times at your holiday house."

How wonderful it would be to have a holiday home of our own. A place for me and my men and our children where we could relax and invite our friends. Somewhere with a big kitchen and a deck, and views of mountains or a beach or a lake. I explored some beautiful holiday homes with Mom while she was still alive. I usually saw every room because I loved to play hide-and-seek and would find the best hiding spots in the garage or the attic or the...

Chiara? Where are you? You know that the basement is out of bounds.

...basement.

A memory suddenly washes over me. A dark, frightening memory of a cold place filled with strange smells and damp concrete. The smells invade my nostrils and suddenly the raspberry jelly on my plate looks like smeared blood.

I get to my feet as my throat convulses.

Chiara, I know you're down here.

"Chiara, are you all right?" Nicole is staring at me, her brow wrinkled in concern.

The urge to run is almost overpowering. I clench my fists at my sides. "I just need to..."

Without another word, I hurry out of the room. A window. I need fresh air. I head for the window at the end of the hall and fumble with the lock.

"*Bambina*, are you all right?"

I jump as a hand lands on my shoulder. It's Cassius, and he's gazing down at me with concern. I realize I'm still holding my cake fork like a weapon, brandished in my fist.

"I don't know. I just got the strangest feeling."

"Lorenzo!" he calls over his shoulder, and the blond man appears by my side. He feels my brow and presses his fingers to the side of my neck.

"Princess, what's wrong? Christ, why is your heart rate so high?"

A holiday house. A basement. I never saw the videos, but I can hear their screams echoing off concrete walls. Screams of terror and pain that dissipate on the damp air and are blown to nothing in the wind.

"I just remembered something. A place I saw years and years ago."

I can barely see my two men. The memory in my mind's eye is blinding. I know where that basement is. I could be there within forty minutes. This time of year, the house is probably empty.

"A basement. Maybe it's nothing, but I have to know for sure. Will the two of you drive me?"

They stare at me and then exchange glances. Lorenzo speaks first. "If you want to check something out, sure, but are you sure you want to leave your party?"

I glance toward the living room, feeling guilty for running out on my guests. I couldn't even relax for half an hour without thinking about the killer. "This isn't like my idea about Christian Galloway. This feels *real*. I have to know if I'm right."

Cassius clasps my shoulder. "Of course, *bambina*. Just tell us where and we'll take you."

"Thank you." I turn to Lorenzo. "Do you have lock-picks? Or something to break down doors, like an axe? We'll have to break in. If I'm wrong then I'll just have to find some way to pay for the damage."

The sick feeling in my stomach doubles. Please, let me be wrong.

Lorenzo takes hold of my upper arms. "Princess, we'll

do this, but are you sure you're all right? What's come over you?"

I shake my head. "I can't explain it. It's a feeling. A horrible feeling. Maybe this is hormones or indigestion, and I will be more than happy to laugh about it later and you can make fun of me, but right now I'm not going to calm down until I'm in a car and we're on our way." I wipe sweat from my top lip and entreat him with my eyes.

Lorenzo nods. "All right, we'll take my car."

Salvatore is coming toward me and Vinicius is hovering behind him. I need them, too. This is about more than the five of us.

I reach for Salvatore's hand. "Salvatore, I need you and Vinicius to do something for me, and it's really, really important. I think it might be life and death."

"Of course, we will," he assures me. "Just tell me what you need us to do."

I tell them what I told Lorenzo and Cassius, and ask if they'll take all our guests to the compound.

Vinicius nods, and adds, "Sure, we can. But it might sound better if the request was coming from you."

He means Nicole might be unwilling to go anywhere under their orders, which is a fair assumption. I head back into the lounge where the women are sitting up with worried expressions on their faces.

"I'm so sorry to do this, but I have to cancel the party."

Ginevra gives a cry of dismay. "You're not unwell, are you?"

I shake my head. "You all remember the Black Orchid

Murders. Nicole, you have first-hand experience at pretending to be one of the victims. I've remembered something that might lead us to the killer, and I have to go now and see if I'm right. It's all I can think about."

Ginevra's expression changes from worried to fearful, and she nods.

"Could you all please go with Salvatore and Vinicius to Lorenzo's compound and wait there? We'll be an hour, maybe two. That's all I ask of you, to wait there until it's safe and we know if I'm right or not."

Rosaline stands up and comes toward me, her brow wrinkled with concern. "Of course we will, but you're going to be all right, aren't you? You and the baby?"

I'll be able to calm down when I know what I'm dealing with. "I'll be fine, especially once I know you're safely on your way to the compound."

Candace and Sophia are getting to their feet, along with Ginevra. They all implicitly trust Salvatore and would follow him anywhere. Nicole, however, seems hesitant.

I go over and sit down next to her. "I promise I'll tell you everything as soon as I can. Will you go with Salvatore and Vinicius? I know you might not trust them, but I hope you trust me."

She glances at the men and then back at me. "I trust you. And you know what? After everything that's happened, considering the people who have let me down and the people who haven't, I trust them, too."

19

Lorenzo

Beside me in the front seat, Chiara has both her arms around her belly and she's hugging it tightly as she gives directions. We drive for forty minutes north of Coldlake to a wooded, hilly area that I don't know well. It's where the wealthy residents of the city build holiday homes, so it's not somewhere I ever went as a kid.

Finally, we head down a deserted road, turning into a driveway and stopping in front of a house.

It's a lake house. An immaculate, sprawling weatherboard lake house with a broad veranda all the way around. A triple garage off to one side. An immaculate garden with the lake just glimpsed through the trees.

We get out of the car. I heard about places like this as a

boy, but we never took a holiday, let alone considered having a whole other home to use only a few weeks of the year. This is the world that Chiara and Salvatore grew up in. That Cassius would have grown up in if he'd been raised in Coldlake instead of Italy. Pristine. Perfect. Children playing. Wives in dresses and husbands discussing investments and stocks.

Even deserted and with dusk creeping in, it looks idyllic, only Chiara is staring at the house like it wants to eat her.

"It doesn't look like anyone's home," I tell her.

"I would have been surprised if they were. How do the two of you feel about some breaking and entering?"

Fog is rolling in off the water and it's getting dark. I dig the lockpicks out of my pocket and grab a flashlight from the trunk of my car. "Fine by me."

A sticker in the front window of the house declares that there's an alarm system.

"Give me a minute," I tell the other two, and wade into the bushes until I find the electricity meter. I lever off the locking tab with the lockpicks and get to work switching it off. A few minutes later, I return to Chiara and Cassius.

"I turned the mains power off so hopefully the alarm won't go off," I tell them, heading for the back door. "There's a chance the backup battery in the alarm is flat seeing as this house is only used for part of the year."

"And if it's not?" Cassius asks.

Then the alarm is definitely going to go off. The alarm

panel will be hidden somewhere in the house where I can't reach it. But we'll cross that bridge when we come to it.

I hunker down in front of the back door and start working with the lockpicks.

"You've led an interesting life," Chiara observes.

"Who, me? Vinicius taught me all these tricks, the sneaky criminal that he is."

He's better at picking locks than me, and fifteen minutes later I'm sweating and starting to get frustrated. "Fucking stupid fucking lock," I growl under my breath.

"Take a breather and try again," Cassius suggests. He's leaning against the veranda railing holding the flashlight, directing the beam at the lock so I can see what I'm doing. "Or we could just break the door down."

I take a deep breath and stare at the lock. Breaking shit has always seemed like a perfectly acceptable way of getting what I want, but I can picture Vinicius' smug expression if he hears that the back door of some suburban asshole's lake house defeated me.

I shove the picks back in the lock and try again, and two minutes later, the lock tumbles open. Thank fuck for that.

I get to my feet, my hand on the doorknob, and turn to Chiara. "If the alarm goes off, we shouldn't stay for longer than five minutes."

"That's fine. What we need to do won't take longer than two."

"Okay, here goes." I push the back door open—

And silence. The battery's dead. I toss the lockpicks up

and down in my hand as I swagger through the door into a sparkling, expensive kitchen. People shouldn't make this so easy. "Okay, princess, where now?"

"The basement."

Suddenly, all the hairs stand up on the back of my neck.

Chiara shoots me a tense, apologetic look as she heads past me, down the hall and over to a door. She opens it and there's only darkness beyond.

My stomach's suddenly churning and I'm rooted to the spot, which is ridiculous as Chiara never saw the basement where our sisters were killed. She doesn't know more about that basement than what I told her. Does she?

"Did you watch those videos?" I demand. "Tell me the truth. Why this basement?"

She shakes her head. "I don't even know where you keep those videos. I suddenly had a feeling and a few things connected in my mind. I thought we should find out for sure. Please don't be angry with me if I'm wrong."

"Of course I won't be angry." As much as I want to find out who killed our sisters, I feel an almost overwhelming desire to bolt out the back door and never look back. Whatever gut feeling Chiara has, I hope in a few minutes we'll be laughing it off.

I want to go home.

I want to be anywhere but here.

With a grim expression, Cassius moves past me and shines the light through the doorway as he begins to descend. Chiara tries to follow him but I grab her arm.

"Stay behind me," I mutter and pass through the door. The steps are steep and it's a long way down. "Hold on to the rail and be careful," I tell her over my shoulder.

Ahead of me, Cassius' back is blocking my view. At the bottom of the steps, he moves aside and passes the flashlight beam over the walls—and I feel like someone's punched me in the guts. I step forward, and my ears are filled with terrified screaming. Women beg for their lives and make pitiful, inhuman noises.

Memories hit me like a tidal wave. I stagger back, fall on my ass and sit there, one arm raised in front of my face and panting for breath. Slowly, I lower my arm and take another look. The patterns made by the different shades of brick in the walls. The narrow vent up by the ceiling. The slightly askew light fitting. Every detail is the same. Useless fucking information that I branded into my mind along with our sisters' torture, hoping in vain that I might recognize something. Discover something. Do *anything* with the nightmares I witnessed, again and again.

Someone crouches down beside me and touches my arm. "Lorenzo?"

I get to my feet and move back a pace, and then to the left. "Here. This is where the camera must have been positioned." My voice doesn't sound like mine, as if I've been half strangled. I look around wildly and see the door. "He always entered from the right. There was a..." I move my arm back and forth, remembering how the table looked, four feet high and human-sized. Long enough to fit a man. Or woman.

"There was a chair," I say, my voice reaching my ears from a long way away.

I can see the ropes binding my sister to the chair, her blonde hair tangled and falling over her shoulder. Her tear-stained and mascara-streaked face and the terror in her eyes. Terror and total confusion. She didn't understand why any of this was happening to her and her captor never bothered to explain. Maybe Sienna went to her death never knowing why, or maybe in her heart of hearts, she knew.

She was tortured and killed because of me.

"Is this the place?" Cassius demands, his voice rough with emotion. "Were they killed here?"

The walls still hold the echo of their screams. The air is dank with their misery. I can smell their blood in the concrete. "This is where our sisters were killed."

Chiara moans. "I didn't want to be right. This isn't the man I knew. This isn't the face he showed to everyone."

"*Bambina*, whose house is this?"

"Mom and I came here the summer after your sisters were murdered. It rained all week and Nicole and I were bored. There was nothing to do but play hide-and-seek. The basement door was always locked and I was told never to come down here, but one day I tried the handle, and it opened." Her eyes grow unfocused at the memory. "The smell. I was too young to know what it was, but I know now. It was death. There was something terrifying about his face when he found me down here. Just for a second, he looked like a monster. Something out of a nightmare. I was only ten years old and you're full of make-believe when you're ten, and I told myself I'd imagined it. I forgot all about that day until just before when Nicole and I were reminiscing. Do you remember what we talked about, Lorenzo? I thought that the man who murdered your sisters was a doctor, or someone medical. While I was going through all the cold cases Vinicius dug up, I thought to myself, this killer must travel a lot. He must have a good excuse to be away from home so often."

Chiara takes a deep breath and looks around the basement.

"The man who owns this house is a medical researcher. He travels all the time for medical conferences. He knows Dad. He's a *really* good friend of Dad's and he has been for years. To look at him, he seems weak and harmless, but I saw who he really was the day he found me in this basement. I saw the monster in his eyes."

My fists clench so hard that my nails cut into my flesh. "Who is it?"

She swallows hard, and whispers, "Mr. De Luca."

Just outside the door, there's the sound of a footfall. For a split second, we all freeze and Cassius and I stare at each other in horror as we realize what we've done. We've brought Chiara to a serial killer's house.

I lunge for the door just in time for it to swing closed. Someone on the other side has pulled it shut and locked it.

I pound against the door. "De Luca? Open this door. Open this fucking door!"

A menacing voice travels through the door, so

different from his usual weak, whiny tone. "I told you to stay out of my basement, Chiara. You think I haven't learned by now? This house is protected by a silent alarm."

"All those years ago, I saw your true face and I told myself that I imagined it," Chiara says, her eyes wide and terrified. "You're a better actor than Vinicius realized. You've been acting all your life, pretending to be a weak and timid father and researcher."

"Who's in there?" De Luca says in a sly voice. "Is it Vinicius Angeli? I strung your junkie sister out before I killed her. The withdrawal was so terrible that her whole body was on fire. How it made me laugh. I barely needed to torture her myself."

I beat on the door with both my fists. "*Open this door, you murdering fuck!*"

"That sounds like the crude tones of Lorenzo Scava. I made your sister so beautiful. Aren't you grateful? Perfect on the outside. A filthy piece of trash on the inside, just like her brother."

I pull out my revolver and fire three shots into the wood. The bullets penetrate but don't pass through.

Chiara calls out, "Mr. De Luca, why did you do it? What did these men and their sisters ever do to you?"

"Chiara, you're so naïve it hurts. Of course you flocked to four broken men, the goody-goody politician's daughter. This was all your father's idea, and I was happy to oblige. What does he do to people he doesn't like? He makes them suffer. He made your mother suffer, or were you so wrapped up in yourself that you didn't notice how much he'd broken her by the end?"

Chiara puts her hand over her mouth and sobs. "You did all this for Dad?"

"For the price of his silence. Your father found out about my artistry and he agreed to turn a blind eye on the condition that I found my victims outside Coldlake, and if I performed a little favor for him. Four sweet little favors. How he hates the syndicate for their power and lawlessness. The mayor let your men play in his city, but they were going to be happy over his dead body."

Cassius steps up to the door without a word, lifts his foot and kicks it hard. The door barely shakes under the force of the kick.

"You'll never make them happy, Chiara, no matter how many times you let them fuck you."

Chiara has tears streaming down her face. "How could you? All those women were innocent."

"I don't need to justify what I do to those who crawl about on the surface of this earth like worms." De Luca sounds crazed as he shouts, "I'm above you all! I'm better than all of you. You're cattle. You're nothing, and so were your sisters."

"Shut your fucking mouth, you *stronzo fiammeggiante*," Cassius roars between kicks.

"Those videos are some of my finest work. I hope you've enjoyed rewatching them as often as I do."

He's there. He's *right fucking there*, just inches from me, and I can't get my hands on him to tear him apart. I push my fingers through my hair and growl in frustration.

There's the sound of footsteps disappearing back up the stairs.

Chiara screams after him, "You can leave us here to die, but our friends will still find us. It's all over for you, Mr. De Luca. Everyone's going to know what you've done. Your wife. Nicole."

The footsteps stop. "Will they, though?"

He gives a cold laugh, and then he continues walking up the stairs.

"Don't you dare! Leave them alone!" Chiara screams, but there's no answer.

Cassius goes on kicking the door and ramming it with his shoulder, but we're trapped like fucking animals.

I pull my phone out of my pocket and glance at the screen. "Does anyone have any reception?"

Chiara and Cassius check, but they've got nothing, the same as me. I go over to Chiara and put my hands on her shoulders. Tears are flowing freely down my face.

"Princess, look at me."

"I should have known something was wrong with Mom. I didn't see it until my birthday. I could have—"

"Hey. Stop that. Cassius and I are going to get you and the baby out of here safely, but I need you to take a few deep breaths. Nothing that piece of shit said is worth the oxygen he fucking steals to say it." I take her face in my hands. "Okay?"

More tears trickle down her face and she whispers thickly, "I'm so sorry I brought you here."

I shake my head. "I needed to find this place, and you found it for me, princess."

Chiara takes a deep breath, and then another.

"Good girl. Everything's going to be fine."

Cassius is still throwing his body against the door. Meanwhile, I search the room for any other way to escape. Trapdoors. Manholes in the ceiling. There's fucking nothing.

"Can you guys smell smoke?" Chiara asks.

Cassius stops kicking the door and I inhale deeply. There is something smoky about the air all of a sudden. And is that a faint crackling I can hear?

Cassius and I exchange glances. A locked basement in a burning house. Even if the fire doesn't reach us, we're fucking toast as soon as all the oxygen is sucked out of here by the flames.

I push the table beneath the vent in the wall and climb up on top of it. I've got one sliver of a bar and I try calling Salvatore, but the call keeps dropping out. I type a text and send it to the group chat instead.

Message sending failed.

Message sending failed.

Message sending failed.

"Jesus fucking Christ," I growl, and beat the wall with my fist.

I remember Chiara's terrified face the day she found out she was pregnant and realized that from now on, the four of us would do whatever it takes to keep her and the baby safe, even if that meant dying for them. Cassius and I are facing the possibility that we won't get the privilege of sacrificing ourselves.

We're all trapped. We'll all die together.

Chiara has her arms wrapped around her belly and she's gazing up at me with a face so pale and scared that my heart is on the verge of shattering into pieces.

"We're going to get you out of here, princess," I tell her, with more bravado than I feel.

I just don't know fucking how.

20

Salvatore

"Wow, this place is crazy. Like a nuclear bunker or something," Rosaline says as she steps out of the white SUV and gazes around the basement of Lorenzo's compound.

At Chiara's request, I've brought Nicole, Rosaline, Candace, and Sophia to the compound. Vinicius pulls into the garage behind us with Mrs. De Luca in his Ferrari and we all head upstairs. Chiara insisted that she be brought here, too.

"It's a bit like a prison, but it's safe," Nicole assures the other girls and takes her mother's hand.

Of all of them, Mrs. De Luca is being the most difficult.

Her expression is impatient as she exclaims, "But I still don't understand what we're doing here!"

Neither do I, but I've seen enough dead women to last me a lifetime. If Mrs. De Luca tries to leave before we know it's safe, I have no qualms about locking her up.

Vinicius and I get them settled in the lounge and then stand together in the kitchen trying to keep calm.

"Do you think Chiara has figured out who the Black Orchid Killer is?" Vinicius wonders.

"Chiara said before that she might have met the killer without knowing it. I haven't seen her turn so pale since she found out she was pregnant."

There's nothing we can do but sit and wait. I receive a text forty minutes later from Cassius with their location and the message, *Just to keep you in the loop.* At least we know where they are.

Half an hour goes by. And then another half an hour. I try calling all their phones but the calls aren't going through.

"Something doesn't feel right. I think one of us should go out there," Vinicius says.

Just then our phones light up with a text message from Lorenzo.

With Chiara and Cassius locked in basement, 42 Lakeside Drive, 35 miles north of Coldlake. House on fire. Call 911. De Luca is the BOK. He's going to try and kill his family.

I read the message out loud. "Holy shit."

Vinicius comes to his senses first. "You go to the De

Luca home and see if he turns up there. I'll call 911 and drive out to the lake house."

Sweat breaks out on my brow. Vinicius has the fastest car and he drives like the devil, but it will still take him thirty minutes to get out there, and meanwhile, Chiara and our baby are trapped in a burning basement.

I turn toward the lounge to tell Chiara's friends that they need to stay here, only to see Nicole standing in the doorway.

"Did you say 42 Lakeside Drive? That's my family's summer house. What's going on?"

I stare at her blankly for a few seconds. *Your father is a sadistic serial killer and he's put the people I love most and my unborn child in danger.*

I force myself to keep my shit together. "Chiara's at your lake house but she wants you and your mom to stay here. Vinicius is going to get Chiara and the others and I have to go out. You're all safe here, I promise."

I don't wait to see whether she believes me. I bolt for Cassius' car and start heading across Coldlake. It's peak hour and there's so much goddamn traffic. The Black Orchid Killer has eluded us for nine years. My hands sweat on the steering wheel as I picture him slipping through our fingers once again.

When I reach De Luca's home, all is quiet. I park farther down the street and walk back, breaking into the house through the ground floor study window.

So, this is what my sister's killer's home looks like. Cream carpet. A water tumbler full of pens standing on a computer desk. I walk through to the lounge and study all the family photos that looked so innocent just a few days ago. Now I know what he is, there's something off about De Luca's smile in all the happy lake house, beach house, and theme park photos. His smiles look forced and his eyes are dead, but I would never have noticed if I wasn't looking for it. No one would ever have noticed. He came home after torturing my sister and his family hugged and kissed him. Mrs. De Luca put a plate of meatloaf in front of him and after dinner, he went upstairs and read his daughter a bedtime story.

I want to rip all these photos from the walls and crush them under my heels while I scream at the top of my lungs.

I have a gun, but I could use some backup so I text Acid. *Can you spare Alecta and another hunter? I'm at the De Luca residence waiting for the BOK to show up. It's De Luca.*

Acid replies a moment later. *De Luca is the BOK? What a fucking trip. Two hunters on their way.*

A few minutes pass and then I hear a car pull up at the house. I peer through the front curtains to see De Luca getting out of a black SUV. His expression is composed and he approaches the house at a normal pace, but there's something hidden behind his back.

I go and stand behind the lounge door, and I wait, blood pounding in my ears.

De Luca lets himself in and calls, "Honey? Are you home?"

I hear him stop at the lounge door and then continue

down the hall. Moving silently, I follow him. He's got a knife hidden behind his back. He really is planning to murder his family. The wife and daughter wearing Mickey Mouse ears with him at Disneyland.

The world turns red. I have a gun in my hand but I don't want to use my gun.

I want that fucking knife.

I want to shove it through his neck while he looks me in the eye. I want him to know it's me who's killing him.

With a roar I lunge at De Luca and tackle him to the ground, wrestling the knife out of his grip. I'm yelling at the top of my voice. He's yelling.

I need to stab. Need to *hurt*.

"You," he gasps, and the surprise and horror in his wide eyes is the gift I've been waiting for. Nine years of pent-up rage and grief break through me as I plunge the knife into De Luca's chest.

For a second, there's no blood. There's just him and me and the realization in his eyes that he's been forced to the ground in his own home and something's happened, there's an ache in his chest, but it can't be the knife, it *can't* be.

I yank the blade out and show it to him, covered in his blood. He stares at it, eyes huge.

I stab him again.

And again.

Blood gouts up all over me. "*You fucking murderer. You piece of fucking shit. I knew I'd kill you one day.*"

I can't stop shouting, and I can't stop stabbing. The

knife sticks in his sternum and my hand slips on the bloody handle of the knife.

I stay where I am, watching the handle moving slowly up and down as De Luca struggles to breathe. His face is filled with rage.

"It's me. Salvatore fucking Fiore. I've killed you, you worthless piece of shit."

He opens his mouth to speak, but I don't give a fuck what he has to say. I pull the knife out of his chest and slash it across his throat with a roar. Blood gouts all over me. Hot, viscous blood. The blood of my worst enemy.

It feels like victory.

It tastes like vengeance.

And he's dying. This piece of shit is dying before my eyes.

I rip his shirt open, take the knife in my hand and carve a word into his chest as his blood gurgles in his throat.

KILLER.

I grab a fistful of his hair and yank his face up to mine. "Everyone's going to know what you are. You know who found you out? Romano's daughter. She would have liked you to stand trial, but I couldn't wait to send you straight to fucking hell. Say hello to the devil, courtesy of the Cold-lake Syndicate."

With the last of his strength, he glares at me. Then the light leaves his eyes and he goes limp.

Distantly, I'm aware that my phone is ringing. I take it

out of my pocket and see that it's Vinicius. "What's happening? Where are Chiara and the others?"

Vinicius gives a weak laugh. "I'm still on the freeway. The neighbors noticed the fire as soon as it started and called it in. I've just been talking to Chiara. She's fine. The baby is fine. They're all fine. The firefighters got them out of the basement."

I close my eyes in sheer relief. Oh, thank fucking Christ.

"Here's the kicker," Vinicius adds. "Do you know who the neighbor is that called 911?"

"Of course I don't. Who is it?"

"Christian Galloway."

The man we suspected of being the Black Orchid Killer. Coldlake's running corpse-fucker joke. "You're fucking kidding me. Christian 'corpse-fucker' Galloway for mayor."

"He gets my vote."

I can't help myself. I laugh, feeling like a maniac with this knife in my hand but too happy to care. "De Luca's dead. I just killed him. I've got to go and I don't know, sort myself out? I'm covered in blood."

Vinicius breathes in sharply. "He's dead? He's really dead?"

I stare at all the blood covering me, the walls, the carpet. De Luca's thin chest with the word KILLER scored across it. "He's so fucking dead. Go get our girl, okay?"

I hear the determination in Vinicius' voice. "On my way."

I hang up and take myself into the kitchen and wash the worst of the blood from my face and hands. I could take De Luca's body with me, wrapped in a rug. I could burn the house to the ground to cover up the evidence, but I think of all those other brothers, sisters, and parents of young women who this bastard killed. I killed him for all of them. They should get closure too.

I wipe my fingerprints from everything I've touched, take the knife and walk out of the house.

It doesn't feel right to go back to the compound and face Nicole and her mother wearing the remnants of De Luca's blood. It doesn't feel right to go home, either. Instead, I find myself driving into the heart of Coldlake and past all the casinos I own. I keep driving to a hotel with a casino that I don't own, one with a beautiful marble fountain out front. The place I took Chiara after our first date and she was too tipsy and grief-stricken to deliver back to her father.

The last place I saw Ophelia alive.

The last place I saw my sister smile.

I park and head over to the fountain. It's dark now, but some people give my bloodstained shirt strange looks as the colored lights wash over me. The water sprays high in the air in a beautiful display.

He's gone, Ophelia, and he'll never hurt anyone else ever again.

I close my eyes as bittersweet relief washes over me. I've carried my sister's ghost with me since the day I discovered she was dead. She's always been with me. My love for her. My grief. My rage. All the pain ebbs out of me until there's just her left. Just Ophelia, whole and unharmed.

And she's smiling at me.

My phone buzzes in my pocket. Lorenzo has left a message for me in the group chat. *Where are you, Salvatore?*

At the Maxim, I type.

His reply comes through a moment later. *Wait there.*

He doesn't need to tell me that. I'm not going anywhere. I sit and watch the lights and listen to the water. I think I could sit here forever.

Sometime later, a car door slams and a female voice I know and love calls my name. Chiara rushes into my arms, a warm, soft bundle with a protruding belly. I hold her tight as she exclaims at the blood all over me.

Lorenzo glares at me over her shoulder. "You fucking idiot, sitting around here covered in bloodstains."

I give him a lazy grin, and a moment later, he smiles, too. His voice is rough with smoke and emotion as he says, "Good job, Salvatore."

Cassius is covered in soot but his dark eyes are glittering. "You did us all proud."

Vinicius seems dazed but happy as he embraces me. "Single-fucking-handed."

"The firefighters managed to put the fire out and most of the house is still standing," Chiara tells me. "I hope they swarm that place and Mr. De Luca's home. If he's a serial killer, there must be evidence inside."

"I hope so, too, baby." Either way, he's dead and we

know who murdered our sisters, and that's the most important thing.

Chiara looks around at the fountain. "This is where you used to bring Ophelia," she whispers. "How are you feeling?"

I kiss her smoky forehead, still smiling. "Everything I ever wanted is right here. I'm so fucking happy, baby. Now, come on. Let's all go home."

THREE DAYS LATER, we're all sitting in my house watching the news together. De Luca's picture is in one corner of the screen with the caption, *Dead man suspected to be the Black Orchid Murderer.*

The news anchors are reporting on forensic evidence found in De Luca's lake house that links him to our sisters' unsolved murders. They then cut to the mayor who's giving a faux-bewildered interview outside city hall.

"He was one of my acquaintances. I had no idea he could be capable of something like this. My heart goes out to his wife and daughter in this terrible time. I hope that the victims' families will find consolation from the reopening of this investigation. The people of Coldlake deserve answers."

Lorenzo swears loudly. "You fucking snake."

"I guess Dad asked the chief of police to give all the evidence back to the detectives," Chiara says, her expression bitter.

The news anchor goes on to say that De Luca is also suspected of being involved in other unsolved murders across several more states.

Chiara's expression softens. "That's some good news. I hope Kira Campbell's family and all the other families will get some closure now."

I put my arm around her shoulders and kiss her forehead. "I hope so too, baby."

So far, no police have come knocking on my door asking my whereabouts at the time De Luca was murdered. Mrs. De Luca and Nicole told the police they were out shopping when Mr. De Luca was killed and they don't know a thing. They're doing remarkably well considering they just found out they've been living with a sadistic killer. Chiara's told me that their home has never been a happy one. He never mistreated them but he was cold and evasive over the years. Now they know why.

Lorenzo is watching the mayor with glittering eyes. "Now that we know who killed our sisters, there's no reason this son of a bitch should go on breathing."

Vinicius sits forward, his elbows on his knees as he gazes at Chiara. "How very true. What do you think, Chiara?"

She's still gazing at the screen. "I thought maybe Dad might get pulled into this investigation, but it looks like he's covered his tracks."

Cassius cracks his knuckles. "How about we take care of this ourselves? A little more vengeance after all we've been through could really take the edge off."

I don't care what anyone says about revenge not being satisfying. Murdering De Luca with my own hands was exactly what I needed. I'll happily shoot Mayor Romano full of bullets or stab him in the throat. Whatever Chiara wants.

"Dad has a campaign rally next week," Chiara tells us. "What do you all think of some public vengeance?"

I give her a broad smile. "Baby, tell me more."

21

Chiara

A *new beginning for Coldlake!*

The mayor's campaign banner in shades of black and gold stretches across the stage. The podium stands empty and waiting for him.

All around me, people are buzzing with excitement and waving little black-and-gold flags and cardboard signs like this is a parade. They're energized in anticipation of an easy win. Dad's opponent has been torn apart by the press and on social media, and his rallies are a flop. I'd feel sorry for Christian Galloway if he hadn't refused to pull out of the race and let his running mate, a composed and intelligent woman, take his place. His career is over but he's too stubborn to realize.

I'm three rows back, right in front of the podium. A brown wig conceals my hair, and I have dark sunglasses over my face. The loose black dress I'm wearing can't conceal my bump, so I sit with my arms wrapped around my belly.

Can you feel where we are, little one? We have an excellent seat for grandpa's demise.

Somewhere behind me, my four men are concealed among the crowd, dressed inconspicuously and concealing weapons.

A few minutes later, loud music plays and Dad strides out onto the stage, confident and smiling. I saw him like this so many times. In earlier years, Mom and I would be up there with him, applauding with everyone else.

Dad launches into his speech and he's polished and engaging as always. He draws many cheers from the crowd.

"There's a bright future for Coldlake. A new beginning! But first, let's see just how far we've come."

Dad steps aside and smiles up at the huge screen over the stage. A trailer starts to play with energetic music and sweeping shots of the city.

Suddenly, the music cuts out and the picture changes. In place of the smiling family riding bicycles around the lake is a stark basement with rough brick walls and a concrete floor. Two people are tied to chairs in the middle of the shot.

One dark-haired man. One blonde woman.

There are gasps from the crowd as they realize who they are. The mayor, only he doesn't look anything like the mayor they know and love, and his daughter. Mayor Romano's normally so friendly and open expression is cold and closed, and his heart is closed to the daughter weeping quietly beside him.

And then they hear their conversation.

I suppose you thought you'd impress the Coldlake Syndicate when you killed Mom.

Slitting that woman's throat is the best thing I ever did.

The whole time the video is playing, the mayor frantically tries to have his audiovisual people turn it off, but for some reason, they're not listening to him.

A few minutes later, the screen goes black, but not because the video has been turned off. We've shown everyone what they needed to see, for now. The full video is being emailed to every newspaper in the city and posted all over social media.

Everyone in Coldlake is going to have watched this video by the end of the night.

They'll see how Vinicius and I tricked Dad into speaking, but they'll understand the truth of what Dad said. He knew who the Coldlake killer was all these years and did nothing.

And he murdered Mom.

There's shocked silence from the crowd, and then the murmuring begins.

I stand up and take my wig and glasses off. I'm the only one standing, and I feel people's attention pulled to me. I do nothing except stand and watch Dad.

And wait.

It doesn't take long, just a few seconds. Dad's panicked gaze lands on me and his eyes narrow. "You did this, you spiteful bitch."

Everyone who wasn't already looking at me turns to me. People are suddenly recording us on their phones. I smile up at Dad.

Yes, I did this. Mayor Romano's daughter.

Not kidnapped.

Not held against her will by the Coldlake Syndicate.

Standing on her own two feet and facing the man who murdered her mother.

This secret has been hell to keep, and I feel it pouring out of me in an unstoppable tidal wave. The people at this rally know the truth. It's spreading out across the whole of Coldlake. Everyone is going to know the truth. *Everyone.*

There's nowhere to hide, Dad.

His expression flickers with an emotion I've never seen from him before.

Fear.

I hold his gaze for a moment longer, and then turn and walk away. I squeeze past people who are still reeling from what they've seen.

At the end of the row, Cassius and Salvatore close in on me from either side and we walk quickly away from the crowd. We're the only three people in the vicinity who have their heads held high, while everyone else gapes at Dad or mutters in confusion. A few whispers of vindication reach my ears. *I thought there was something they weren't telling us about the way the mayoress was murdered.*

Now you know. I've torn the mask from your mayor and shown you the killer that he is.

I've done my part. It's up to Coldlake what happens next.

As we leave the building, I make a call on my phone. A deep, deadpan voice answers. "Yes?"

"Thank you, Thane. That was perfect."

"You're welcome. You and the Strife men, are we square?"

I smile. "We're square, but I hope this isn't goodbye. I might need you in the future and you might need me. I hope we can start fresh."

"No targets on our backs courtesy of your boyfriends?"

"No targets. We're...friends?"

The word *friends* hovers awkwardly in the dead air between us. I can feel Thane's wariness and mistrust, or maybe it's just Thane being Thane and he doesn't care one way or the other.

Finally, in his usual flat voice, he replies, "Cool. Later."

I hang up with a smile.

A black 4WD Mercedes is waiting out front and Vinicius jumps out of the back seat to hold it open for me. Once we're all settled inside, Lorenzo guns the engine and we race down the street and away.

"It's not too late for me to go back and shoot him in the face," Lorenzo says as he drives.

That was the first plan that was floated, but murdering my father never felt like enough. I don't want him dead. I wanted him exposed.

I shake my head. "Thank you, Lorenzo, but this is better. Everyone in Coldlake hates him now. This is his worst nightmare."

Let him live his nightmare, as he made me live mine.

Vinicius reaches back and squeezes my knee. "I'm proud of you, kitten."

Cassius wraps a hand around the nape of my neck and kisses my forehead. "We all are."

I relax back on the seat, safe with my men in a fast car on the streets of Coldlake. Streets that are mine now. Streets that are ours. Me, them, and this little one inside me.

"How did vengeance taste, baby?" Salvatore asks, his blue-green eyes bright and his handsome face radiant.

I smile at Coldlake Bridge in the distance that divides the north from the west. At the skyscrapers of the city center where Cassius lives and Salvatore works. At the waters of the lake itself. I got vengeance on my own terms, without a drop more blood spilled. For the first time in nearly two years, my heart is lighter than air.

Mom is happy. I can feel it.

I smile at each of my men in turn, admiring their handsome faces burnished by the afternoon light. I cup my belly with my hands, feeling the strong kick of the little one within.

"Vengeance is sweet. But being here with you all is even sweeter."

EPILOGUE

Chiara

I run my fingers across the white daisy petals and smile. Daisies are such sunny flowers. Mom always loved them, but because they looked cheap and common, she wasn't allowed to grow them in our garden.

I get slowly to my feet, one foot and then the other, and then, it seems, I have to haul my huge belly up last of all. There's a sea of daisies in the garden, as well as dahlias, poppies, and chrysanthemums. It's slow work, gardening while you're eight and half months pregnant, but since the day of Dad's rally, I've needed soothing work. Gentle work. A place for my mind to wander over the memories, good and bad, like a bee wanders over a flower bush.

Within a week of the rally, Dad was charged with

Mom's murder and as an accessory to the sisters' murders and was refused bail. He's currently sitting in jail awaiting his trial. I have no doubt he'll plead not guilty, and he might be acquitted of Mom's murder seeing as the only witnesses are four mafia men and their girlfriend. I've given my statement to the police about the night of my seventeenth birthday, and my men have, too. I'll give my evidence in court when the time comes and I'll hold my head up high when I do. I have no reason to be ashamed.

Lorenzo told me an interesting thing a few days ago. One of Zagreus' bounty hunters watched police divers in the canal by Bleaker Street. They were there for an hour, pulling out slimy shopping trolleys and muddy sneakers, before finding what they seemed to be looking for. A knife. Lorenzo's knife that he threw into the water the night he first kissed me, and the one Dad used to murder Mom. Lorenzo told the police about it when he was interviewed. Maybe it will help in the case and maybe it won't, but it lightens my heart to know that people are talking about Mom at last and investigating her murder.

For the sisters' murders, I'm more hopeful. Thane tells me there's interesting electronic forensic evidence to corroborate what Dad admitted in the basement at Strife. Evidence that shows Dad knew about many of De Luca's murders before he committed them and incited him to kill the syndicate's sisters. It was a perfect arrangement for them. De Luca could sate his bloodlust and Dad could punish the men who were keeping him from wielding ultimate power in Coldlake. De Luca was frightening, but

Dad's cruelty and pettiness leaves a sick taste in my mouth.

Ophelia, Amalia, Evelina, and Sienna will get their day in court. Everyone in Coldlake and beyond will hear how Dad was complicit in their murders, and the murders of many other women.

My men have mixed feelings about this. It's not the kind of justice they normally take comfort in, and they still don't trust Coldlake's officials. The story is too big and too scandalous to be swept under the rug. Secrets were what allowed Dad to get away with murder. Secrets and power, and now he has neither to hide behind. All of his influential friends melted away once the story hit the news and, it turns out, Dad wasn't as solvent as he pretended to be. He had to sell the house to cover his legal expenses.

So, I bought it with my own money. Money I didn't even know I had.

When Mom died, I was so sunk in grief that I didn't hear when her will was read. I was underage so it was easy for Dad to keep the truth from me. Mom married Dad with a small fortune of her own and she'd changed her will when I was thirteen to leave everything to me. The Black Orchid Murders happened when I was nine and De Luca continued to kill outside Coldlake through all my teen years. Dad grew more ambitious and must have felt untouchable. I wish I could ask her what happened in the years between when I was nine and thirteen to make her change her will. I don't believe she knew Dad was involved in any murders, but perhaps she felt something evil growing in the man she loved and quietly made plans to protect me.

I feel her in the rooms of this house, especially at night when the lights are low and soft music is playing. I stripped away the few things that reminded me of Dad and now it's all Mom.

Me and Mom.

I filled in the swimming pool. With the pool gone, the house feels completely different, and I planted a garden in its place with all her favorite flowers.

Daisies and dahlias. Poppies and chrysanthemums.

I GO into labor three days early. I feel calm as I announce to Salvatore and Cassius that I think I've had a contraction, but they turn so pale it's as if they forgot I was pregnant.

While they're still reeling from shock, touching my belly, and grabbing my shoulders, I take out my phone and call the midwife. Then I video call Vinicius and Lorenzo and tell them what's happening.

"Kitten, oh my God. How are you feeling?"

"A little nervous, but I'm all right." I glance at the other two. "You'd better get here quickly."

"Why? What's wrong?" demands Lorenzo. From the way his screen is jumping around it seems like he's broken into a run.

"Oh, I'm fine. But Salvatore and Cassius could use some emotional support."

Seven hours later, the contractions are a fierce band around my belly. I feel like my muscles are going to squeeze me and the baby to mush at any moment.

"Breathe, baby."

I'm no longer calm.

"You fucking breathe!" I shriek at Salvatore, and his eyes practically cross as I squeeze his hand so tight that the bones creak.

"Cassius, take my place for a minute, will you?" Salvatore gasps.

Salvatore's hand pulls out of my grasp and a larger one takes his place. Cassius murmurs soft words in Italian in my ear and dabs a damp cloth against my sweating brow.

"*Bambina*, you're doing so well. Look at you. So strong. You can squeeze harder. You won't hurt me."

The contraction passes and I suck in a huge breath. I thought this would hurt, but I didn't anticipate the immense pressure my body would suddenly be exerting on itself. "How much longer?"

"We're nearly there," the midwife tells me from between my thighs, her attention focused on the baby. "The next contraction, you're going to push as hard as you can, okay Chiara?"

"Okay," I gasp, taking a firmer grip on Cassius' hand. It's nearly three in the morning. My eyes are burning and my men all look disheveled and tense, but they keep smiling at me and saying encouraging words.

Lorenzo is down by my legs and watching the midwife like a hawk. He's read every book about babies and the delivery process he could get his hands on and was insistent he would deliver the baby himself. I put my foot down and told him I was having an experienced professional, and that was the end of the discussion.

"The next baby, then," he conceded. "This one, I'll just watch. We're practicing this first time around, princess."

Vinicius is opposite Lorenzo, holding my other hand and compulsively running his fingers through his hair. For once, he hasn't got anything to say. The midwife hasn't complained that the master bedroom in Salvatore's house that has been turned into a birthing room is crowded with men. Her expression didn't even flicker when we told her that all four men are the father. All she said was, *This baby is going to receive a lot of love, isn't it?*

We would love to love it, if only it would arrive.

I'm opening my mouth to ask for a sip of water when I'm gripped by another contraction.

The midwife pats my thigh. "Here we go. Time to push, Chiara."

I barely have a choice in the matter. Everything in my body is screaming, *Down, push down, get this thing OUT.*

I feel a slithering sensation. Everything seems to happen at once.

"It's a boy!" Vinicius cries out, finding his voice at last.

A boy. *I have a son.* I barely have the energy to sit up. "Let me see him. Is he all right?"

A moment later an indignant cry pierces the air. The midwife lays the baby on my breast and my eyes fill with tears as I feel his weight on my heart.

"Baby," I whisper. "Hi, baby. We're so happy to meet you."

My men all crowd around me, their hands on me, their fingers gently touching the baby. Their son.

The midwife checks the baby's reflexes, cleans him up and weighs him, and wraps him in a blanket. Lorenzo is hovering by her the entire time and as soon as she's finished, he holds out his arms.

"Can I hold him?"

"Of course you can."

The men all huddle around Lorenzo, smiling at the baby in wonder.

"Can you take a picture of them?" I whisper to the midwife, and she takes out her phone and snaps some photos. I want to remember this moment forever.

"I've sent them to you," she tells me. "Congratulations on your beautiful boy."

A few minutes later, Vinicius collapses into the chair next to me. "I don't know about you, kitten, but I'm exhausted."

"Oh, you poor thing," I tell him with a grin. "How does it feel to be a father?"

He reaches out and takes my hand, and his golden eyes are glowing. "Absolutely wonderful."

Several hours later, after the midwife has gone and I've had my first go at breastfeeding the baby and fallen into a doze, I wake up to see Salvatore walking up and down the room with the baby in his arms. The baby is sound asleep.

"I thought you only have to do that when he's crying."

"I just want to," Salvatore murmurs and comes over to drop a kiss on my mouth. "Good morning, clever mama."

The sun is up and morning light is filtering through the tree outside the bedroom window. Vinicius is asleep in the chair next to me and Cassius is sitting on the window seat, looking tired but peaceful. His white shirt is wrinkled under the arms in a rare moment of not looking runway perfect.

Lorenzo comes in a moment later with a tray of mugs and passes out coffee. I take a grateful sip of my latte and listen to Lorenzo reassert to everyone that he could definitely deliver a baby, it didn't seem that hard.

I remember screeching at Salvatore when the contractions became too much. Delivering the baby wouldn't be hard for *him*, anyway.

"I could deliver the next one. I know I could. If you still want a midwife, princess, they could supervise."

I must be high on birth hormones because I smile and say, "If you really want to, you can deliver our next baby."

He grins. "I can't wait. For the knocking up part and the delivery part."

I nod at the baby. "You might change your mind about another one right away. He could give us all hell for the next twelve months."

"This little angel? He would never." Lorenzo holds out his arms for the baby and Salvatore puts him gently in the other man's arms.

I drink my milky coffee and consider how spoiled I am to have four fathers to help me with the baby. They won't all be here all the time, and I don't know how useful they'll be at feeding, changing, and bathing the baby, but seeing as they're all keen for a big brood, they'll learn. The next few weeks will be exhausting, but for now, I enjoy being waited on and called clever mama while they fuss over the baby.

I notice that Lorenzo's gazing down at the baby, his eyes shinier than usual.

"Is everything okay?" I call to him.

"You sneaky bastard, Vinicius. You beat me to it," Lorenzo whispers, smiling at the baby. "All my careful planning, and he's yours."

Vinicius sits up in surprise. "What? Are you serious?"

Lorenzo comes closer to the bed. "Look at his eyes."

The baby has opened his eyes and they're a bluish-gray color, but with distinctive shards of gold and green among the blue, in the same shades as Vinicius' golden-hazel eyes. In time, his eyes seem like they'll turn even more hazel.

Salvatore bursts out laughing. "That's the cherry on the sundae. Nice work, Vinicius."

Vinicius rumples his hair back and forth, his smile delighted. "And I wasn't even trying to win for a change." He takes the baby in his arms and holds him close. "You sneaky little man, you take after your dad, don't you? Clever *and* handsome."

"What are we going to call him?" Cassius asks.

I've been running shortlists of names through my head and the men have been discussing—arguing—names back and forth, but I knew I wouldn't be able to choose until I met the baby.

"Vitali," I say. "Vitali Angeli Romano." I look up at Vinicius and then the others to see what they think. "My children should all have the same last name because I want them to feel like full brothers and sisters, but your family names could be their middle names."

Vinicius smiles and kisses me. "I think it's lovely."

"Vitali. It means *life*. That's beautiful," Cassius murmurs, stroking the baby's cheek with his forefinger.

I don't think it's just lovely or beautiful, I think it's perfect. Five of us have become six and we're ready to move forward with the next part of our journey. We're ready to begin.

Life starts now.

BONUS CHAPTER

This chapter took on a life of its own, so settle in. In many ways, it's more of an extended epilogue than a bonus!

I got so many lovely messages about the bonus chapter included in Second Comes War. *You guys have been telling me how much you enjoyed it and asking for more with* Third Comes Vengeance. *My answer was only if I can think of something good for them.*

I'm happy to say I did! One morning I was going over the aftermath of the Black Orchid Murders in my mind and imagining how the boys coped during those awful months that occurred ten years before the end of this series. As you saw in the last book, and the chapter when Ginevra's baby was born, Lorenzo was hella messed up after watching the videos of the murders. It made me wonder how he pulled himself out of that self-destructive hole he was in.

But he didn't do it alone. In the Coldlake Syndicate, no one has to do anything alone if they don't want to, which is why I love them so much. Vinicius was there for Lorenzo. Vinicius, who has always been in love with his harsh, violent, clever, "straight" best friend.

For extra atmosphere, listen to "idfc" by Blackbear as you read.

This bonus chapter contains hardcore MM and MMF content, so if that's not your thing, give it a skip—though you might want to read the non-smutty sections as they complete Chiara's journey with the Coldlake Syndicate.

And don't forget to grab your free download! There's a link to Contestant: A Dark Reverse Harem Prologue Novella *at the end.* Pageant: A Dark Reverse Harem Romance *is my next book and it's coming Spring 2022.*

Vinicius

Ten years ago

"Acid. Hey."

"Hey," Acid says on the other end of the phone line. I can hear how tired he is. Not physically tired.

Fed-fucking-up.

I sigh and rub a hand over my face. "Is he there again?"

"Yeah. He caused a fight in the bounty bar. Things got smashed up. People got hurt."

"I'm sorry. I'll make sure he pays for any damage and medical bills."

"It's not about the money," Acid growls. "How many more times is this going to happen?"

I know it's not about the money, but what else can I

offer Strife? Their boss is circling the drain and I don't know how to pull him out of this. I can't stop Lorenzo from showing up there. Strife is in his quadrant, not mine. Acid talks like I should know how to pull Lorenzo out of this. A few months ago, Lorenzo was their take-no-prisoners boss who walked around with his head held high, ordered everyone to get in line or get the fuck out of western Cold-lake. The Strife men hated the blond man for laying down his law at Strife, but over the months, I think they gained a grudging respect for Lorenzo.

Now they're losing it again.

"I'll come and get him."

"Thanks," Acid replies and hangs up.

I head for my car. It's not like I haven't got my own shit to deal with right now. Amalia's death is a raw, bleeding wound in my heart. A part of my soul was ripped away when I learned that I'd never get my beautiful, broken sister back. Even when she was trapped within a prison of drugs and self-hatred, I hoped that one day I'd be able to pull her out of it. Death of hope is the cruelest grief of all.

When I reach Strife, Lasher and Zagreus are standing in front of the locked office upstairs, shoulder to shoulder. Big men, one blond, one dark, more than capable of beating a drunk Lorenzo to a pulp and throwing him into the alleyway out back. If it were anyone else but Lorenzo causing trouble, they would have.

I begin apologetically, "He's going through—"

Lasher waves a hand. "You don't have to explain. We know why he's like this, but, Vinicius, if you could do something to help him we'd really appreciate it. Strife has enough on its plate with the gangs up our asses."

"Sure," I say, my throat so tight it's burning. Fix my traumatized best friend who never listens to anyone, won't talk about what he's been through, and who never accepts help.

I'll get right on that.

Inside the office, Lorenzo is passed out on the floor. A bruise is forming on his jaw. Someone gave him a good slug.

"Up. Come on, Lorenzo. Let's go." I haul his arm over my shoulder and pull him to his feet. He's not blackout drunk yet and I'm able to walk him over to the door.

He opens his bleary eyes and tries to focus on my face. "Vinicius? Let's have a drink. Acid, get us some vodka."

"You don't need any more vodka."

"I need a fuckin' drink!" he roars in my face, blasting me with stale alcohol breath.

I wince and angle my face away. "Fine. Acid's downstairs in my car."

"Is he? Let's goooo."

Out front, I pour Lorenzo into the passenger seat of my car and buckle him in. When I turn around, a figure has appeared noiselessly in front of me, and I jump. I recognize the man's black clothes, black hair, and silver jewelry. "Jesus, Thane. Are you part fucking bat?"

Thane looks balefully from Lorenzo to me, his eyes very dark in his pale face, and his voice even darker. "He's a disaster waiting to happen to us."

If the gangs in the southwest find out that he's like this, they'll get ideas about expanding into his territory. The Strife men are doing their best to hold the line, but it's Lorenzo the gangs have learned to be afraid of.

Salvatore and Cassius haven't said anything to my face, but I know they're wondering whether Lorenzo is washed up and if we should partition his territory among the three of us. The only thing stopping them is the hope that Lorenzo will pull through this—that and the fact that they don't know how to run the roughest quadrant in Coldlake or manage the Strife men. Only Lorenzo can do that. The Strife men don't respect Cassius or Salvatore's lineage, and as well as we know each other they don't respect me enough, either. I'm not a leader and I don't want to be. I work by myself or as part of a team.

If Lorenzo can't recover from Sienna's death we might be forced to give this quadrant to Acid, though my mouth sours at the thought of him strutting into Salvatore's house, Cassius' penthouse, or my converted factory as a fully-fledged member of the Coldlake Syndicate and our equal. Lorenzo once quipped that he's called Acid because he gets under your fucking skin.

I glare at Thane, but he doesn't move back. He's got five inches on me but I'll be damned if I'll be intimidated by him. I put my hands against his chest and shove. He moves back half a pace, but that's all.

"Lorenzo's still your boss. You keep your mind on your job, which is running Strife and putting down every gang member who steps into your territory. Now, get out of my fucking face." I push past him and get into my car, my heart pounding in my chest, but I refuse to let Thane see how much I'm rattled by the state Lorenzo is in. I rev the engine and roar away with a squeal of tire rubber and a cloud of smoke.

It takes a lot of arguing and shoving to get Lorenzo inside his apartment. The place is a mess of empty vodka bottles, but I'm surprised to find he still isn't smoking. He started when he was fifteen and was a solid pack-a-day man until just after Sienna died. If he can kick that habit, why can't he kick the binge drinking?

"Fuckin' hate this place!" Lorenzo shouts, and a neighbor bangs on the wall and tells him to shut the hell up.

"Then move," I growl, and push him toward the bedroom. When he's collapsed face down on the bed, I do a lap of the apartment, collecting every bottle of alcohol I can find and pouring it down the sink.

Back in his room, I sit down on the mattress beside his prone body, and he stirs. "Lorenzo, you've got to cut this out."

"It's my best fr—" He hiccups and rolls onto his back. "My best friend. What are you doing here?"

I've been asking myself the same question.

He strokes a clumsy hand down my cheek and smiles. "You're so pretty. Every time I look at you, I think, you're so fucking pretty. I bet your dick is pretty, too."

My stomach swoops. It's not the first time he's talked about me being attractive or good-looking. His flattery, if

you can call it that, has become cruder and more sugges-
tive the more I haul his drunk ass out of Strife. He stuck
his hands beneath my shirt last week and wondered aloud
about how I taste. Drunk Lorenzo touches me.

Sober Lorenzo can't even look at me.

"In the morning I'll be drunk, but you'll still be pretty."
He frowns. "You'll be pretty but I'll...how does that
saying go?"

"Idiot," I mutter.

Lorenzo has always been fiercely beautiful. A vital,
proud man who energizes me just by being in his presence. Seeing him so broken shatters my heart.

My throat thickens and my eyes burn. If the others
have been doing any crying, it's been in secret. Either
they're too proud, or they're too miserable to even cry. As
for me, I've been sobbing my guts out and I don't have the
strength to hide it any longer.

"I shouldn't have let you watch those videos alone. I'm
so sorry." My voice cracks and tears slip down my face. If I
hadn't been such a coward then, Lorenzo wouldn't be like
this. I could have shared that horror with him and then I
would understand what he's going through. "You shouldn't
have been alone. No one should be alone with something
like that."

I think of Amalia tied to a chair, shaking and
screaming and slowly dying over days and days in pain,
fear, and misery, and I really start to cry. I put my hand
over my face and just let it out.

"Fuck, please don't cry. I won't drink anymore."

"We should just give it all up," I say thickly, swiping tears from my face. "I don't want to do this anymore. Salvatore and Cassius can run Coldlake. They already know what they're doing. You and me, we're just a couple of street brats and we're fucked. Look at us."

I can't do this anymore, but even as I try to stand up I can feel my heart being ripped in two.

"No, Vinicius, no, no, no." Lorenzo grabs a fistful of my shirt and drags me down onto the bed with him. "You have to stay. I won't drink anymore."

His arms lock around me tightly.

"You always say that. You never mean it."

Lorenzo's face is wedged against the pillow. His eyes close slowly and he passes out, still with his arms around me. Exhaustion sweeps over me and I lay down beside him. I'll get up and go in a minute but I need to rest my eyes.

The next thing I know, a shard of light stabs through the open curtains and right into my bleary eyes. Lorenzo has rolled onto his back and he's snoring, his blond hair tangled on the pillow.

I sit up and pull the curtains closed, then move to get up.

Without opening his eyes, Lorenzo grabs my shoulder and pulls me back down. In a voice like gravel, he says, "Don't get up. If you get up you'll be mad at me."

I end up with my head on his shoulder, and I hate myself for liking how it feels to have his heart beating beneath my cheek and his arms around me. My eyes close once more. "I can still be mad at you while we're laying down."

"Shut up," he mumbles.

Tentatively, I rest my hand against his chest. He cups the nape of my neck and tucks me tighter against his shoulder. Is he sober? I'm aching to enjoy this and so I tell myself he is.

Hours later, I'm awoken by the sensation of someone drawing out from beneath me. My cheek hits the warm mattress where Lorenzo was laying just a moment ago. He's sitting up on the side of the bed, head and shoulders bowed.

"Do you remember anything about last night?" I ask.

He groans and scrubs his hands over his face. "Yeah. No. What did I do?"

"You picked a fight in the bounty bar."

"Oh, Jesus. Acid must be pissed as fuck."

I sit up and swing my legs over the edge of the bed until I'm sitting next to him. "He is. They all are."

"Great, just great." He takes a deep breath and peers at me as if trying to focus on something a long, long way off. "Did I say anything else last night?"

I bet your dick is pretty, too. "You talk so much shit when you're drunk."

"You're mad at me." He fumbles around on his night-stand and then feels on the floor by his feet.

"I'm not mad at you, I'm worried that..." I realize what he's looking for and anger races through me. Is he fucking serious? "Don't bother looking. I threw all your vodka out."

Lorenzo freezes, and then sits up, both hands clenched on the mattress. I stare at his tangled hair and the dark smudges under his eyes. I remember what Salvatore told me he said after Sienna was killed.

Fuck off. Let me kill myself in peace.

If he doesn't do it himself or provoke a bounty hunter down at Strife to put a bullet in him, the alcohol will finish him off. I don't want to watch another person I love slowly poison themselves to death.

"Do you even remember what you promised me last night?"

Lorenzo gets to his feet and crosses the room, standing by the wall with his arms crossed tightly over his chest and his fingers tucked into his underarms.

"*Do you?*"

He shrugs, not meeting my eyes. He can't look at me.

Can't touch me.

Can't stand to be near me.

"You told me you weren't going to drink anymore," I say, raising my voice. "You begged me not to leave. You used to be so strong, but you've just given up."

I'm shouting now, and he winces, but there's so much more I want to say. Everything I'm not saying is screaming in my head.

You make me think you want me. You only ever touch me when you're blackout drunk. I just want my friend back. I hope and I fucking hope you're getting past this, and then in the morning you treat me like I've got the plague.

I'm not doing this anymore.

I can't watch you kill yourself when I love you so much.
I HATE YOU SO FUCKING MUCH.

I shoot to my feet and grab him by his T-shirt and shove him against the wall, my teeth bared, my chest heaving. Even hungover Lorenzo is stronger than me and a better fighter and he could crush me like a bug, but he doesn't fight back. His body is limp against the wall and his head hangs down.

I shout at the top of my lungs, "I had to watch Amalia fade away before my eyes on smack, and now my best friend is drinking himself to death. I can't do this again; do you hear me? Ask me to help you while you're sober. *Fucking ask me. Right now.*"

His lips are pressed stubbornly closed. His gaze is fixed on a spot past my chest like he can't see me. Like I'm not even here.

I count a whole sixty seconds in my head, and then I let him go with a shove. "Fuck you. I've had enough."

I storm out of his apartment and try to slam the front door behind me, but it's still loose on its hinges from when I broke it down six months ago in a vain effort to stop him from watching the video of Sienna being tortured to death.

I slam it with my foot and yell, "And fix your front door."

∾

Without Lorenzo, life is quiet.

I hate it.

I hate myself. *We* did this to him. We let him take those flash drives and fill his head with nightmares. I want my old friend back, just as he was. The skinny, blond teenager, smiling with a cut lip and blood dribbling down his chin, eyes so bright and dancing with mischief. An older, stoic but patient Lorenzo who sat crossed-legged next to my sweating, vomiting sister on the many occasions she tried to go cold turkey. She cried in his lap and apologized for all the horrible things her body was doing. And he just gently wiped her face with a cloth and murmured to her softly, *You're all right. It's okay. We're not going anywhere.*

His eyes would meet mine, and for just a moment, gratitude would blaze in my heart, louder than the overwhelming misery that my twin was suffering like this.

And sometimes, on days with peach-colored sunsets or on black velvet nights encrusted with stars, his eyes would latch onto mine and a spark would kindle in their depths. A flicker of heat, there and gone before I could capture it.

Now, his eyes are dead.

Slumped on the sofa, I flick through television channels. The news is broadcasting one of the mayor's rallies. He's standing at the podium with his familiar black-and-gold branding all around him. There's a beautiful woman standing just behind him, hand in hand with a pretty blonde girl aged nine or ten. The girl's solemn blue eyes are fixed on the mayor. This will be his wife and daughter, I presume.

Mayor Romano launches into his speech. "Too long, organized crime has been allowed to flourish in Cold—"

I roll my eyes and switch the television off. A moment later, Lorenzo's name lights up on my phone. He surely isn't blackout drunk on a Wednesday—not yet, anyway—and so I answer it. "What do you want?"

"Hello to you, too. What are you doing on Saturday night?"

He's not slurring. Makes a change. On Saturday night I imagine Acid will be calling me to drag his drunk ass out of Strife. I can't wait. "Why?"

"I'm throwing a house party."

A house party. I blast him for his drunken bullshit and he invites me to a *house party*. "What do you have to celebrate?"

"Will you come?"

"Will you be drinking?"

"No."

"I don't believe you," I snarl, and hang up. No apology, no explanation, no asking for my help. Nothing that I actually want from him.

On Saturday morning, I get a text from Lorenzo with an address and a time. Seven o'clock at a residential address in western Coldlake. I frown. It's a house, not an apartment. Lorenzo bought a house? I shrug it off and throw my phone aside. That asshole can do what he likes. I need time off from his bullshit.

But when evening rolls around, curiosity is gnawing at me. I call Acid and his phone rings and rings before he finally picks up.

"Yo." He speaks over pounding music and loud voices. It sounds like Strife is busy already.

"Have you seen Lorenzo lately?"

"Yeah, yesterday. Maybe the day before. He was down here meeting with Zag over some bounty."

"Was he drinking?"

"For once he fucking wasn't."

I stare across the room, sunk in thought.

"Is that all? I've got four deep at the bar."

"Have you seen him drunk since the last time I came to Strife?"

"No. And I better not ever again, or I'll have a few fucking things to say to the Coldlake Syndicate." Acid hangs up.

I tap my phone with my forefinger. Curious.

I wait until it's past eight o'clock and then get in my car and head over to the address Lorenzo gave me. I'm not in the mood for a party, but I want to know what he's up to. I expected to see a load of cars parked along the street, but there are only a handful of cars, and none of them are outside Lorenzo's address.

The man himself is standing in the driveway with his hands shoved in the pockets of his jeans. He looks annoyed as I pull up next to him and roll the window down.

"Fashionably fucking late," he tells me.

There's not a trace of a slur in his voice. "You know me, always fashionable. Where is everyone?"

"Who's everyone?" He turns and walks up to the front

door, and then shoots over his shoulder, "You coming or not?"

I guess I am. As I step out of my car, I notice how the perimeter of the block has been dug up and there are pallets of bricks and concrete on the front lawn. The house itself seems to be undergoing renovations. New front door. New windows with heavy metal shutters being installed. It's an austere two-story building and it looks like Lorenzo's throwing all the security he can at it.

"Are you building a fortress?"

Lorenzo gazes around. "Yeah. Fortress. Compound. Whatever you want to call it. This place is going to be impenetrable once I'm finished with it. No one gets in or out without my say-so."

A pang goes through me at the thought that this is the kind of place where we could have kept our sisters safe if we knew they were in danger.

There's not much to see in the hall. There are paint tins and plastic sheets everywhere. "Nothing says house party like heavy renovations."

Lorenzo ignores my quip and heads for the stairs, heading down rather than up. I follow him, curious to know what he's got in the basement.

But it's more than a basement. It's like there's another house down here. Cold, bare concrete, well-lit with strip lights and so much space. All four of us could fit our cars down here. Lorenzo heads down a corridor and pushes open a door.

"I'm thinking a shooting range here." He points to another door. "Armory there."

I perk up. A shooting range? Lorenzo knows I love weapons of all sorts. There's nothing more satisfying than target practice with a sleek gun after a long day.

He moves back up the corridor to another door and disappears through it. Curious, I follow him. It's a big, open space with nothing but stacks of boxes marked with "Medical Equipment" and pharmaceutical-sounding names. It looks like Lorenzo's kitting this place out to be some sort of med room.

"What's this? Are you finishing your degree?"

He shakes his head. "You remember my great-uncle Tomaso?"

Tomaso has been retired for about two decades but he used to be a surgeon. "Yeah. How old is he now? Eighty?"

"Eighty-three. He's moving in and he's going to teach me some shit."

My eyebrows shoot up my forehead. I don't hear from him for three weeks and suddenly he's bought a house and is covertly learning medicine. "Surgery?"

"The basics. Stitches. Transfusions. Thought it might come in handy."

It would definitely come in handy. Since Mayor Romano kicked off his tough-on-crime policies, finding a doctor who'll treat our men without asking questions or calling the cops has been nearly impossible.

Lorenzo stares at my incredulous expression. "What, you think I can't do it?"

"Of course you can do it," I hesitate and add, "if you're sober."

I haven't seen one bottle of vodka anywhere. Lorenzo smells like plain soap without a whiff of alcohol on his breath.

"Will you..." He scowls and clears his throat.

I wait. I want to hear him say the words. I want this on the record in case I see him going off the rails again and I have to do something drastic like tie him to a chair.

"Help me," he mutters.

I punch his shoulder. "Are you kidding? Of course I will. What do you need me to do?"

Lorenzo glances around the room and then back to me. "You already did it. You came."

My throat feels suddenly thick. "Were you worried that I wouldn't?"

"I wouldn't fucking blame you."

After everything he's done for me, I can find it in me to be patient with him. I will make myself find that patience because I'm not going to let myself come that close to giving up on him again. My voice is hoarse as I say, "Please get better, because I need you to do something for me, too."

"What's that?"

"Forgive me."

Lorenzo flinches and moves like he's going to grab me but changes his mind. He speaks through clenched teeth. "Don't fucking say that. There's nothing to forgive. I don't regret watching those videos and I'm grateful that you didn't. If you had, there'd just be two of us fucked up and I'd feel even worse."

His complexion is still gaunt and unhealthy, but there's a fire burning in his eyes again. A small one, but I think it might get brighter.

"I have new plan. I couldn't stop thinking about what I saw and heard unless I got blind drunk, so I've decided not to try and block it out."

I frown, not understanding. "What do you mean?"

"I think I've just got to let those thoughts come. Just..." He makes a sweeping gesture with his hand. "Pass through me and then let them keep going. I don't know. I'm not good at expressing this shit."

Lorenzo heads over to a box and pulls out a stack of dog-eared notebooks. "This is where I wrote everything down that I saw. Fat lot of fucking good that did us, but I haven't thrown them out. I still need these books. I'm adding to them. Weirdly, if I write all the gore and screaming down, I feel better." He flicks through one of the books. "After you shouted at me the other week, I started writing, and I haven't touched a drop since."

I stare at the notebooks in his tattooed hands, horror and grief warring inside me. Those pages are filled with our sisters' suffering. They should be burned. They should be destroyed—

I swallow down my pain. If writing in those notebooks gives Lorenzo relief from what he put himself through for us then I'm not going to stop him.

Lorenzo lifts his bright eyes to mine. "So, yeah. Thank you for yelling at me, you asshole."

He tosses the notebooks back into the box and gazes at them. "Whoever he is, he's not going to win. One day we're going to find him, and we're going to make him suffer."

"The place is finished. Want to see?"

I grin at the sound of Lorenzo's voice on the other end of the phone. "You know I do. I'll be right over."

It's been six weeks since I visited Lorenzo in his new house, and he's stayed sober the entire time. Brick by brick, he's rebuilt his sanity.

When I pull up to the house, there are two security guards in fatigues who ask for my name. I feel like I'm being allowed entrance into a military facility as the gates roll back. The garage door opens, and I drive down into the underground garage.

I park next to his Challenger and get out in the cavernous space. From down the hall, Lorenzo emerges from the med room with blood spattered all over his white T-shirt.

"Been cutting up bodies, doctor?"

He glances down at himself as he walks toward me. *Prowls* toward me. My mouth waters. He shouldn't look that good covered in blood.

"Just had my first patient. Bounty hunter with a stab wound. I think Strife's going to be my best customer, except no one pays. I'm doing this shit for free; can you believe it?"

"I don't know if I'd pay for a psycho college dropout to cut me up, either."

He punches my shoulder. "Come on. I'll show you the rest of the place."

Lorenzo's face glows with pride as he takes me upstairs and shows me the finished kitchen and lounge. He's chosen minimalist furniture, but the place is comfortable. There's plenty of room for all of us around the coffee table.

"Top floor, bedrooms. There are five. This place will fit all four of us if we need somewhere secure to hole up," Lorenzo tells me as he climbs the stairs.

I follow him up and he leads me to the master bedroom. Lorenzo doesn't do décor, but the wooden furniture he's chosen has a simple charm. The bed looks big and comfortable and the wardrobes are mirrored.

Sober Lorenzo isn't going to touch me or tell me my dick must be pretty. He's regarding me with a solemn expression, hands shoved in the pockets of his jeans.

"The place is great. You've done an amazing job on it."

He takes a step toward me but doesn't say anything, and my heart starts to stutter.

"You're looking good, too. Healthier. Have you been working out?" I'm running off at the mouth, trying to hide that he's making me flustered. I can chat up women all goddamn night, but my best friend staring at me while his enormous bed is right there makes me trip over my own words.

We're standing eye to eye, just staring at each other.

"It's good to have you back. You don't know how much I —" I break off as Lorenzo grasps the neck of his T-shirt at the back and pulls it off, ruffling his hair.

"Did I show you these?" He spreads his arms, inviting me to look at his tattoos.

He's been working out aggressively and the muscles of his chest and stomach pop beneath the ink. Lorenzo's body has always been beautiful. He has heavy, muscular shoulders and narrow hips. The tattoos cover his torso and arms and disappear down inside his jeans.

I put my hand out and touch his cheek, turning his head so I can admire the tattoos on his throat. I haven't looked at him closely since his ink was finished. "These are great."

Lorenzo swallows against my fingers. "They're hers."

Sienna's drawings. The beautiful work that she poured her heart into, now decorating her brother's body.

"She was a beautiful artist. You're a beautiful canvas."

He glances at me from beneath his lashes. "Me? I'm not the good-looking one."

I bet your dick is pretty, Vinicius. Was that a case of *in vino veritas*? *In wine, there is truth.* Or was he just spouting nonsense? Now he's watching me, letting me touch him. I keep on tracing the ink patterns on his throat.

"Will you rip my guts out if I try something?"

He shrugs, but he doesn't move away.

I guess I'll find out. I trail my hand down his chest, which lifts and falls with a breath. I keep going over his stomach and past his navel, and I hook a finger into his jeans, right by the button.

Lorenzo's eyes are glittering as he watches me. If he didn't want this, he'd be shoving me away, but he's not making a move on me, either. I feel a flash of confusion because Lorenzo isn't the sort of man to let someone else take the lead in any situation.

I glance around the room. He brought me up here. He stood me right next to his bed and took off his T-shirt. Maybe he's enjoying the way I squirm, the sadistic bastard.

Wondering if I'm about to get my teeth punched out, I slide my hand down to cup his cock over his jeans. He's thickening under my touch. His lashes flicker, and he swallows, the strong muscles of his throat moving.

Who says Lorenzo isn't good-looking? To me, he's always been ferociously beautiful.

I lean in to kiss him, but he turns his face away. My teeth clench in irritation. "What? It's not gay if we don't kiss on the mouth?"

"Have you ever seen me kiss anyone on the mouth?" he counters.

"It's nice. You should try it sometime."

Lorenzo slides his hands around my waist. "Do you want to talk or do you want to fuck?"

Being invited to touch him, have sex with him, I've been craving this for so long, but I love to kiss. Half my foreplay is usually kissing.

Lorenzo takes my head in his large hands and slides his

thumb over my lower lip. "How does this work? I've never fucked a man before."

My disappointment washes away on a wave of arousal. Maybe I don't need kissing if he talks to me and looks at me like this while he's standing so close. His breath is on my mouth. His chest is brushing mine.

"That's the hardest part figured out. Who goes where," I say, and I can hear how husky my voice is. In most of my fantasies about Lorenzo, he's the one screwing me. "I thought I might have to beg you to go on top."

A heated smile slides over his face and he runs his thumb over my lip again. "You can beg me if you like, but can I go down on you first?"

Oh, Jesus Christ. My hands come around him and I explore the smooth, hot skin of his back. "You never have to ask."

Lorenzo undresses me, stripping off my clothes with unhurried movements. Then he shoves me back onto the bed and takes off his jeans. He's fully hard now and while I've seen him butt naked at various times over the years, I've never seen him like this.

My brain barely has time to catch up with what I'm seeing before he's kneeling between my thighs and gripping my shaft.

His hand. Around my cock.

I sit up on my elbows and stare at him.

"How do I do it?" he asks.

"Do it how you like it."

"Fair point." He lowers his head and takes my cock in his mouth, sucking before drawing up slowly.

I groan and my head falls back. Lorenzo, naked and hard, and he's sucking my dick. Maybe things will get better. I never thought they would when I've been trapped in a hellhole for months.

"You're really good at that," I say through gritted teeth, but Lorenzo stays focused on what he's doing. Heat floods my body as he works me up and down with his mouth.

I'm on the verge of coming when he stops and sits up. He watches me, hair falling into his eyes and a mischievous smile on his reddened lips. "I wondered how you looked like that."

I breathe hard, no thoughts in my head except for Lorenzo screwing me until I come. "Please tell me you have lube."

He jerks his chin at the bedside table. Thank fucking Christ. I lean over and get it and throw it to him.

"I want to look at you." He grasps my thigh and pushes it up to my chest.

Suddenly this feels way too fast. I don't understand why we're doing this. I feel like I should understand what's going on in his head before we fuck.

"Wait, wait. When did you first think about doing this?" I want to know why this is happening. Why now.

The smile dies on his face, and my heart plummets. Maybe he doesn't even know.

"It's not a happy fucking story. You want to do this now?"

I nod. He puts his hand on my thigh and another on my hip. Heavy, possessive hands, holding on to me.

"We were about...fourteen? I stole a car and drove us into the southwest."

My eyes widen. I remember that day. Skinny, fierce Lorenzo, who wanted to go on searching for Amalia even when I was too tired and filled with hopelessness. We went to every dive bar. Every brothel. Every squat. Anywhere in Coldlake where a pretty runaway might hole up. Every rumor we heard that might be her, we went to check it out.

It could be her. Come on, Vin, I'll drive.

Drive what?

Uhh...wait here.

"I remember." I was huddled in the front passenger seat, swamped with misery as we headed into gang territory.

"I wanted to reach out and hold your hand. But I just..." He shakes his hand and shrugs.

It was never her, but Lorenzo never gave up on trying to find Amalia, and in the end, he was the one who did find her. I had a few short, painful years with her before she was killed, but as hard as it was to see her like that, at least I knew where she was.

"That killed the fucking mood," he mutters.

I reach up and touch his face, then wrap my arms around his neck and pull him down to me. I can't kiss him, but I can hold him.

"Don't you ever leave me," I whisper harshly in his ear. "Don't go where I can't reach you ever again. You're my best friend before anything else and I won't survive in this life without you."

He pulls back, his face just inches from mine. "You, too."

He looks down between us. Strangely, we're both still hard. Wordlessly, he reaches for the lube. The mood hasn't been killed. It's intensified. He rubs my asshole with his slippery finger and then pushes inside me.

"Fuck, Lorenzo." I close my eyes and grasp the backs of my knees.

I watch him apply lube to his cock and time slows down. His movements are unhurried, focused, but as the head of his cock pushes inside me, he lifts his blue eyes to my hazel ones.

Lorenzo's lips are parted as he breathes harshly. I've never had sex with anyone who loves me. He'll probably never say it, but he doesn't have to.

His hands are on me as he works himself deeper. I grab hold of his shoulders, his blond hair hanging down between us. I feel the groan in his chest more than I hear it. Every sense is overwhelmed by him, but I still want more.

He grasps my cock with his slippery hand and works me slowly up and down. I can't fucking cope. He thrusts deeper and keeps up his slow pace, like he's savoring every moment. I've never felt so seen. There's nothing I can do, nothing I can say, I just hold on to him and moan as he deliberately and methodically overwhelms me.

A moment later I come, spurting all over his hand and my chest.

Lorenzo groans. "Fuck, that's hot. You look so good when you—" He hisses through his teeth, and then his head falls back and his thrusts are deep and fast. Finally, he opens his eyes.

"I hope I fucked you all right," he says as he eases out of me.

A lazy grin spreads over my face. "Fishing for compliments?"

I reach for him, but he's already heading to the bathroom to clean up. Then he's back, pulling on his jeans and heading for the door.

"Do you want some coffee? I bought this huge coffee machine."

Disappointment plummets through me. No kisses, and it looks like I'm not going to be allowed to hold him either. I fall back with a sigh. An hour of Lorenzo's devoted attention and then he's back to his normal self.

Downstairs, I stare at him in his jeans, steam from the coffee machine billowing around him and the light playing over the ink on his muscles.

It's not just that he's incredibly sexy.

I've just always loved him.

I imagine saying that to him now, *I've always loved you*, and the words turn to ashes in my mouth. That moment between us upstairs was fleeting, and it's already gone. I gaze out the window at the walls that he's building around his house. Thick. High. Impenetrable.

"You've been bi forever, haven't you?" he asks me.

I turn back and see he's holding out a cup of coffee. I take it and nod. "Pretty much. What about you?"

Lorenzo shrugs. "I don't know. I just like you, you pretty motherfucker." He takes a mouthful of coffee and smiles at me.

He's standing three feet away from me on the other side of the counter, but he's smiling at me. He's not going to say I love you or shower me with affection, but there's no comparison. One hour of Lorenzo's fierce attention and rough adoration is better than a lifetime of some lesser person's.

I finish my coffee and stand up. "Call me if you feel like drinking, and I'll come around and slap the bottle out of your hand."

Lorenzo nods, his expression serious. "I'm sorry about the last couple of months."

He doesn't need to apologize. I'm just relieved he was able to pull himself out again.

A week later, I'm driving over Coldlake Bridge when Lorenzo calls me. We've been in touch every day and he seems to be doing well. "Hey, what's up?"

"I've been thinking. We need something," Lorenzo says.

"We do?"

"A woman."

I flinch. I've been thinking about him and he's been thinking about a woman. "Then go get a woman if you want one."

"Don't sound so pissed off. I don't mean me. I mean us."

"You and me?"

"Maybe. But wouldn't it be better with all of us?"

I shake my head at the road. "What are you talking about?"

"The four of us. Sharing one woman. Not a sex thing, though we would all have sex with her—"

"What are you on?"

"Paint fumes. I'm finishing the basement. Stone-cold sober and I have too many goddamn thoughts in my head."

At least he's thinking about things that aren't our sisters. But a woman for all of us to share? Sounds like a recipe for disaster. Who would have the patience to put up with the four of us?

"We're the Coldlake Syndicate. We're not easy to kill, but a woman is. That's what I was thinking about."

Three nights later we all have dinner at Lorenzo's house as Salvatore and Cassius haven't seen it yet. I can tell from their expressions that they weren't expecting much from the scruffiest man in the syndicate, but both of them are impressed by how practical and secure Lorenzo's new home is.

Cassius puts bags of Chinese food on the coffee table and holds up a bottle of white wine. "Who wants a glass?"

Lorenzo shakes his head and rips open the bag of prawn crackers. "None for me. I'm not drinking right now."

Salvatore holds out his glass and Cassius fills it. "Good. You're a mean drunk. Ginevra is still terrified of you."

"Oh, yeah. Sorry about that. Where are the soup dumplings?"

Soup dumplings are Lorenzo's favorite. I find them in the bag and pass them over, along with the rest of his order, a box of Singapore noodles.

As we eat, we discuss new developments in our quadrants until conversation dwindles. Inevitably, talk turns to our sisters but I don't want that tonight. I think we need to put that behind us for now and think about the future.

I nudge Lorenzo with my elbow. "Tell them about your idea."

He raises a brow at me. "Really? I thought you thought it was stupid."

Not stupid, but it's strange and caught me off guard. "Tell them anyway."

Lorenzo shoves a soup dumpling into his mouth, chews for a moment and then starts to speak around it. "The four of us, all in a relationship with the same woman. That's the idea."

"Are you sure you're not drunk?" Cassius asks.

"I'm stone-cold sober."

Salvatore shoots me a look. *Is he?*

I nod. "It sounded crazy when he told me about it the other day. It still does, but sharing Coldlake is crazy, and that seems to be working."

Lorenzo hunts through his noodles with his chopsticks. "It's going to get fucking lonely if I don't share a woman with someone. I can't imagine being in a relation-ship without the three of you."

"Figure it out, because I'm not going to fuck you," Cassius says.

"Vinicius already did that."

I choke on my wine and nearly spit it up. I assumed Lorenzo would be one of those *I'll fuck you, but don't tell my friends* kind of men.

Salvatore grins at me. "Did you two finally have sex? About time."

A hot feeling steals over me, halfway between a blush and a glow of pleasure. I dart a look at Lorenzo who has a smile playing over his lips. An affectionate smile. A moment later it's gone, but it was there.

"Congratulations on fucking," Cassius deadpans. "Now explain your crazy plan or I'm changing the subject."

"If I had a woman, I'd always be worrying that she was in danger the second she was out of my sight. Wouldn't you?"

The three of us glance at each other. None of us deny it.

"This place is secure. If I left a woman here and went out, I'd feel okay about it, but women don't stay where you put them." Annoyance flickers over his face. "They want to go out. They want to see their friends, their family. She goes off by herself, and then the next thing you know, she's fucking dead. She might have a baby with her, she might be pregnant, and then they're dead, too. I'm not fucking doing that again."

He drops his box of noodles and chopsticks onto the coffee table with a clatter and shoves his hands through his hair.

Bleak silence fills the room. Salvatore and Cassius look at each other, and then at me.

"Think of it this way," Lorenzo mutters. "I don't want the whole of Coldlake. I want to share this city with the people I trust. And I want the same with a woman, too."

Salvatore sits back, his eyes narrowed as he considers this. "Maybe I'm drunk, because that almost makes sense."

Cassius swirls the wine in his glass. "What would she be like? What kind of woman is going to suit all our tastes?"

"What crazy woman is going to look at Cassius and Lorenzo and decide she wants both of them?" I ask.

"We're not that different," Lorenzo says with a shrug.

"That's the problem. You're both assholes."

Lorenzo gives me the finger.

"What about sex?" Cassius asks. "Would we take turns, or would we all have sex with her at the same time?"

A heated smile spreads over Salvatore's face. "All at the same time? Fuck, I hope so. Can you imagine?"

There's a short silence as we picture it. Vividly.

"I want someone clever," I say. "Someone I can teach a few tricks, and who can teach me a few tricks, too. I want to walk down the street with the four of us flanking her and feel so fucking lucky that we have her."

"Someone classy," Salvatore says. "Someone who's strong and understands family and loyalty."

Cassius thinks. "Someone sweet. I miss sp—" He breaks off and clears his throat. He misses spoiling someone like he spoiled his little sister. Cassius acts gruff and severe, but he's got the softest heart of all of us.

"Someone screwed up," Lorenzo says.

"Don't stick your dick in crazy," Salvatore replies.

"Not that sort of screwed up. Someone who's been through some shit so she won't fall to pieces when we put her through it, too."

"You're not going to torture the poor girl," I tell him.

"Not on purpose. Well, not much. But she's going to see some shit just by being with us."

He's not wrong there. I muse on our list of requirements. "Clever, strong, classy, sweet, loyal, screwed up. Does such a woman even exist in Coldlake? The world?"

Salvatore looks from one of us to the next, his eyes bright. "I don't know. We could be waiting a year to find her. Two years. Maybe ten years, but when we do, we'll all know that we've found the right one."

Someone we all want, and who wants us, too. Someone for all of us.

A woman who's worth the wait.

Present day

I press my mouth against Lorenzo's. A slow, heated kiss, our tongues tangled together. Sunlight from the big windows in my loft spills over us. He wraps his arms around me and pulls me closer and deepens the kiss.

How is this real? We don't have the right to be this happy.

In the next room, the baby starts to cry. I'm in such a good mood that the piercing wails make me smile. That's my son. Listen to the lungs on him.

"I'll go," I murmur between kisses, but Lorenzo pats my shoulder and gets to his feet. He heads into the next room and comes back with Vitali in his arms.

"What a little screamer you are," he murmurs, kissing the baby's forehead. "Is it time for your feed?"

I glance at the clock. Chiara won't be home for another ten minutes, but Vitali's impatient today. "I'll make him a bottle."

Before I can get to my feet, I hear footsteps on the stairs and Chiara pushes the front door open. She's dressed in leggings and a black crop top and her cheeks are flushed from exercise. She dumps her gym bag on the floor and hurries over to the baby, her arms outstretched.

"Baby, baby, baby, I'm here. Did you miss Mommy?"

She settles down with him in her arms. As soon as she starts to breastfeed him, he quietens down.

Lorenzo settles his back against me as we watch her. I play with a strand of his hair as Chiara nurses our son. All I've ever wanted, right here.

"How was the gym?" Lorenzo asks her.

She puffs her cheeks out. "Exhausting. Cassius is such a beast."

She's not wrong. I've been working out with him, too, and he's as punishing as a personal trainer. "Does he shout at you that you're a miserable worm when you complain your legs are rubber and your arms are like cooked noodles and you can't go on?"

Chiara blinks in surprise. "No. Cassius always tells me how wonderful I'm doing."

I sit up so fast that Lorenzo falls behind me. "That bastard! He swears that he trains you the same as he trains me, but all he does is shout at me."

Lorenzo scowls, pushes me back on the sofa, and settles against me once more. "Maybe the difference is Chiara does as she's told for Cassius."

Chiara gives us her sweetest smile. "Of course I do. And when I get tired, he brings me cups of water and tells me to take a break."

I roll my eyes. Cassius would only bring me cups of water if he were going to dump them over my head and tell me to work harder. "Disgusting. Next time, I'm coming to your training session and he can bring me cups of water, too."

Lorenzo laugh-snorts. "You fucking wish."

"Why don't you come and train with us, Lorenzo?" Chiara asks him.

Lorenzo gives her a sardonic smile. "Do you want World War Three to break out? Because that's what will happen if Cassius tries shouting at me."

"Good point. You keep doing whatever you're doing. It seems to be working for you."

He lifts his shirt and pats his muscular stomach. "Thank you. I know it is."

I pull my T-shirt off and hold my arms out. "What about me? Is all this suffering at least working? Am I enduring that bastard's bad temper for a reason?"

"You look fantastic," Chiara tells me. "You always did, but the training has made you look even better."

"Thank you, kitten." I glance at Lorenzo, one brow raised.

He stares back at me. "What?"

I throw my T-shirt at him. "I want a compliment! I know you're capable of them. Princess, you're adorable. Princess, you're so cute. Chiara gets them from you all the time."

"Give him a compliment. He's dying here."

Lorenzo shrugs, fighting a smile. "Chiara already complimented you."

"He wants a compliment from *you*."

Damn right I do.

He settles his crossed arms over his chest and regards me critically. "Your muscles look cut. Good tone. Good gains." Then he smiles and grabs my chin. "And you're more handsome than you've ever been. Look at that fucking smile."

"Thank you," I mutter, my cheeks heating. I look between the two of them, Chiara smiling down at the baby and Lorenzo relaxed against the sofa with his arm draped around my shoulders. In the bleakest days of my life, I never imagined we would get here. I don't think they did, either.

Vengeance is a strange thing. I thought I'd never feel better than the day Salvatore killed De Luca and avenged our sisters in blood. We were flying high that day, our hearts in a turmoil of grief and gratitude. A weight lifted from my shoulders and I felt that Amalia was finally put to rest.

Then, ex-Mayor Romano went on trial for his wife's murder and as an accessory to the Black Orchid Murders. Chiara testified about the night her mother was killed in front of her. She held her chin up and she never cried, in public at least. The sight of her breastfeeding afterward with tears running down her face almost made Cassius put his fist through the wall, and he cursed the ex-mayor to hell and back.

We gave testimonies too, though I don't know if anything we said was particularly convincing to the jury. The defense lawyer made a lot out of the fact that Lorenzo's knife was used to kill Chiara's mother, and Lorenzo later threw that knife away. The lawyer tried for hours to make Lorenzo lose his temper in court, to try and show that he could have been the murderer, but Lorenzo kept his gaze either on the jury or on our baby, and didn't raise his voice once.

What convinced the jury in the end, I believe, were deleted text conversations recovered from De Luca's "lost" phone and a burner phone that was found in Romano's safe. They discussed Mayoress Romano's murder in detail and they talked about our sisters and De Luca's other murders.

Romano was found guilty on all charges and sent away for life. Chiara was ecstatic with relief and happiness that she finally had justice for her mom. I was thrilled for her and our sisters, but not even Romano's sentencing gave me the release that I didn't know I needed.

It was a news article I read online about the families of De Luca's other victims. Desperate and grief-stricken families across many states who finally knew who had taken their loved ones from them. Reading about them talk about their daughters and sisters. I felt like I was connected to something bigger. Their grief was my grief. I didn't know them, but I understood them, and I loved their daughters and sisters, too.

Lorenzo and I took Chiara to the prison to visit her father a few weeks ago. She didn't sit down. She didn't say hello. All she did was pick up the phone, look her father in the eye through the glass partition and say, "You'll never see your grandson, and you're not my father."

Then she put down the receiver and calmly walked away from the man who shattered her heart.

Since that day, she's been thriving. It was Chiara who came up with the solution to our living arrangements. She has her own home and we're all able to stay with her there. There's always at least one of us with her, and usually two or three. She also stays with all of us and has cribs at each of our places. She brings the baby to meetings, especially with Cassius, who loves to show the baby off, and down at Strife. Acid loves to hold the baby. Thane held Vitali, once, out in front of him at eye level. They stared at each other for a few seconds, and then the baby started to cry. Alecta rolled her eyes and took the child away from him and gave him a proper cuddle.

"How long until you're done breastfeeding?" Lorenzo asks Chiara.

"Just a few more minutes."

"I mean, how long until he's on solids?"

"Soon. Why?"

A heated smile slides over his face. "Because once you're done breastfeeding, you can get pregnant again."

"And what Machiavellian scheme do you have to get me pregnant this time?"

"It's a fiendish one. I plan on screwing you a lot."

Chiara shoots him a skeptical glance. "Just that?"

"Either that or give the rest of them vasectomies in their sleep. I've been looking up how and it's easier than I thought to cut—"

"Don't even think about it, Doctor Evil," I tell him.

Chiara finishes feeding the baby and goes to put him down for his nap. When she returns, Lorenzo follows her path across the room, his eyes glued to her ass that Cassius has been lovingly sculpting.

"Speaking of screwing..." He nods his head in the direction of the master bedroom and glances at the two of us. "Who wants to be screwed?"

"Me," both of us say at the same time.

As Chiara reaches for my hand, she asks me, "Do you ever fuck Lorenzo?"

"I have once or twice. But he doesn't like it."

"Who says I don't like it?" Lorenzo says, strolling ahead of us and pulling off his T-shirt, the tattoos moving over his muscles.

"You never ask for it. A couple of times I've tried and you've pushed me off."

He shrugs. "I'm the one who fucks."

I roll my eyes and shoot Chiara a look. "Lorenzo's too alpha to take it in the ass, kitten."

Lorenzo turns to us in front of the bed and folds his arms, his gaze narrowed. "You're damn right I am. But not for the reasons you're thinking."

"What reasons, then?" Chiara asks.

"If I'm doing the fucking, I can keep an eye on things. Eyes open. Brain switched on. The one getting fucked always has their eyes closed and they get lost in it. They're fucking useless."

Chiara bursts out laughing. "Useless at what?"

"Looking for danger. Intruders. Anyone not having a good time. You think I'm thinking about just my dick when we're all screwing you, princess?"

"That's very thoughtful of you, but..." Chiara and I exchange glances, and she turns to him with a smile. "Seeing as we're safe in Vinicius' loft and the baby is asleep, will you relax long enough to let go for a little while?"

He stares at her, and then the corner of his mouth twitches. "Maybe."

She walks her fingers up his chest. "Would you like Vinicius to rail you senseless while I go down on you?"

He smiles wider, and then holds his hand out to me. "Give me your poppers."

I retrieve them from a drawer and slap them into his palm. "Enjoy."

He unscrews the cap, pinches off a nostril, and inhales sharply.

"You haven't even taken all your clothes off yet," I point out.

He tilts his head back and groans. "I just like the way it feels. If I'm going to let go I may as well do it properly."

My eyes lock onto the muscles of his throat as he arches his neck. God, he's sexy. Chiara helps him out of his jeans while I peel the leggings down her legs.

Lorenzo takes Chiara by the chin and tilts her face up to his for a kiss. "Sure you don't want me to fuck you first?"

She glances at the baby monitor and shakes her head. "You relax. I'll go if he cries."

"Whatever you want, princess. Let me go down on you, though." Lorenzo kneels down on the floor and pats the mattress. "Spread your legs for me."

She does as he asks, but she glances down at the floor. "If Vinicius fucks you there, you're going to get rug burn on your knees."

"Good. Fuck me up." He pats the spot next to her on

the mattress and then looks at me. "I want to go down on you, too."

Chiara and I sit pressed against each other, and I watch as he licks first her, then me. He hooks one of her legs over his shoulder and one of mine over the other. He takes me deep into his mouth and pushes me to the back of his throat, and I groan. He sits up long enough to push two fingers into Chiara.

"Good girl," he murmurs, and goes back to blowing me.

Her eyes pop open. "Wait, weren't we supposed to be topping him?"

Chiara and I are both leaning back on our hands while Lorenzo sucks me and pounds her with her fingers.

"Oh, yeah. How does he do that?"

Lorenzo starts to laugh around my cock, his shoulders shaking as I draw him up and off me. He's kneeling at our feet, a mischievous smile on his face. "I do it because you two are just so fucking easy to top, even from down here."

"Are we?" Chiara asks me.

"We are. Look at us." But I get to my feet and reach for the lube while Lorenzo goes back to going down on her. I watch them for a moment, their golden hair, her gentle beauty, and his savage good looks. I drip lube down Lorenzo's ass, and he shivers at the cold. When I push one finger slowly into him, he lifts his head, his eyes closing.

His grip on my finger is intense. Fuck, yes, I need to be inside him. I replace my finger with the head of my cock, pausing to give him a moment before surging deeper.

"Go slow, I'm not used to—" He groans and buries his face in Chiara's thigh. "Fuck. Me."

I exchange glances with Chiara. We never get to see Lorenzo like this. It's fucking beautiful.

Chiara threads her fingers through his hair. "Look at you getting fucked in the ass, you dirty cock slut. You love that, don't you?"

Lorenzo gives an unintelligible answer. His cheeks are flushed and his eyes are almost closed. He goes back to licking Chiara, his movements clumsy but persistent. I hold on to his hips, loving the way the muscles of his back bunch and flex. He's stretched tight around my cock, a grip so delicious that I can't help but pound him harder.

"Kitten, you're going to come in a moment, aren't you?"

Her teeth are sunk into her lower lip and she nods rapidly, staring at Lorenzo.

"Good girl," I purr. I need her help with Lorenzo and I slow down my thrusts, letting him concentrate on getting her off.

She tips her head back with a wail and arches her back, breasts thrust upward.

When she relaxes, panting for breath, I tell her, "Kitten, come down here and stroke him for me, nice and slow."

Chiara nestles on the carpet beside Lorenzo and takes his cock in her hand. "You're rock hard and leaking pre-cum," she tells him. "You want to come so badly, don't you?"

He buries his face in the mattress. "Yes. Fuck. You two are going to make me lose my fucking mind."

She plays her fingers over the muscles of his back and his tattoos, and then reaches down to cup his balls, rubbing them gently as she keeps pumping his cock up and down.

Lorenzo is breathing hard and bracing his knees against the carpet so I can pound him harder. I'm so used to Chiara's slender frame that Lorenzo's body feels like heavy machinery.

He comes with a shout, his body flooding with heat as his muscles clench in pleasure. The sight is so beautiful that it drives me over the edge as well.

When I lift my head, Chiara is sitting up and pressing kisses to Lorenzo's chest. I ease out of him and he wraps his arms around her and they go tumbling onto the carpet.

I leave them lying there and go take a shower. When I come back, Chiara's alone on the bed, and I get beneath the blankets and cuddle her.

"Where's Lorenzo?"

"Bathroom? Baby?" She doesn't open her eyes as she snuggles into me. Between broken nights of sleep, breast-feeding, and training with Cassius, she's exhausted.

Sometime later, we're roused by Lorenzo shaking our shoulders. "It's a beautiful day. I want to go out into the countryside. Can you two move?"

"Mm, do we have to?" I mumble.

"Yeah, you fucking have to. Get up. I've got the baby. We're going out."

I crack open an eye in time to see Lorenzo, dressed in jeans, pulling a T-shirt over his head and disappearing out the door. Just because it's a beautiful day doesn't mean he has to deprive us of sleep.

"That man is a sadist," Chiara says, burrowing into my chest. "We could just ignore him and sleep."

"Wanna bet?" I say, pushing myself upright. Lorenzo never wants much, but when he does, he's a pain in the ass until he gets his way.

We get dressed and pile into his 4WD, and he takes us to the freeway heading southwest.

Chiara's sitting in the back and she wraps her arms around his shoulders from behind. "Is everything okay?"

He reaches up to cup the nape of her neck. "Everything's perfect, princess. I just thought of something I wanted us to do."

Whatever he wants, it seems to be at the compound. When we pull into his basement, he digs a set of keys out of his pocket, heads down the corridor, and unlocks a door. There's a small room beyond, with nothing inside but a safe the size of a small fridge. He enters the combination and pulls it open, hunting through the contents until he finds what he's looking for.

When he turns around, he shows us something sitting in the palm of his hand. Four somethings. Flash drives with labels stuck to them, each one bearing a name.

Ophelia.

Evelina.

Amalia.

Sienna.

Chiara opens her eyes wide. "Those are the videos."

The recordings De Luca sent each of us, showing him torturing and murdering our sisters. I wondered where they were but I never wanted to ask. Lorenzo closes his fist around them and nods, then glances at me. "Call the others. Tell them to meet us at the gas station at exit twelve on I-28."

That interstate heads out into the wilderness, and I start to get an inkling of what he has in mind as I pull out my phone.

"Can Ginevra watch the baby?" Lorenzo asks Chiara.

"I'm sure she can. Let me give her a call."

"We'll swing by her place. Vinicius, I need your help with something from the armory, and then we'll get back in the car."

Forty-five minutes later, we're waiting in the gas station lot as Cassius' white SUV and Salvatore's Maserati pulls in. They each kiss Chiara and then turn to Lorenzo for an explanation.

Wordlessly, Lorenzo shows them the flash drives, and then opens the trunk of his car and shows them what we loaded inside. It's a grenade launcher, the same one that Salvatore almost killed Lorenzo with the night De Luca tried to trap us.

"What do you think?" Lorenzo asks, gazing around at us all.

Salvatore blinks rapidly and nods. His voice husky as he says, "Yeah. Blow them to smithereens."

We pile back into our cars and drive for another hour into the hills. Lorenzo seems to know where he's going and takes us to a deserted quarry. There's not a soul around, and standing at the bottom feels like we're cut off from the rest of the world.

Lorenzo takes a red gas can out of the trunk and walks it across the quarry before coming back to us. "Who wants to pull the trigger?"

"You have to do it," I say. "You've been holding on to them for us. But let's all take a flash drive over there."

One by one, each of us picks up the drive with our sisters' name. Cassius kisses his and makes the sign of the cross, his eyes suddenly overbright as he turns away and walks up the slope. We follow him, and Salvatore and Lorenzo place their drives at the base of the gas can.

I grip the small metal object in my hand fiercely, thinking hard about Amalia. The happy girl she once was, long, long ago. This is the last physical piece of her tethering her to this earth, and it's bittersweet to let it go. But in the end, I do, because I still have the best of her in my heart. Always.

I kiss the drive and whisper, "Your nephew is going to know all about his brave sister. I love you, Lia."

We all walk back and stand in a row behind Lorenzo as he hefts the grenade launcher onto his shoulders.

"Stick your fingers in your ears," Lorenzo says, bracing his feet against the ground. We do, and a moment later, he pulls the trigger. The force of the explosion knocks his shoulder back, and a split second later the gas can explodes. Flames and black smoke erupt into the sky.

I step forward and clasp Lorenzo's shoulder, and he

covers my hand with his own for a moment, still staring at the flames.

I turn and look at the others. Cassius has his arms wrapped around Chiara, who has silent tears running down her face, but she returns my smile.

Salvatore nods to himself and says, "That's better. Now they're free."

Lorenzo tilts his head back and breathes deeply. They're free, and now he is, too. He gazes at the clear sky, the grenade launcher still propped on his shoulder, and then turns and looks at each of us in turn.

His brothers.

And the mother of our child.

His gentle smile is lit with peace and burnished by sunshine as he says, "What a beautiful fucking day."

ACKNOWLEDGMENTS

Thank you to you, dear readers, for coming on this journey with me. Writing this series has been the most fun I've had in years. I'm delighted that you've embraced Chiara, Salvatore, Vinicius, Cassius, and Lorenzo along with me.

Thank you to my editor Heather Fox, who has been amazing to work with. Your encouragement and energy have been wonderful. I couldn't have done it without you!

Wrapping up a series means tying up all the loose threads, but there are a few story threads that some of you will have noticed I left hanging. The gang problem in the southwest of Coldlake is one. How the Strife men and the Coldlake Syndicate will cope with each other going forward is another. Thane was so *curious* about what it's like to share a woman, and was he asking Vinicius about it to be an asshole, or is he genuinely curious?

The short answer, both.

The long answer... We'll be returning to Coldlake for a new series where you'll really get to know Acid, Thane, Zagreus, and Lasher. It will be a reverse harem! You haven't met their heroine yet, but she's really something. Though they won't be the focus of any new books, you'll be seeing more of Chiara, Salvatore, Vinicius, Cassius, and Lorenzo in those books, plus plenty of new characters as well.

Meanwhile, I have a brand new duet for you beginning with *Pageant: A Dark Reverse Harem Romance*. And I mean *dark*. Please remember to read the lengthy trigger warning at the beginning of the book. There are many themes that are typical in dark romances but some that aren't as well. But there will be a happily ever after ending!

In *Pageant*, we're traveling far from Coldlake and into the world of the Russian mafia. The anti-heroes are cold and cruel and live by a strict criminal code. Crossing them means punishment or death. Our heroine is only twenty-one, but she's clever and resourceful and knows all about their world. She tried to escape, but they've dragged her back in.

I can't wait to hear what you all think of this new book! I love to chat on Instagram, TikTok, and in my shared Facebook group, which are all linked at the end of this book.

Thank you for reading *Third Comes Vengeance*. If you enjoyed this book, please consider leaving a review on Amazon and Goodreads.

ALSO BY LILITH VINCENT

Steamy Reverse Harem

THE PROMISED IN BLOOD SERIES (complete)

First Comes Blood

Second Comes War

Third Comes Vengeance

THE PAGEANT DUET (complete)

Pageant

Crowned

FAIRYTALES WITH A TWIST (group series)

Beauty So Golden

M/F Romance

BRUTAL HEARTS SERIES (stand-alone)

Brutal Intentions

Brutal Conquest

ABOUT THE AUTHOR

Lilith Vincent is a steamy romance author who believes in living on the wild side! Whether it's reverse harem or M/F romance, mafia men and bad boys with tattoos are her weakness, and the heroines who bring them to their knees.

Follow Lilith Vincent for news, teasers, and freebies:

TikTok

Instagram

Goodreads

Amazon

Facebook group

Newsletter

Printed in Great Britain
by Amazon

41842801R00205